Close to the Secret . . .

"I asked you, where am I?" Cal croaked.

The man removed a cigarette from his lips. "I heard you." An amused look flitted across his stony face.

"You aren't listening," Cal grated, wrapping his thick fingers around the steel-framed cot.

"I'm a good listener."

Casually, Cal slid his feet under his weight. He groaned, but he had them where he wanted. He measured the distance. "What are you? A cop?" He launched himself in one sudden motion. Surprise opened the man's mouth. But before he could react, Cal was on him, fingers straining for his throat. "Now," he snarled, ignoring the throb in his head, "how about an answer?"

The man brought his forearms up swiftly. At the same instant, he jammed a hard knee into Cal's lower chest, sending him sprawling backward onto the cot where he rolled quickly, ending up half-sitting. He stared into the round, black bore of a heavy automatic pistol.

"One little move, Sanders, just one. And you'll never ask another question."

THE LAST HUNTER

FRED CEDERBERG

BERKLEY BOOKS, NEW YORK

This Berkley book contains the complete
text of the original hardcover edition.
It has been completely reset in a typeface
designed for easy reading, and was printed
from new film.

THE LAST HUNTER

A Berkley Book / published by arrangement with
Stoddart Publishing Company, Limited.

PRINTING HISTORY
Stoddart edition published 1986
Berkley edition / October 1987

All rights reserved.
Copyright © 1986 by Fred Cederberg.
This book may not be reproduced in whole or in part,
by mimeograph or any other means, without permission.
For information address: Stoddart Publishing Company, Limited,
34 Lesmill Road, Toronto, Canada M3B 2T6.

ISBN: 0-425-10400-1

A BERKLEY BOOK® TM 757,375
Berkley Books are published by The Berkley Publishing Group,
200 Madison Avenue, New York, NY 10016.
The name "BERKLEY" and the "B" logo
are trademarks belonging to Berkley Publishing Corporation.

PRINTED IN THE UNITED STATES OF AMERICA

10 9 8 7 6 5 4 3 2 1

This story should have been told in the mid-1960's. But for reasons which will become apparent, it could not.

                              (signed)
                              Cal Sanders

Prologue

✻

3-5-45   1530 hrs GMT

File AH 1945

For Prime Minister's eyes only, to be hand delivered on receipt.

TO: MI 5 (Operation Alois Sibling desk)

Saviours departed Celle 2300, 29-4-45, returning 0410 30-4-45. Alois Sibling an isolated guest. As per instructions, Saviours Carpet airborne at 0712, 30-4-45. Field source reported Carpet destroyed, 0921. No survivors. Keepers in place, 1530, 3-5-45. Travel itinerary completed.

                                        Control.

15-5-66   2200 hrs GMT

File: AH 1945

For prime ministerial and presidential eyes
only, to be hand delivered on receipt.

TO: MI 5, CIA, RCMP (Operation Alois
Sibling desks)

Society member departs Stuttgart.

Destination Toronto via New York.

                              Control.

CHAPTER 1

✸

No one saw Klaus von Hagen leap out of the fifteenth floor window of the Royal York Hotel.

But a stout, middle-aged businessman, emerging from the cool depths of Union Station into the warm sunshine flooding Front Street, glanced upward to see his fatal descent.

"It looked at first as if he was swimming," he said, his eyes reflecting shock and horror. "Or just hanging there, up in the sky. Except his arms were waving in a kind of lazy motion. For an instant, I couldn't believe what I was seeing. Then he began to drop. Straight down, turning slowly. Until he struck the roadway. Do you know, he actually bounced!"

He shuddered. "It was a sickening sound."

The tall policeman scribbled notes. "Anything else you can think of, sir?" he prodded, quietly.

"The cab driver"—he motioned toward the row of hacks at the curb—"the one with the cigarette hanging out of his mouth, he jumped, then ducked behind his vehicle."

He sighed, switching his briefcase from his left hand to his right. "Heavens, it was a sickening sound! The poor man . . ."

• • •

The city room was almost deserted. And the incessant chatter of the teletypes was muted.

Cal Sanders sat in his shirtsleeves, his jacket hanging carelessly over the back of his chair, watching Limey Lewis. Limey had a head too large for even his wide shoulders. He stared through his glasses across the rewrite desk. "You got nothing better to do than hang around here?" he asked Cal. "And where-in-hell's Emmerson?"

"Emmerson was through at three. So I guess he's headed home."

Limey lifted a thick wad of copy paper out of the city desk in-box and shuffled the pages slowly, one by one. "Everybody goes home. Except you."

Cal ignored the remark.

The make-up editor hunched over his elbows behind the middle of three desks lined up end-to-end. His chin rested in his two hands. A smoking cigarette stuck straight out from his lips.

"We move that last page on time?" Lewis asked.

"Yep."

"Well, something went right today."

The make-up editor glared.

Waist-high wire baskets jammed with streamers of teleprinter copy, newspapers, foam cups and fist-sized balls of brown bags stood forlornly at either end of the rim, by the section desks and outside the teletype room.

Cal sighed. Clogged with deathless prose, he thought. Stories from Bangkok to Boston and all points between. Every one of them rated good enough for the wire services—Reuters, Associated Press, United Press—to move. And most of them end up in battered wire baskets standing in city rooms from Bangkok to Boston and all points between.

The sounds from a bank of teleprinters had fascinated him from day one. It had been music. Sometimes discordant, sometimes almost in a kind of four-part harmony. But their rhythm was always insistent.

The copy boy hesitated in the doorway, then scurried between the desks dropping off copies of the opposition *Times* at the make-up desk. Then Limey Lewis. Two on the rewrite desk, another to the rim. Finally, he slid one across Cal's desk.

THE LAST HUNTER 3

"You got it, Mr. Sanders," he said cheerfully. "Still warm!"

Cal scanned it briefly. Brush fire wars. Accidents. And the city council. Dog days, he reflected, we're heading into the summer dog days. When everything goes sideways.

"We got a matcher for that council story?" Lewis called to make-up.

The make-up editor was on his feet, leafing through the pages. He flipped them back. "Yep," he grunted.

The telephone in Lewis' small office rang. Once. Twice. Again. He stared at it, then, as if he had made up his mind he would answer it, crossed the room and went inside.

Cal could hear him growl "Hello" before he reached behind his shoulder and closed the door.

The make-up editor was staring wistfully at Cal. "You going to the Press Club for a bolt or two?" he asked. His voice was as sad as his face.

Cal shrugged. It was a long sentence coming from Barney. He liked Barney, even if he didn't know whether that was his first name or last.

He was shrugging his coat on when Lewis swung his office door open. "Where are you going?"

"Over to the club with Barney."

"Well, the Royal York's on the way. How about stopping off and checking out a fatal." Lewis handed Cal a note.

Fifteen-one-seventy-seven, it read.

"What kind of fatal?" Cal asked.

Limey Lewis' sarcasm was the kind that begged for a punch in the mouth. "There's only one kind of fatal. Dead. How-in-hell would I know? My contact said there was a fatal. The guy was registered in 15-177."

"I'll get my car. An' drop you off," said Barney.

Cal was in the hotel lobby when he saw the knot of plainclothes officers picking their way through clusters of guests toward the elevators. He recognized the taller man in the lead, Inspector Charles Cowan from Homicide. Angling quickly across the carpeted floor, Cal moved alongside him. The inspector nodded. Cal fell into step. They halted in front of a harried-faced younger man. His eyebrows threatened to come completely together over his small nose.

"Inspector Cowan?" he asked, tentatively extending his hand. "Brittain, sir, hotel publicity."

He glanced at the three policemen then, recognizing Cal, added, "Is Mr. Sanders with your party?"

"Obviously," Cowan replied, impatiently. "Do you have some information for me?"

Brittain flicked a sliver of lint off the inspector's shoulder. Cowan shied away.

"Well?"

"No, sir. Just that it's . . . ah, on the fifteenth. Room 15-177." He smiled lamely. "And you probably know that already. The unfortunate gentleman is—was—from West Germany. Checked in today, an hour or so ago. His name was Klaus Hagen."

The chief elevator dispatcher, grey haired and soft voiced, motioned them toward an open door. "Over here," he said, "gentlemen, please."

"Fifteen," Inspector Cowan said brusquely. Cal filed in behind them. The door slid shut, leaving Brittain, hotel publicity, standing on the foyer's carpet. The car rose almost noiselessly.

Cal was as tall as the inspector, and as broad. But rumpled. He turned his head and glanced at the other officers; he didn't recognize them. It had been too long since he had covered the police beat, exclusively. But there was no doubting they were police: their faces were too scrubbed, too shaved, too square and their frames too bulky. The detectives he had known were now inspectors, like Cowan, or pensioned off.

"You coming up for the ride?" one of the detectives asked, facelessly.

Cal ignored him. "What's up, Charles?" he asked Cowan, a man who never liked "Charlie" or "Chuck" and had made the more formal "Charles" stick.

The inspector shoved his hands in his suitcoat pockets, and said, "You just happen by, Cal? Or did someone tip you?"

"We have our methods too, Charles."

"Yes, but you didn't get this one on the blower. We

didn't use radio after the constable's call because the papers would've picked it up."

"Okay, I just happened by."

"I don't believe you."

The elevator stopped. "Fifteen," the operator said, staring up into the inspector's face. "Watch your step, please."

The inspector swung to his left. The thick carpet muffled their footsteps. They marched in pairs, Cal and Cowan leading, toward the new wing of the cavernous hotel.

"A murder?" Cal hinted.

"Not necessarily. How about a suicide?"

"Pills or gun?"

Cowan shook his head.

"He jumped?"

"That he did," said the inspector. "Or at least he fell fifteen storeys and it was fatal."

The corridor turned. A uniformed officer was waiting. It was a short hall, ending at a curtained window. There were four rooms leading off either side. The officer's hands were locked behind his back. He stood aside as the inspector neared.

"No one's been inside, sir," he said.

"Are the lab men here yet?"

"No sir, not a soul."

The inspector turned to the two detectives, detailing them to find the woman in charge of the floor, the cleaning help, bell captain, maids. "Get anyone who might have been on the floor, particularly this wing, since three o'clock," he said, rapidly. "And check out the telephone operators. See if any calls were made out of 15-177 since Klaus Hagen checked in. Or if there were any incoming calls. Tell that publicity guy, Brittain, I also want the key to 15-175 because I'll need another room for questioning the help."

Both men nodded and left. Cal followed the inspector into 15-177.

"I don't have to tell you not to touch anything, do I Cal?"

Cal smiled. "It hasn't been *that* long since I was covering your cases."

It was a typical hotel bedroom, quietly furnished in

"modern": two, long matching day-night beds made up as chesterfields were on either side of the beige-colored room. A television set, its grey eye sightless, peered out of one corner at the chest of drawers and top mirror. A can of shaving soap, razor, mouthwash, toothpaste and soap sat on the chest. Two clean ashtrays were on the low end-table in front of one day-night bed, an open pack of cigarettes between them, revealing a neat row of filter-tips. A pair of dark-grey trousers was hung neatly over the back of the heavy, cloth-covered chair that sat to one side of the open window. The bright May sunshine filtered through the wind-ruffled curtains. One closed piece of lightweight, metallic luggage stood by the wall near the closet door; a second was atop the aluminum cross-legged rack.

"No sign of violence," the inspector said more to himself than Cal.

There was a faint odor in the room. Cal couldn't make up his mind what it was. He sniffed loudly.

"Yes," said Cowan, "I smell it too. Some kind of deodorant, I think."

"More like a cologne."

Cowan wrinkled his nose. "Could be. Care to guess what kind?"

"Could be shaving lotion. But I can't imagine a German businessman lathering himself with after-shave. Particularly in mid-afternoon," Cal responded. He took a stride toward the bathroom. "Mind if I take a look?"

"No. Just don't touch anything."

Cal returned to the bedroom. "No signs that he shaved after he arrived."

Inspector Cowan smiled thinly. "Your point, Mr. Sanders?"

Cal's nostrils picked up the scent again. "Just that it isn't after-shave."

"Then it's probably cologne," said Cowan.

Cal could hear the uniformed officer padding up and down the hall through the half-closed door.

Inspector Cowan pursed his lips. "We received a call at 3:38," he began. He sat down heavily on a day-night bed. "Someone had jumped out of an RY window and landed on the sidewalk." He lifted his right hand and gazed thoughtfully at his fingernails, then slipped the hand into his suitcoat pocket and brought out a slim, dark-green passport. "This," he said, "was in his pocket. Klaus Hagen, Federal Republic of Germany, aged forty-seven, businessman. And being a conscientious, thorough German, he had dutifully checked in with the consulate by phone when he arrived. And he is, or was, a very real person in good standing. This I learned with a quick phone check. He's a steel salesman, or again I should say, *was* a steel salesman. Married, with a home in Stuttgart. But what he has done—except die—since he came to Toronto, I do not know."

Cal shifted his 210 pounds from his left foot to his right. "I don't see any fare-thee-well note."

"No, there wasn't any note. At least, one hasn't been found."

Cal held his hand out. "Mind if I have a look at the passport?"

Inspector Cowan passed it to him. "Why not? Everybody from the investigating officer to the ambulance attendants has played with it."

Except for the stamped seal of the German eagle, it looked like any other passport. Cal opened it. The head-and-shoulders shot couldn't have flattered Hagen. It revealed a face with a hard, thin nose over tight lips and under slitted eyes.

"Looks like he might have been a World War Two army officer," noted Cal, returning the leather-bound document to the inspector.

"He was forty-seven. That makes him very eligible."

Cal nodded and stared out through the gauze-like curtains where the shoulder of the western wing of the hotel blocked the sky. The rows of windows in its massive face gleamed dully, like a hundred doped eyes. From below he could hear rush-hour traffic.

There was a sharp rap on the door. Chic McGregor, one of the identification department veterans, entered. Chic was so thin he was barely visible, even face on. And when he smiled it was so broad, Cal always expected the lower half of his jaw might drop at his feet.

"Chic," he asked, "you losing weight?"

"Rubber head!" snapped Chic.

"You bring the crew, Chic?" asked the inspector. "Chic's got work to do," he said, turning to Cal, "and there's no room for you."

"You get snarly as you get older, Charles." Cal mimicked the inspector's snappy tone.

"Ah Cal, you don't have an edition until tomorrow . . . and by that time it'll more than likely be just another routine suicide."

Cal moved toward the door, then stepped into the bathroom to permit a file of ID men to walk into the room. He paused on his way out. "I'm going over to the Press Club, Charles. Can I call you here in about half an hour? Just to check?"

"Better make it an hour."

"And if you're not here?"

"We still have an office and a telephone in it, Cal."

As Cal walked down the hall toward the bank of elevators, the two detectives appeared, herding two obviously frightened maids and a poker-faced front boy ahead of them. No one spoke.

Outside the hotel, the air was warm, and a mild breeze fanned Cal's face. A group of cabbies was standing around one of the small maples almost embedded in the pavement at the shoulder of the street. Cal turned to the freckle-faced commissionaire and asked: "Where'd he land?"

The commissionaire knew what Cal meant. "Over there, sir. By the cabbies."

"You see him hit?"

"No sir, but I heard him. It was flat noise, like a water bag bursting open."

A yellow squad car, its motor idling, was double-parked beside the row of standing cabs. The cackle of its two-way radio was faint in the noise of moving traffic.

"Chee-riste," Cal heard one cabbie exclaim. "There I was, trying to pick a couple of winners at Woodbine when this bird lands in. Another couple of feet and he'd a crumpled my fender."

"Yeah?" remarked a second. "Maybe he should've had the courtesy to ask first?"

THE LAST HUNTER

Cal turned and began to walk down York Street, laughter in his ears.

Barney wasn't among the regulars and two advertising men in the Press Club when Cal arrived. He nodded impersonally because he recognized the faces but couldn't recall the names. Ordering a vodka martini—despite his doctor's orders—he sat down in a large leather chesterfield. He tried to relax and enjoy the tart chill of the drink. But something vague and indistinct nagged him.

He considered the name: Klaus Hagen. It evoked a faint response in his memory bank, nothing more. It was, he allowed, like trying to recall his childhood days; he needed a key expression or sound or smell to trigger a recollection.

Carefully, he set his drink on the low table in front of him and reached for the telephone. He dialed the newspaper. Switchboard put him through to the record room.

"Willie," he said, recognizing William Muncie's hoarse voice, "it's Cal. Do me a favor, will you? See if we've got anything on a Klaus Hagen: K-L-A-U-S and H as in Harry A-G-E-N. Yeah, it's German. What's up? I don't know. Maybe nothing. But see what you can find. No, I'll wait. Okay, so you're a few minutes. I'm not going anywhere."

Cocking his head and lifting one shoulder, he jammed the receiver against his right ear and with his hands free, lit a cigarette. He smoked and sipped. Minutes passed. Finally, he heard Willie's voice. "You still there, Cal?"

"Yep."

"We got nothing on Klaus Hagen, but we have a file on a Klaus von Hagen, born in Koenigsberg, Prussia, former colonel in the German Wehrmacht."

"When was he born?"

"Lemme see. Nothing here. But this is dated 1946 and he was twenty-five. That'd make him about forty-seven, depending on when his birthday was."

Cal allowed a smoke-cloud to escape from his lungs.

"Not much else. Cleared by a de-Nazification court in '46; once believed to have been involved in the generals' plot to assassinate Hitler. Married. That's all."

Cal hung up. He peered across the room at his reflection

in the wall-length mirror. It was a nondescript face in a nondescript bulky forty-one-year-old frame stuffed in a rumpled two-piece suit. He had gone to fat after he married and stayed that way despite his divorce. Self-consciously he tightened and straightened his tie, but not enough to be accused of wearing it snugly. Enough to look "a bit more presentable" as his ex used to suggest.

He sighed and picked up his drink. He knew more about Hagen than he had a few minutes earlier, yet not enough to satisfy the round-and-round feeling inside his head. Hagen's a suicide, Hagen was murdered, he thought to himself. Which? A suicide didn't make much sense. When ex-Prussian officers killed themselves, it was with a pistol and one of the old Kaiser's colored flags draped over their shoulders. Like Kapitan Hans Langsdorff after he scuttled the *Graf Spee*. And they never jumped out of windows, especially North American windows. So, it had to be murder. Why?

He puffed on the cigarette and reached for his glass. He tipped it up and the last drop rolled down his tongue. And he idly wondered why the death of a former German Army officer bothered him. He had fought them, but even then had never entertained any kind of feeling for their fate. So long as he survived.

But something about von Hagen's end was out of whack. It simply didn't fit any pattern he knew or understood. Perhaps, he mused, patterns shouldn't be disturbed. Never. For a second he considered phoning the Lombard St. morgue, then decided against it. The duty attendant won't give me any info anyway, he consoled himself. He dialed the desk. Limey Lewis was still in. "Got something?" he asked.

"He was a German. And he's dead," replied Cal.

"What else?"

"Muncie says he was ex-Wehrmacht. A colonel."

"Suicide?"

Cal chewed on his lower lip. "I don't know. Yet."

"Where are you? In the Press Club?"

"Yep."

"Well, I suggest if you're interested in finding out, you won't get any answers where you are. Okay?"

THE LAST HUNTER

"Yep."

"I'll tell the desk you'll be leaving an overnighter."

The line went dead. Cal looked up, staring at Alf Williams, a chain paper political columnist.

"You going to spend all evening on the phone?" Williams asked.

"Nope."

"Good. I want to call my wife. She's going to meet me for dinner."

As he stepped outside into the sunlight, the vodka martini bubbled in Cal's stomach. He made a face. "If you've got to maintain your drinking habit," his doctor had said, "stick with beer. Or a small scotch with lots of water. Because you're burning out your gut . . . if not your liver." Ah, God, he reflected morosely, someone is always giving me orders. Walking briskly, he ignored the office workers who were crowding the sidewalk, marching relentlessly to subway and streetcar stops or parking lots. Once he halted abruptly, stepped into a glass telephone booth, fed the machine a dime, talked briefly, then hung up. Outside, he headed for the Peloponnesian Palace where he ordered a beer and T-bone steak, medium rare.

While he ate, he pictured Williams, sitting across from his wife. For a second he envied him. "Everything okay, Cal?" It was Potoula, the lithe little Greek-born waitress. And even though she was almost four months' pregnant, she still had a slim figure. He wondered what had ever happened to the hearty, full-bodied women who used to immigrate to Canada. "Couldn't be better, little one," he replied absently, before realizing she had already left his booth to serve other diners.

His mind was in neutral. Again, he thought of Williams. Cal liked the one-time navy sub-looie, ever since he had talked him into attending an almost bizarre weekend "friends and enemies" reunion at the King Eddy almost two years earlier.

"There's going to be quite a gathering," Williams had said, casually. "And because I'm told you also served during the war as a sub-looie in the North Atlantic, you should find it more than mildly interesting."

Cal had backed off. "Ah, Alf, I'm not into looking

back. Hell, I don't even go to college reunions. The guys who were rah-rahs at school are still pretty much rah-rahs—only older."

Williams sat on the corner of Cal's desk and lowered his voice. "This one is going to be different," he intoned confidentially. "Remember those damned cold nights when U-boat wolfpacks harried and hunted us? Well, how would you like to meet some of their survivors?"

Cal frowned. "You suggesting we fly to Germany for a U-boaters' get-together?"

'No, no I'm not." Williams hiked his trouser legs higher to protect their perfect creases. "It'll be here . . ."

"Here?" Cal knew his mouth was wide open.

"At the King Eddy."

"F'r God's sake!"

Williams looked slowly around the city room. "Very few people know this, but there are some twenty-five to thirty ex-U-boat officers now residents of this city. And they're all bona fide citizens. So, a group of us thought it would be a fine idea to throw a kind of weekend bash where we could talk the bad old days over."

Cal shook his head. "There's been no advance publicity in the papers . . ." he began.

"God in heaven! No!" Williams blurted almost in horror. "You want every lib-left zealot in North America picketing the hotel? They'd go out of their skulls! Hell, they'd give up copulation to get at the guest of honor!" He lowered his head and whispered, "We're bringing in the lion of them all—Korvettenkapitan Otto Kretschmer."

Kretschmer had been the consummate U-boat officer whose U99 had been credited with sinking forty-five Allied bottoms before his boat was sunk by HMS *Walker* the wild night of March 17, 1941. He and most of his crew had been taken prisoner.

The chance to meet Kretschmer had hooked him. And the "reunion" had begun in an atmosphere of strained politeness, almost eighty one-time bitter enemies who had fought each other to survive in howling gales or starlit nights across the vital North Atlantic trade routes. Cal hadn't needed a program to identify the almost stiff-backed

Germans from the Canadians and Americans, even if they all wore three-piece suits.

Yet it hadn't been Kretschmer who intrigued him as the drinks and wine and fresh Pacific Coast salmon eased the initial tension that had left him with the distinct feeling everyone was fencing or maneuvering for a better position. Instead, it had been former Oberleutnant Carl Heindemann who had moved to Canada "to find a new start." Cal sensed that there was more to the man than showed physically; he had either seen too much or knew too much. And he had held his brandy like a veteran (or slyly watered it down) because while that first night dissolved in a welter of boozy camaraderie, Carl Heindemann continued to talk clearly while watching the proceedings through cold but amused blue eyes.

Cal had concluded Heindemann's mask was one of carefully contrived indifference, until late that Saturday night after an almost ceremonial banquet, they had gone to his room for good night cigars and French brandy.

"Korvettenkapitan Kretschmer was the best, if one measures performance by statistics," Heindemann noted affably. "But then it was, as you people say, 'like shooting fish in a barrel.' Later, much later, when a U-boater had to be skillful merely to survive, those of us here tonight sailed and fought." His eyes glittered. He exhaled a thin cloud of bluish cigar smoke. "That was when the criminal element ruled exclusively in my Fatherland." He bit his words off.

The German's quick tack, the sudden and brittle venom in his voice startled Cal. He grunted in self-defense, switching his drink from one hand to the other. "Very few people—even in Germany itself—ever understood there was a resistance movement as early as 1938," Heindemann continued. "Major Ewald von Kleist-Schmensin went so far as to visit Lord Vansittart in London in 1938 and told the British Foreign Office that—and I paraphrase—'There is an absolute certainty of war if Hitler and his extremists are not stopped now.' No one would listen."

"That's hard to believe," Cal said, aloud, adding to himself: What are you driving at?

"I referred to the Nazis as a criminal element. Do you

know what they did to the officers who finally tried to eliminate them—and their leader—after the 20th of July bombing failed in 1944 at the Wolf's Lair in Rastenburg? They hung them like carcasses on butcher's hooks in the Plotzensee prison while the cameras rolled, catching them on film while they slowly strangled.

"My friend, the world will never remember the names of the men—Beck, Canaris, Stuelpnagel, Stauffenberg, Tresckow—who paid with their lives in vain attempts to rid Germany of such animals.

"Ah, Tresckow! General Henning von Tresckow! It was he who in 1942 and 1943 convinced the older members of the original resistance that Hitler must die if the Nazis were to be stopped. Along with a trusted friend, he smuggled a time bomb aboard Hitler's personal plane after an army conference in Smolensk. It was March 13, 1943. Tragically, it did not explode. The detonator failed when the firing pin struck it. As a consequence, the criminal element thrived, blackening Germany's name for all time."

"Ah but those Nazis are all dead, *kaput,* as your people would say," lisped Cal out of a mellow alcoholic haze.

The glitter never dimmed in Heindemann's narrow eyes. "Are they?" He looked up at the ceiling. "Are they?" he repeated, almost as if he was talking to himself.

"It is true that many died in the final days. Others would be executed following the Nuremberg trials . . . the Keitels and their ilk. Some, of course, committed suicide. Heinrich Himmler for one. But what of the others? Those who planned or ignored the crimes which have marked all Germans as traitors to the memory of Goethe and Beethoven?" Heindemann closed his eyes and brought his fingers together as if praying.

"It was easy to arrange their own disappearance during the final days. They had seen the debacle coming. And their power was beyond imagination—power to obtain new identities which could not be classed as fake for the simple reason the existing bureaucracy produced them on demand. Just as they would for honest, God-fearing, legitimate citizens."

Cal settled deeper in his chair, wondering, dryly, why Germans were so infatuated with that word: legitimate.

THE LAST HUNTER

Heindemann opened his eyes. "But history has always insisted there be a reckoning . . . that every piper be paid no matter what the tune," he said, slowly.

Cal crossed one leg over the other. "True," he replied, "but as history also points out, often the reckoning is too late for the involved generation." He sipped his brandy.

"Ach, so. But today history marches to a much quicker drummer. We are in the age of instant communications when man can span oceans in hours."

"Meaning?"

"Meaning, my friend, that those who seek, shall I say, retribution . . . such men can achieve in a few months what took our immediate ancestors years of diligent probing."

Cal abruptly wished he hadn't had so much to drink. He had the vague feeling the former U-boater was telling him something. But he couldn't get his mind into focus. "You're talking about revenge, aren't you," he said at last.

Oberleutnant Heindemann rose to his feet and spilled a splash of fresh brandy into each glass, then sat down again. "You could use that term. I prefer correcting the record . . . Germans forcing Germans, to pay for the shame they brought on their nation."

Ah, hell, Cal thought, he's just another Squarehead trying to impress a one-time enemy that he had nothing to do with anything. What was the expression? "I saw nothing, I heard nothing, I knew nothing."?

Heindemann lifted his glass. *"Prosit!"* he intoned. Placing the snifter down carefully, he looked at Cal. "I apologize, my friend, for boring you with such, ah, flights of fancy."

Cal straightened up, returning the toast with a nod of his head. "You're not boring me," he said. "But I'm not sure whether you mean some people are trying to hunt down these ex-Nazis. Or should be." He waved the German quiet. "Because I've always been under the impression the police forces of the world—even the KGB—are doing that."

"The KGB? Its concern is espionage," Heindemann smiled, cryptically, "except of course when the capture of an important ex-Nazi can be of a propaganda value. But to return to your remark, yes, Western police do look for Nazi criminals. *But not as a priority.*"

Cal decided he didn't need any more brandy. His stomach was growling. "Then who is making it a priority? The Israelis?"

Heindemann sighed. "They are. But they do not count."

"Why not?"

"Because they are not Germans. And it must be Germans who capture Nazi criminals."

Cal shook his head. The conversation had left him confused. And now he had heartburn. He stood up. "It's getting late, Carl."

Cal paid his bill and stepped outside the Peloponnesian Palace, shaking his head at a cabbie cruising slowly along the street. I'm walking this evening, he said to himself. Walking. In his apartment, he flopped his bulk into a chair and rang Cowan.

"Charles? It's Cal. Anything new?"

The inspector cleared his throat noisily. "If you mean did Hagen commit suicide, then yes, there's something new. He was dead before hitting the pavement. Shot in the head with a 9mm pistol. By an expert. Probably a Russian-made Skorpion or Makarov. And no, we don't have a suspect."

"Interesting. A West German gets shot to death by an expert here in this city. What kind of game was he in? Or do you know that yet?"

"Only steel. As in s-t-e-e-l. He had a series of appointments scheduled for Hamilton tomorrow and the next day," Cowan said, evenly. "Arrived in town before noon, registered at the hotel two-three hours later."

"So, you have some time to check out."

The inspector grunted. "You should've been a policeman, Cal," he said dryly.

"Was that a compliment, Charles?"

"Take it any way you want."

"Out of curiosity, Inspector, was there a scent of cologne on von Hagen's mortal remains?" Cal asked.

"I can only repeat what I just said: You should've been a policeman."

"Yes or no?"

"No. Not that we could detect in his clothes," Cowan said, his voice tired.

"That sounds like goodnight."

"It was meant to be." There was a click and the line went dead.

Cal stood at the window. It was dark, the night punctured by thousands of lights. He stared down onto the street seventeen storeys below and watched car headlights chasing each other through the concrete canyons like so many fireflies. He wondered if Williams and his wife had finished their dinner. Or were they making family talk over a last glass of wine? Then he thought of Carl Heindemann, the ex-U-boater he had met at the reunion Williams had arranged two years earlier.

Heindemann's a German, he mused. And Klaus von Hagen *was* a German. In steel. And up until three o'clock today, both were in this city. Did they know each other? Ever? Quickly he crossed the room. Heindemann was still listed in the phone book. "It's a long shot," he said aloud to himself. Deciding against driving his Merc, he caught a cab on the street.

16-5-66   2210 hrs GMT

File: AH 1945

For prime ministerial and presidential

eyes only; to be hand delivered on receipt.

To: MI 5, CIA, RCMP (Operation Alois

Sibling desks)

Third Party people eliminate Society

messenger. Prize at stake?

                                            Control.

CHAPTER 2

✱

THE THREE-STOREY, narrow house stood behind the greening trees in the almost total darkness. Two cars were parked in the driveway—a green Volkswagen in front of a Chev. Cal climbed the steps to the small verandah and rang the bell. The sudden light framed the spare but wide-shouldered man in the doorway.

"Carl Heindemann," Cal said, extending his hand.

The German kept one hand on the brass doorknob and leaned forward. "Who is it?" he asked, peering at Cal until recognition lit his face. "Ach, Mr. Sanders! Or should I say former Sub-Lieutenant Calvin Sanders of the Allied naval forces! It's been quite a long time . . . too long! Do come in."

They shook hands, firmly. "Come in, come in, then I'll ask why you're here."

The pale blond-haired woman stood on the second step of the hall stairway, a housecoat wrapped around her long body, her blue eyes curiously bland.

"My good wife, Margaret," said Heindemann, introducing Cal. "This is Mr. Sanders. I told you about him when I returned from our, ah, reunion two years ago.

Remember? The corvette officer who drank and talked with me one entire evening. Remember?"

Cal noticed she had perfect white teeth, but a slight overbite. "Reunion? What reunion, Carl?" She slipped her small hand out of Cal's after a perfunctory handshake.

"Ach, Mrs. Heindemann, you are getting forgetful. But, perhaps, I should have said it was a get-together. Yes, a get-together." There was only the faint hint of an accent in his words and Cal recalled Heindemann telling him how he had taken speech lessons to rid himself of both his German and pseudo-British accents. "It was the three-day weekend when we former German naval officers enjoyed ourselves with our counterparts in the British, American and Canadian forces. Otto Kretschmer, himself, was the guest of honor."

Margaret Heindemann nodded. "I remember now, Carl, but you didn't tell me Korvettenkapitan Kretschmer was there. Of that, I'm certain."

"It's not important, now, Margaret, but we have a guest. And I'm sure Mr. Sanders would appreciate a drink, even if the hour is getting late. Is that not so? Good schnapps, perhaps? No? Then a small whiskey and soda? Good. We'll have them in the study, Margaret, if you please."

Heindemann showed Cal to the study off the main floor hall, then excused himself. It was a small room, made even smaller by three walls of hardcover books, one of which was built around a polished rack holding three rifles. Cal lit a cigarette and sat in a heavy chair.

"Are they hunting rifles?" Cal asked when Heindemann returned to the room. He pointed to the rack. "They certainly can't be General Service issue."

Heindemann remained standing. "No. Two of them, the first and second, are handmade. Both are Anschutz. From my father. 8.57 calibre. High velocity. The other? A Walther 7.46. Fine weapons made by the craftsmen of old Germany. They were particularly effective against the *wildschwein*—the wild boar, in English. Do you like to hunt, Mr. Sanders?"

"I haven't fired so much as a .22 in anger since I was a

boy when I took a shot at a squirrel. And missed. I walked away, feeling somewhat glad I had."

"You should raise your sights and try again, my friend," Heindemann said, amiably. "You would discover it has its rewards. Particularly on a day when hunting the wildschwein on foot."

"In what way is it a challenge? You've got the rifle. What's the boar got going for it?"

Heindemann's pale blue eyes reflected another time and place. Slowly, he said: "He is a tusker, weighing perhaps 175 of your pounds. And he has the ferocity of a tiger and the heart of a rogue elephant. The first shot must count when he bursts out of the brush and woods. There is rarely time for a second." Suddenly, he chuckled. "If you do not have a nearby tree and you are not an excellent climber, you are in serious trouble. Good men, perhaps with a brandy or two to ward off an autumn morning's chill, have been badly gored. Even killed."

"It doesn't appeal to me, either way, I'm afraid."

"It challenges a man's brain. And his stamina, pitting him against such a formidable, wily opponent. Others hunt the mountain lion or grizzly. I prefer the wildschwein. Remember, you must hunt on its grounds. And try to out-think its survival instincts. That requires dedication. One must also accept the fact there is considerable danger involved."

"Do you hunt often?"

Heindemann smiled. "When it suits me. Or I can find the time." The smile was fixed on his thin lips. "What do you do with your spare time?"

"I'm a reader."

"Ah, you like books." The ex-U-boater followed Cal's eyes to the section lined with war books, from Heinz Guderian's *Panzer Army* to Marshal Zhukov's *Greatest Battles*.

"Yes, Carl, I'm a reader. And I wish you would call me Cal. By the way, I see nothing on naval history."

Heindemann sat down and stretched his lean legs, staring pensively at his slippered feet. "I don't need to read about that side of any war. I studied it at naval school until I could recite every book ever written."

"Still, it's good to read how someone else saw it."

Heindemann shook his head, ruefully. "I cannot agree. It's too recent. One can only learn from the distant past. It provides men with a time span in which to recognize and correct glaring mistakes." He pulled his knees up. "Would you give me a cigarette? Margaret discourages my using them. But I enjoy one now and then."

Cal held a match for Heindemann.

"You said you were a reader, Mr. Sanders . . . ah, Cal. What do you prefer?"

"Ancient history. I'm into Egyptology now."

"And what do you learn from such texts?"

Cal chuckled. "That we haven't got any smarter over the aeons. We've got more tools, but still we struggle against the same old enemies . . . ignorance . . . inflation . . . unrest . . . violence . . ."

"Your drinks, gentlemen," Margaret Heindemann interrupted, gliding across the floor. Cal stood up. "Sit down, please," she said, softly. She turned and faced her husband. "And you shouldn't smoke, Carl." But she smiled. "Good night to both of you, and it's been nice to meet you, Mr. Sanders, because now I do recall my husband telling me about you . . . and that . . . ah, reunion."

"I gather," Cal said, after Margaret had left the study, "your wife didn't really approve of our get-together, as you called it."

Heindemann spread his hands, the smoking cigarette standing straight up between his long fingers. "Her woman's intuition said it would lead to nothing but trouble. So far, she has been quite in error."

"You attended anyway."

"Exactly. Perhaps, just perhaps, I am a man, one who cannot forget comradeship—even, no especially, comradeship formed in war."

"That's not against any law I know of. And there are Brits, Yanks and Canadians who feel the same way."

"Ah, but they did not lose."

Cal balled his left hand and took a puff on his cigarette. "What's the point?"

"Losers cannot discuss losing, unless they are planning to wipe out the past with a final victory," Heindemann said, slowly. He stared at his smouldering cigarette, abruptly crushing it in an ashtray. "Still our evening was a fine time. Otto made it so. Cal Sanders made it so. It was even a time to forget we had been on different sides." He shrugged. "But you did not come to see me to discuss a fine party." He lifted his schnapps: "Prosit!" He threw back a mouthful, gasped, then set the glass down. "Nein?"

Cal tilted his glass of scotch at the greying German. "No, I didn't."

Heindemann smiled thinly. "Then it must be the Klaus von Hagen death. A suicide, the radio report indicated."

"It wasn't suicide. It was murder. In fact, my sources stressed it was an execution-style killing."

Heindemann's face was inscrutable. "What do you want me to say?"

"Did you know Hagen?"

"Should I?"

Ah, thought Cal, it's the stonewall treatment. "Okay," he said, trying another tack, "Hagen was an officer with the German armed forces . . . cleared by a de-Nazification court."

"As I was," interrupted Heindemann.

"And he worked for a West German steel company."

"If you say so, it must be so."

Cal nodded. "And our files suggest he was involved in at least one attempt on Hitler's life."

"That is quite possible."

Cal picked up his drink only to find it was empty.

Heindemann stood up. "I shall recharge our glasses," he said, affably. He returned with fresh drinks, setting Cal's on the table next to his chair. "Now my friend—and I trust you do not object to my calling you a friend—where were we?"

"I thought we were something more than speaking acquaintances ever since the reunion. So, friends it is," Cal answered. "We were discussing Klaus von Hagen's death."

"And where do I fit in?"

Cal lit a cigarette. "Somewhere, but I can't put my finger on it." He coughed. "Today," he went on, "a former German officer was murdered by a person or persons who used Iron-Curtain-manufactured pistols. That, to me at least, makes it an international killing. And here in Toronto. Espionage? I don't believe that. In Washington D.C. or California, okay, I'd buy."

Waving aside Heindemann's effort to interrupt, he continued: "Almost two years ago, you talked about the necessity of hunting down ex-Nazis. I didn't take that too seriously, then. In fact, I'm not convinced there's any kind of unofficial Nazi hunt going on right now. But it's a more plausible theory than it was. Do you follow me?"

The one-time U-boat oberleutnant gazed at his fingers, drumming a silent tune on the arms of his chair.

"Did you know Klaus von Hagen?" repeated Cal, gently.

Heindemann rose and shut the study door softly. Returning to his chair, he lifted his glass, drank half the fiery liquid, then sighed.

"Ach, but that is good!" He blinked his eyes like a man who has finally made a critical decision, and opened them slowly.

"The hunt has become too deadly," he said, almost absently. "And now one of my good and trusted friends has died."

For the first time, Cal noticed a Dutch-made clock against the only wall without shelves. Its hands pointed at 10:22. Effortlessly, his mind soaked up the evenly paced words formed by Heindemann's thin lips.

"I shall begin at the beginning. You may believe me or not. I only ask you to listen for I have never spoken to anyone on this matter. Not even to Margaret. And it is not for a newspaper article for I would deny I had even talked with you. Yet, because I sensed from the evening we met that you were a man to be trusted, I can speak." He broke off, as if about to change his mind. Then he continued.

"Klaus von Hagen was one of a handful of former German officers dedicated to exonerating its class and country of complicity in the crimes perpetrated in the name of all Germany during Adolf Hitler's regime."

And Carl Heindemann, too, is one of them, Cal decided.

"Such officers hunt down all surviving former Nazis, from camp guards to the highest party elite who were guilty of such crimes," Heindemann said, tonelessly.

"Their modus operandi was simple: Locate these survivors, acquire the evidence, then inform the proper West German authorities. Anonymously, of course."

Suddenly Cal recalled Heindemann's words said during that long-ago night at the King Eddy: *The Israelis do not count . . . they must be Germans who capture Nazi criminals.*

"Men such as von Hagen, a world-travelling steel salesman, heavy machinery experts, had perfect covers. They could move freely without creating suspicion anywhere in the West."

Time stood still in Cal's mind while the Dutch clock ticked.

"And by the autumn of '59, they realized the magnitude of their task would be greater than expected . . . that many hundreds of Nazis, equally vicious because they had carried out orders without a twinge of conscience, had escaped the Allied post-war dragnet. It became a great hunt . . . the final act of the search for personal respectability."

Cal shook his head.

"You don't believe me, Mr. Sanders?"

"I gave you the wrong impression."

So, it grew out of a guilt feeling because they, as officers, had failed to overthrow Hitler, thought Cal.

"Armed with private funds, referred to as 'conscience money,' and tapping personal contacts, they had access to unrevealed personnel files and records. In addition, big business connections helped establish 'agents' in every country—North and South American countries where former Nazis had slipped through immigration screens, and even France and Spain."

Heindemann coughed behind a pale hand. "Genuine immigrants, Germans who had fled the Polish and Czech and Soviet seizures of the eastern German provinces, proved willing to cooperate. They checked out rumors, assembled facts, supplied details as to the whereabouts of virtually every German-speaking male or female in their particular locale."

Like drones, Cal mused, functioning like so many drones.

"I said anonymity was originally thought to be imperative. But it was inevitable—as one reflects—that it could not last. The Western world's major police forces . . . West German security . . . the FBI, the CIA, Interpol, Scotland Yard's Special Branch, the Sûreté in Paris, the RCMP—became aware of the operation. Unfortunately, the Soviet's KGB, and its counterparts in the satellite countries, also realized 'the hunt,' as it had become known, was being acted out."

Cal's cigarette burned out. He dropped the dead butt in the ashtray.

"This posed a particular problem for the Russians. Why? Because a carefully orchestrated Soviet bloc propaganda effort had insisted their former Western allies had deliberately made no real effort to track down and prosecute former Nazis. Thus, each ex-Nazi who appeared in a West German court contradicted their design."

Cal glanced at the Dutch clock, thinking abstractly that he hadn't heard it chime the half hour.

"Far better, the KGB decided, that any Fascist criminal appear in a people's court, proving to the free world that the British and Americans, aided by the West Germans, were deliberately protecting those Nazis who had mindlessly murdered millions of pathetic men, women and children in concentration camps."

Slowly Cal brought his glass to his mouth and drank. The scotch and soda was warm.

"The KGB dealt itself into the 'hunt,' as they did in Spanish Huelva two years ago. Do you remember that incident? Yes? No? Well, one Heinz Feglein, a former Belsen senior officer, had been tapped for an 'unofficial' arrest by an ex-Wehrmacht hauptmann when two Bulgarian secret police arrived on the scene. In the ensuing fire fight, all four men died." Heindemann licked his lips. "It was reported in the Spanish press—and elsewhere—as a falling out between two Basque rebel factions fighting it out after an 'internal' disagreement.

"There have been others. You may check that one out should you wish."

Cal slipped an unlit cigarette between his lips. He sat upright.

"Certainly I'll check it. But that's quite a confession, even if it's not *all* true."

THE LAST HUNTER

Carl Heindemann smiled benignly. "They say open confession is good for a man's troubled soul."

"I'm not your confessor. And are you troubled?"

"Yes. Because Klaus von Hagen was more than a friend. I can tell you in strictest confidence, he was a colleague."

"In business?"

"The hunt."

Cal's lower jaw dropped. "F'r Chrissakes!"

Carl Heindemann smiled. "You North Americans always swear when you are surprised. Even when the surprise is not really a shock . . . for you had already suspected that he was. Is that not so?"

"Then you are a member of this . . . ah . . . hunt?"

"I shall deny it if I must, but the answer is yes."

F'r Chrissakes, Cal repeated to himself. Right here in good old Toronto. He shook his head slowly. And I'm sitting on the story. Or at least the beginnings.

"You do believe me?"

Cal grunted.

"Why did you bother to contact me, if you did not sense a connection? Or is your doubt born out of cynicism? Perhaps, Cal, your world is composed of liars and storytellers. If so, you have been exposed to too many such people and now you can no longer tell one from the other."

"I don't think so." Cal tried to grin, only managing a smirk. "But there have been days . . ."

Outside, a car raced along the dark street. Its tires squealed shrilly when the driver took a corner.

Heindemann turned his head slightly, staring at the book-lined wall. "A young man who lives up the street," he said, quietly. "He always drives very fast. And his tires are always underinflated."

"Let's get back to von Hagen, please."

The ex-oberleutnant's mouth was a slash in his jaw. "I cannot tell you anything more."

Cal sighed, impatiently. "Well, we both know he was murdered . . . on 'hunt' business."

"I am sorry for von Hagen. And his children."

Blind alley, mused Cal, then changed the pitch. "Do you have any children, Carl?" he asked.

There was grim humor in the ex-U-boat commander's voice. "Unfortunately for the Heindemann family tree, my crew and I had taken refuge in Calais during the summer of '45. And when Hitler decreed that the port be defended to the last German, we sailors were involved in that decision because the SS took over," he recounted. "We fought as infantry. In the final Allied assault, I was wounded in, ah, a most peculiar area, leaving me incomplete, so to speak." He watched Cal with quiet amusement. "It's not as intolerable as today's sexicologists would have everyone believe. Particularly as one ages, with an understanding woman at one's side."

Cal fleetingly wondered if the comely Margaret could look at the situation with such casual diffidence. He plucked the unlit cigarette from between his lips, breaking it off before dropping it in the ashtray. "So, Klaus von Hagen was a member."

Heindemann nodded almost imperceptibly.

"Then, von Hagen was closing in on an important catch, meaning somewhere in this city, there's a criminal Nazi, living behind forged identification. Isn't that a fair conclusion?"

"If you understand the rules of logical deduction, then your conclusion is sound," the German replied. "But there's always the possibility Hagen had become a nuisance to others in the 'hunt,' if you like. Even children's games, no matter how nobly conceived, often take a deadly turn. All players react differently. Some cannot handle defeat, others cannot live even with victory. Then again, von Hagen could have been en route to a pickup—or information drop—and was eliminated by Eastern agents who were waiting for him," Heindemann concluded, shrugging.

Cal coughed. If you're only a player in this dedicated "hunt," or "society," he thought, you, Carl Heindemann, know one helluva lot of detail. "Do you travel much? In your position as an auditor, I mean," he asked.

Heindemann's lean face was expressionless. The Dutch clock chimed the hour, snapping the brief, heavy silence. "Eleven," he said, matter-of-factly. He stood up. "I do not wish to be discourteous, my friend, but I am rising

THE LAST HUNTER

quite early tomorrow. At 5:30. I will be travelling out of town for an eight o'clock appointment with a small business owner who urgently requires refinancing. It's my duty to audit the possibilities.''

The handshake at the door was friendly.

17-5-66   0815 GMT

File: AH 1945

For prime ministerial and presidential eyes only; to be hand delivered on receipt.

TO: MI 5, CIA, RCMP (Operation Alois Sibling desks)

Suggest tighten surveillance on Society Leader.

                                           Control.

CHAPTER 3

✱

SUSAN KIMBERLY LAY naked beside him on the queen-sized bed, her damp, long, black hair clinging to her narrow face, her eyes half closed. Languidly, she stroked her pale white thighs. "That was good," she whispered. "In fact, very good."

Lord, he thought, leaning over the side of the bed and rummaging through his trouser pockets for his cigarettes and lighter, can't this so-called liberation of assorted young women come up with a better expression after love-making?

Or is it because this one can't quite shuck off the last vestiges of growing up in a pristine Anglican minister's rectory? "Ah!" he grunted, "got 'em!" Lighting up, he lay back and inhaled.

"You know, Cal, you'd think you'd at least stop smoking when you're with me . . . in my bed," she intoned, plaintively. "It's worse when we kiss. I can almost taste the tobacco you've had all day."

"I don't remember you complaining during the exercise."

Susan giggled and changed the subject. "You weren't in the city room all afternoon," she said. "On a special assignment? That's what the desk said, anyway. Tell me."

"Uh-uh."

"Sometimes, I could swear at you."

But you won't, he thought, because you don't. And he liked that. He had come to dislike the new wave of tough-talking, hard-cursing women who talked like construction workers. He recalled what his ex had said once: "If they want to imitate men, why can't they imitate the good ones, not the foul-mouthed Neanderthals?"

Cal's relationship with Susan Kimberly had been unplanned. With his marriage gone and the divorce settled, he had discovered he had time on his hands. He recalled the night Carolyn Anne said she wanted a divorce. He was still in the shower after throwing off the effects of several drinks. He heard her say in a bitter, but low, controlled voice: "It won't bother you, Cal, because you haven't been 'married' for the last dozen years. You don't even know your daughters . . . and Jennie is almost eighteen and Madge is sixteen. Yes, you pay the bills, and you also pay the mortgage. But I'm a stranger in your life . . . a complete stranger, and I don't consider that marriage." Angry and hurt, he had packed and left, baffled and surly because he couldn't remember where he had gone wrong or why. And he wallowed in a moody silence—sensing the time for talking was over—while the lawyers debated. In the end, it was an amicable parting. Carolyn Anne got the house, Cal the final payments. He had visiting rights, she the station wagon.

In the following months which melded into almost two years, he lived in *The Express* city room between walks to a downtown two-bedroom apartment and a Greek restaurant he had dubbed the Peloponnesian Palace. It was owned by twin brothers—Steve and Chris—who had originally come from Sparta. They cheerfully served inexpensive, solid meals and drinks.

He told himself he was free. He even wanted to brag about it, but always gagged on the words before he could get them out. One night, despite the Greeks' misgivings, he got blind drunk on twenty-five-year-old Greek brandy, called Botry's. He could never recall leaving the restaurant, but he knew where he was when he blinked through blood-streaked eyes at the early morning sunlight, slanting through an open window in his own apartment.

Without looking at his watch, he knew it was early; the sounds of mid-city traffic were almost nonexistent. And he was wondering if the fire in his belly would erupt through the layer of fat that girded his stomach before he realized he wasn't alone.

Susan Kimberly snuggled against him. "I'm cold, lover," she murmured. "Don't you have any sheets or blankets?"

He remembered lurching to his feet, convinced his throbbing head was going to fall off his neck. Afraid to bend over, he snatched the bedclothes off the floor, tossed them over her and staggered into the bathroom. He didn't look in the mirror, but climbed into the tub and sat down, adjusted the hot-cold controls and turned the shower on.

"You're downright rude," she said, joining him later in *The Express* cafeteria where he chewed on soggy toast. "You didn't even wake me up or anything."

Cal looked at his hands and counted his fingers.

"No wonder everybody says you're a loner."

He looked at her. "What else can I say?"

"And you drink too much."

"Tell me something I don't know and maybe we can carry on an intelligent conversation."

"You kept falling asleep, right on top of me," she hissed. "And I just kept prodding you awake until we'd finished our business."

My god, he thought, unhappily, now it's just business. "Did I offer to pay you?" he asked cuttingly.

"You really are gross," she snapped and, getting up, walked quickly away, disappearing at the head of the stairs leading down to the city room. He followed her with his hung-over eyes, conceding that she had good legs even if they were thinner than Carolyn Anne's. The thought of Carolyn Anne made him sad.

Although he saw her occasionally in the city room over the next two weeks, they never spoke. But he found out she was a journalism grad who had paid her dues, working three years in the boondocks. "She's not one of the best writers, but her stories don't bounce, either," said Limey.

"So, she's a solid researcher. How old is she? About twenty-six or twenty-seven."

He rang her up one night. "I owe you an apology," he said, simply. "Why don't you have dinner with me?"

Susan handed him her apartment keys. "I think it's a crock of you-know-what to have the man open the door into your own apartment," she said as they stepped inside.

He dropped the keys in her open hand. "If that's what you believe, then why do it?"

"I'm trapped in a social style I don't particularly fancy," she said. "But it'll change one of these days."

By the time he had turned around after closing the door she was in the kitchen and out of sight.

"I've got rye and gin. And beer. What's your choice?" she called.

"Am I going to get some kind of lecture with my rye and water?"

"No."

She kicked off her shoes, placed his drink on the coffee table in front of his chair and smiled too brightly. "I'm in one of my moods," she said. "But they go with the woman." She lifted her gin and seven to her mouth. "Cheers!"

Cal drank a large mouthful. "It must've come over you on the walk here. You were okay at the Peloponnesian Palace . . ."

"Ah, yes, the Peloponnesian Palace!" She mocked his words.

It annoyed him. He stared out the window into the spring night and across the street into another apartment. Faintly, behind the large window he could make out a woman sitting on a chesterfield. Whatever she was staring at was hidden from his view. He watched a man come into the room and sit beside her. She didn't seem to notice.

"They do that every night. Sit and stare at TV," said Susan. "Have you noticed I don't have television?"

Cal glanced around the room. "Not until just now."

"It turns men and women into zombies."

He grunted to cover up the fact he didn't know where

the conversation was going. He said finally: "Are we going to fight?"

She shook her head and looked into his face. It was as if it was the first time she had seen him since they arrived.

"Well, are we?" he goaded.

"Why?"

"You seem to have ants in your pants tonight."

"I don't have any panties on," she smirked, setting her drink down and moving between his knees.

Susan Kimberly was absolutely correct in that department.

"Are you going to stay for the night?" Susan asked.

"I don't know. I've got a lot on my mind."

She sat up, her small breasts jiggling. "How about me?"

He stroked her bare shoulder, gently. "Come on, woman, don't be so touchy. I thought we had buried the hatchet. You know what I mean."

Susan made a face, reminding him he had forgotten younger women pouted when they didn't get their way. "It's the Hagen story, isn't it. Well, it got front-page treatment. That should satisfy you. Sensation City. Was it all true . . . that stuff about that Hagen possibly being a secret agent?"

Cal had carefully written around Heindemann's story, linking international agents in what he suggested was espionage. "Just about."

"The opposition matched it. So it must've had something going for it . . . after the morning paper buried it under City Notes. And radio and TV jumped on it. What are you going to do for a follow-up?"

Cal laughed. "Now you sound like Limey Lewis. So, I'll tell you what I told him—that I gave it a running start, now his political and police reporters can pick it up."

"I don't believe you."

"Then don't." He sat up.

"You can stay the night," she murmured. "There's shaving cream, a razor, toothbrush and your brand of paste in the bathroom."

"What kind of toothpaste?"

"Pepsodent." Susan smiled archly.

"You noted that the morning I left you, in my apartment. But how did you know I'd be with you here tonight?"

"It was only a matter of time."

"What else do you know?"

"You're forty-seven, divorced and have one helluva reputation as an investigative reporter."

He shook his head and went to the bathroom. My old father was right, he concluded while he stepped into the shower. I won't understand them until I'm dying. And then it will be too late.

It was almost eight o'clock when Cal awoke. He pawed the sleep out of his eyes and stretched. Klaus von Hagen was left buried in the deepest recesses of his mind until he had finished three slices of toast and two cups of black coffee with sugar. He grimaced, remembering a wire he had got off to Kurt Schroeder, *The Express* correspondent in Bonn. Correspondent? That's what his byline stated. Actually, he was a stringer. A hack who worked on a retainer and space bonus for probably three dozen papers all around the world.

"Well," he said aloud to himself, "I just hope to God he got the message. Or I'm going to have nothing and the desk will be demanding blood out of a rock named Sanders."

Susan said nothing so he showered, dressed and unlocked the door.

"See you later?"

"Probably."

Strange woman, he thought, closing the door.

Schroeder had come through, moving 400 words that added up to a soft follow-up. They described von Hagen as an exemplary family man, father and husband, sire of three university student sons. Frau Hagen could offer no explanation for her husband's murder. Bonn civil servants declined to comment on the possibility the dead man had been involved in espionage. Cal wondered if Schroeder had made that up or the desk had thrown it in to reinforce the initial story.

But Limey Lewis was satisfied.

THE LAST HUNTER

Cal was hunched over the morning paper crossword puzzle. Susan stopped in front of his desk. "You've got some hand-delivered fan mail," she said, casually handing him a cheap, white envelope.

"Thanks." He jammed a thick forefinger into the half-glued (hurried?) flap and ripped the envelope open. It was a single sheet of paper, folded once to make fit. He read to himself: Mr. Sanders, please be at the United German Club tonight at nine o'clock.

"Well?" Susan asked.

"Nothing. It's Julie Christie asking me to a party tonight."

"May I see it?"

He handed it to her.

She frowned. "It's to do with the von Hagen murder, isn't it?"

"I get that feeling, too."

"Are you really all ice? Or are you faking it?"

That's what Carolyn also asked, he thought, but she never tried to get inside me. He stared at Susan while the onion sandwich he had foolishly wolfed down at lunch triggered waves of heartburn. "Take your choice."

She ignored him. "Are you going to tell the desk?" He shook his head. "I thought not. Can I go with you?"

"We'll see. Okay?" He returned to his crossword, wracking his tingling brain for a five-letter word for a loser.

17-5-66 1422 hrs GMT

File: AH 1945

For prime ministerial and presidential eyes only; to be hand delivered on receipt.

TO: MI 5, CIA, RCMP (Operation Alois Sibling desks)

Keepers request immediate backgrounder on Printer.

                                              Control.

CHAPTER 4

✶

IT WAS TWENTY minutes to nine when Cal parked his Merc half a block from the United German Club. And it was raining hard enough to shroud the street's old-fashioned brick face behind a watery curtain.

"We're certainly early enough," Susan said. She wiped the thin mist off the window with the side of her hand and stared up at the houses. Each had a set of concrete steps guarded by a wrought-iron railing leading up to ornate front doors.

"When I'm expected to be somewhere, I like to be early. Except for my own funeral," he commented dryly.

"It isn't exactly upper crust," Susan murmured more to herself.

The light shining through the high, curtained ground-floor windows reflected in the puddles on the wet sidewalks, turning them into shimmering bowls of soft silver. The air was fresh and warm, the sky black and forbidding. A cat, its eyes glowing, sat atop a solitary garbage pail beside a hydro pole. And further down the street, the lights signalling a crosswalk filtered through the night.

"Okay, girl, time to move. Out you get and I'll lock your side," Cal said.

Number 29 didn't appear to be a club. Then he saw it—a square, lighted box over a basement door to the right of the steps leading up to the main door of the house. On it in small black letters was **UNITED GERMAN CLUB.**

Moving carefully in the dark, they found the stairs, tilted out of line, and went down them one at a time. Water had puddled them, and Susan squealed every time she placed her open-toed shoes in one. The door was solid with a heavy, iron handle. From behind it, they could hear accordion music. In the inky shadows, Cal halted, and Susan sensed his indecision.

"Let's go back to the apartment," she whispered. "This place turns me off. It's spookier than King Tut's grave."

Cal opened the door with a sudden movement. They were confronted with a small, wooden landing followed by a half-dozen steps leading down to a polished floor. The room was narrow and long, and sported artificial beams across a whitewashed ceiling. On the two, long, dark-brown walls some crude artist had painted imitation pale blue windows with round, white clouds.

Arranged helter-skelter around a shiny rectangle of open floor were clusters of wooden tables and chairs. Most were crowded with men and women who drank beer out of heavy glass steins and talked animatedly through layers of wispy bluish-white smoke. And moving between them, as effortlessly as broken-field runners, were waiters wearing what looked like long, white butchers' aprons over dark trousers and open-necked shirts.

For a brief moment they stood, unmoving. Then Cal closed the door and they moved down the steps. But before they reached the floor, from a table to the right and just below the landing, a stout, grey-haired woman rose. She beamed a broad smile at Cal and Susan. "Come in!" she boomed. "Come and enjoy the music!"

Her face was expansive. When she smiled, she showed off gold-capped teeth right back to her molars. Her plump shoulders were encased in a square-necked red dress, short-sleeved, allowing her thick arms to move freely.

THE LAST HUNTER

"Give me your coats, my friends," she said, this time without the boom.

Cal grinned. "No ma'am, we'll keep them," he said good-naturedly.

She studied him carefully, then placed a hand on his shoulder. She laughed, then glanced at Susan. "And the young lady?"

Susan shook her head.

The woman looked back at Cal. "But you, big man, must leave yours. It's a club rule. Yes, it's a club rule. Now, give it to me, please."

The smile never left her face, but her words were firm. Cal squinted down at her, at the mass of grey hair piled high on her head, puzzled. Then he smiled. "Okay ma'am, you win."

"Are you a member?" she asked as he removed his trench coat.

"No."

"You were invited?"

"Yes. Sort of. And I like beer and good German music." He handed her his coat.

"Good!" she said, softly, turned and walked into a small coat room he hadn't noticed before. His was only one of a half-dozen coats on hangers.

"Here is your check, sir," she said.

Cal slipped it into his pants pocket. "Then I don't need a membership to get into a club like this?" he inquired.

The woman cocked her head slightly but her smile remained fixed. "Not when I say you can come in. And I say you can. Now, find a table and enjoy yourself. We only serve beer, you know."

It was after they sat down that Cal could see where the music was coming from. At the far end of the room, on a small dais, were two musicians, one standing and playing the accordion, the other seated on a low stool, his back to the wall. He had a zither across his lap. While his hands almost carelessly strummed the instrument, he smoked. Both wore short, leather pants and lederhosen. Yet somehow they had neglected alpine hats and white shirts. Instead they sported blue sweaters.

Before Cal could signal, a waiter appeared with steins of froth-topped beer.

Susan watched people while Cal thought: Well, we're here. Now where's the contact? His eyes searched the semi-dark room. Every person at the table, he concluded, was German; the women with their scrubbed faces, homey, beautiful, placid; the men thick-necked, with angular faces, broad mouths and eyes that masked a hundred personal feelings.

"Well, boy," Susan said, looking at her wristwatch, "it's almost time!"

"What's with this 'boy' crap?"

"You call me 'girl.' "

"Drink your beer, woman," he said. "Time for what?"

She smiled as she lifted the stein to her lips. "For the writer of that note to show up."

Again he casually eyed the crowded tables. He sipped. He reflected: I'm here, but who is going to meet me? If anyone? Perhaps the sender of the message is watching me now. But who is it? And why the invitation?

German or Commie agent? he wondered. Short-necked? Bullet-headed? Tight-jawed and smooth-shaven with a pair of narrow eyes? Hair slicked back or close-cropped? One man or two? Or a woman? If a woman, was she beautiful? Blond and Aryan? Short and dumpy?

The smoke began to hurt his eyes. He shifted his gaze from face to face. But he confessed, he was striking out. It looked like a Saturday night in any ethnic club, husbands with wives, men with girl friends. I've been watching too many TV espionage shows, he thought, humorlessly. Then he began to laugh quietly.

"What's the joke?" Susan asked, placing her stein down heavily on the table. "And is it inside or out?"

"I was thinking."

"That's out."

He lit a cigarette. "Promise you won't tell?"

"Promise."

Cal exhaled a cloud of smoke. "I have no idea what this contact looks like."

"How could you?"

THE LAST HUNTER

"I knew you wouldn't understand," Cal said. He picked up his beer.

The accordion player squeezed out a Tyrolean love song and several people began to sing along. The sudden burst of song seemed to startle Susan and she slid one slim hand halfway across the table. "This place still gives me the creeps," she said. "Let's leave, please."

With his free hand, he covered hers, pressing down gently. "Girl," he said, loudly over the singing, "it's only 9:10. Let's wait a while and then we'll go. Promise."

She smiled, moving her face closer to his. Suddenly she changed the topic. "What do you think this contact should look like?"

He shrugged his shoulders. "Let's dance," he said.

The crowd was getting progressively noisier, shouting in German at the waiters, yelling at the two musicians who were trying to keep the patrons swinging and happy. When they stopped between tunes, a half-dozen sing-songs broke out. The smoke thickened until it was banked in low-lying clouds through which the perspiring waiters hurried, carrying metal trays loaded with forests of beer steins.

Several times an unfamiliar face smiled in Cal's direction. The same flaxen-haired girl winked at him, twice. He watched her carefully. He was almost convinced she was the contact when she winked at him a third time and her escort, enraged, turned and glared at him. Finally, he stood up and exchanged seats with the girl.

Ten o'clock came and went. The wet rings from three sweating beer steins left the table-top damp.

Cal glanced at his empty glass. "This is good beer," he said. Then his eyes zeroed in on a group at an outside table—three men and one woman. Funny, he thought, I hadn't noticed them before, didn't even see them come in. Closer inspection left him with the impression they looked like everyone else in the room—except it was the only table where the male-female count wasn't equal.

One of the men, very blond, with a pugnacious expression, was staring intently around the room. As he turned his head, Cal could see a vivid scar that was almost transparent in the light thrown by a small lamp above him. He was about thirty, Cal figured. The man on the blond's right was older, chunky and bald with a fringe of brown hair that clung to the back of his head.

The third man was the oldest. Cal judged him to be nearing his sixties. His face was pink, and when he opened his mouth to talk, he showed gaps in his teeth. The lone woman sat between the blond and the old man. She was thin-faced with high cheekbones and brown hair. She and the older man did most of the talking, with their chunky partner joining in now and then.

The accordionist was playing polkas, loudly, rhythmically. Sometimes off-key. The zither player was smoking again, a tired expression on his craggy face. Many of the men and women had picked up the beat, and were raggedly stamping their feet to the time.

Cal stared at Susan. She had a quizzical look in her eyes. "Polka?" he asked. He really didn't want to dance, but it would revive him, break the dejected mood he was settling into.

She shook her head. "Uh-uh."

From outside, above the din of the stamping feet and the shouts of the dancers jostling in a tight, flying circle, Cal thought he heard thunder. He listened intently. There it was again; this time there was no mistaking the rumbling, booming sound.

"It's raining again," he yelled at Susan, "but with thunder and lightning this time."

She nodded, her head keeping time with the polka's one-two-three beat.

The pairs of dancers, arms locked around each other's waists, whirled wildly. A swinging hip brushed against a table, sending several glasses of beer tumbling to the floor. A woman shrieked, laughing crazily. Once or twice the small wall lamps flickered.

Cal watched, bemused. He had just made up his mind to tell Susan that it was time to go home when he saw the stout woman who had checked his coat. She seemed to be trying to get through the milling couples. Her elbows were high and her head jogging from side to side. Cal couldn't get a good look at her face. Once he thought he did, but a bouncing couple blocked his view. Then she staggered

THE LAST HUNTER

wildly. Through the blur of colors and smoke he saw her face—streaked and grey and lined in obvious pain.

Again she was bumped. Her arms went higher, flailing madly, like an exhausted swimmer reaching for the end of a pool after a hard race. Her lips moved, but in the cacophony of sounds, Cal could not hear her.

Then, as if in slow motion, she appeared to lose her balance. For a split-second she hung, poised like a hummingbird in midflight, her arms beating; then she fell forward, crashing to the floor. Her bare plump arms twitched.

Cal leaped to his feet. Pushing two couples aside, he reached her. The dancers in the inner part of the circle stopped; those on the outside slowed, shuffling aimlessly.

"Shut down the music!" someone called. The music sighed and wheezed to a discordant halt.

The stout woman was face down on the floor, her arms awkwardly stretched over her head. Her once-neat pile of grey hair was askew, long strands running over her shoulders. Cal peered at her. High in her back, a few inches below the squared neckline of her red dress was a widening, wet splotch, a brighter hue than the color in the fabric.

The man standing above the woman's right side disengaged his arm from his girl's waist. Bending quickly despite a thick middle, he rolled the woman over and lifted her head a few inches off the floor.

"Hey, old woman, what's the trouble?" he asked, gruffly. "You hurt yourself?" Then he saw a trickle of bright, crimson blood running from the corner of her slack mouth. "She's bleeding!" he gasped, hoarsely. "She's bleeding from the mouth! *Mein Gott!*"

Cal dropped to one knee. He searched for a pulse in the wrist of the nearest arm. The flesh was warm and fatty, but he couldn't detect a flicker of life. All he could see was a forest of legs, shapely, thick and trousered.

"Susan!" he called as she edged next to him. "You try!"

The silence in the room was disturbed only by the sounds of shuffling shoes as their wearers shifted uneasily. Susan's slim fingers moved nimbly around the wrist, then stopped. Cal watched her pale and intent face. He could almost hear her counting while she stared into the wall of bodies and faces surrounding her.

Carefully, she placed the limp arm on the floor and shook her head.

"I can't find any pulse at all, Cal," she hissed.

A woman standing behind Cal began to moan. Someone moved against a chair or table and its legs scratched the floor.

"Let's get out of here, fast!" a nervous voice shrilled.

Cal straightened up, towering over most of the couples in the suddenly hot, sticky, room. "Nobody leaves!" he said flatly. "And someone call the police three-six-eight-one-seven-one-one. Tell them there's been a shooting. Then phone for an ambulance. Hurry!"

The nervous voice cried out again, high-pitched and clear: "I'm getting out of here!" Several couples began pushing toward the small cloak room. Cal glanced swiftly around the room. The three men and the woman he had been watching were nowhere to be seen. He suddenly recalled he couldn't remember seeing them before the stout woman had appeared and collapsed.

Everybody was moving, bunching up on the landing and stairs. Only the zither player remained sitting on the small wooden platform. His back was to the wall; he was lighting a cigarette off a glowing butt.

"Where's your friend gone?" Cal yelled at him.

"Who? Heinrich?" He had a flat voice, distinctly guttural.

"The accordion player!"

The zither player shrugged his shoulders. "You asked somebody to call the police, didn't you?"

Cal had the waiters stand shoulder-to-shoulder, their backs against the narrow doorway. In the confusion he looked at faces, trying to find one that might strike a nerve. The patrons began to return to their tables. Cal returned to where the woman had fallen.

Cal studied the man standing next to him. His face was lined, framed by a lean jaw.

"You her husband?" he asked, suddenly.

"No! No!" he replied, shakily.

"Then where is he?"

THE LAST HUNTER

"He died. A month ago."

There was a sudden movement at the door. "Police!" someone yelled.

The two uniformed men, bulky in black-blue, blocked the stairs forcibly, then one made his way inside to the landing. The other remained by the door, a big arm barring any possible exit. His partner came down the steps two at a time, then halted. He took in the room. Then he saw the woman's body inside the ring of the tables. He made straight for her and in one motion bent over the body and fumbled for a wrist.

"No sign of life," said Cal. "She must have been dead when she hit the floor. Shot to death."

Straightening up, the officer stared at Cal suspiciously. His eyes were slate-colored, cold and close-set. "And who are you, mister?" he asked evenly. "A doctor?"

Cal produced his police pass. "A newspaperman," he said while the officer gave the orange-colored card a cursory look. He nodded toward Susan. "And you, ma'am?"

"Also *The Express*."

The accordion player didn't wait to be asked. "I'm Heinrich Gemmel. I play accordion here," he said rapidly. "I called the cops. And the ambulance." Cal looked into the face of the accordion player. Up close, he looked much older than he had when he was playing.

Cal nodded thanks.

Half the room was empty. Tables had been knocked over. Broken glasses were splintered and jagged on the wooden floor. At the cloakroom two men were arguing loudly over a dark raincoat.

Susan's hand was on his arm. "Don't get involved, Cal," she said. "You aren't a policeman. And these people are afraid."

"I know, but the murderer is probably walking out of here, right now," he replied, almost stubbornly. Then he looked down at the stout woman. No one stood around her now. It seemed as if no one cared what had happened to her. She was still. Her left cheek flattened against the floor.

Who would want to kill a middle-aged woman in a

rundown German club? he wondered vaguely. What could she possess that was worth killing her for?

"It doesn't make much sense, does it?" Susan said, horror tinging her words.

Cal shook his head. "You know her?" he asked the accordion player.

"Frau Getz," he said, laconically. "She runs the club. Or owns it. I don't know which."

The officer was all business. "You people stay put, eh," he said coolly. "Now, where's the phone?"

The accordionist pointed toward the cloakroom.

The officer glanced down at the dead woman, and clucked something unintelligible, then almost impatiently walked toward the cloakroom. He stopped once, hands on hips, to call to those couples who hadn't made it out of the room: "You people, you might as well sit down. You're going to have to stick around a while!" then moved on. He disappeared from sight, but everyone could hear the clear jingle when his coin dropped through. Then they heard him dial.

Inspector Cowan arrived five minutes later, his light-colored coat rain-splattered and open. He immediately removed it, throwing it carelessly across a table. Behind him came the same faceless detectives Cal had met the previous day in the Royal York.

Inspector Cowan's face registered a flicker of surprise when he saw Cal: the two detectives said nothing.

"The body is over here, Inspector," the policeman said. "Except to check for signs of life, nobody has touched anything since me and P.C. Harris arrived sir."

The patrons, sitting in chairs across the room, watched nervously. One of the men sipped slowly from a glass of stale beer. A woman tapped her escort and, when he turned, whispered in his ear. He grunted and took a pack of cigarettes from his pocket, gave her one and sat back while she picked through her purse. Finally, she found matches and, after three tries, lit up.

The inspector looked at the stout woman, finally moved closer and bent over her. Then he spoke to one of the detectives who had checked her wrists for pulse. "Dead?" he said. The detective nodded brusquely. "Cover her up 'til the ambulance arrives, okay, Morris?" Cowan said.

THE LAST HUNTER

The people in the chairs squirmed visibly when the inspector stared at them. Pivoting slowly on one foot, he faced Cal. "All right," he asked, grimly, "what do you know about this?"

Cal recited the events, introducing Susan before he did.

"Did you hear a shot?" the inspector asked.

"No. There was too much noise, music, shouting, singing."

"None of you?" Inspector Cowan glanced at the accordion player.

He shook his head.

He stared at Cal. "You still haven't told me why you're here, my friend," he said.

Cal should have been ready for the question. But he wasn't. He shifted his gaze to Susan. Their eyes met. Hers were widespread as usual, but curious.

"Chance, mere chance, Charles," he replied. The expression in Susan's eyes changed subtly and he knew he'd have to explain to her later why he had lied.

Inspector Cowan didn't believe him either. And the smirk on his face confirmed it. He shrugged, turned his head and spoke rapidly to the two detectives: "Get the ID and lab men up, then we'll start on the found-ins. Cal, you and your lady stay here. I'll get around to you later."

"Me, too?" asked the accordion player.

Inspector Cowan glanced at the zither player and the waiters, standing behind the beer taps. "Yes. All of you," and, removing a notebook from inside his suitcoat, walked over to the patrons who seemed to shrink together when he approached.

Cal sat down beside Susan. The accordion player remained on his feet.

Cal glanced up at the musician. "Sit down," he said, "and join us."

"Thanks," he replied, pulling out a chair and dropping into it, heavily. "Two years I've been here, since Frau Getz and her husband opened the club and nothing has ever happened," he said. "Oh a few fights. You always get a fight or two when men mix beer with women. But nothing serious, nothing they couldn't handle. Now," and he peered curiously at Cal, "she's dead, *kaput*. And after Herr Getz had his heart attack."

Cal was only half listening. He found himself looking at the zither player, still seated and smoking.

"Your friend," Cal said, finally, nodding toward the zither player, "doesn't he ever get off that chair or stop smoking?"

The accordionist surveyed the zither player briefly, picked up an empty beer glass, hefting it in a boney hand. "Hoepner? Willie Hoepner is different. He has seen too much. He was a machine gunner on the Russian front before he learned to play that instrument. When a man has killed as many men as Willie there's isn't much left of him. Not enough to make him care about life any more. Especially his own. Strange, isn't it? Willie did the killing and it killed him."

Cal said, "He doesn't look old enough to have been in the last big war."

"The Willie Hoepners don't get old. They just exist until they disappear," he said matter-of-factly.

Cal dropped his head into his hands and tried to think. Not about Willie Hoepner, but Frau Getz and von Hagen and an unsigned note with instructions. Somehow, they fitted together, he sensed. But how? If Hagen was killed because he was on the track of an unknown Nazi escapee, if this much was true, where did a stout middle-aged German woman come into the picture? And where was the person who wrote to him?

He wished fervently he had kept his eyes on the three men and thin woman. He didn't know why, but somehow he was convinced, they formed another part of the jigsaw that so far showed two killings in two days, both German, one from the city, the other from distant Stuttgart. He was shaking his head when he felt Susan's small hand touch his.

"A shiny dollar for your thoughts?" she asked, softly.

"Later."

"It's always later."

Cal glanced to his left at the zither player. He was talking quietly to the inspector who was making notes. Startled, Cal suddenly realized the stout woman's body had been taken from the room, the upturned tables and chairs were standing back in their mute places as if nothing had happened. Waiters were stacking chairs atop tables, sweeping and mopping the planked floor; those unable to get out of the beer cellar before the police had arrived were also gone. Only the two detectives and one uniformed man remained, talking in hushed whispers on the small landing.

Cal lit a cigarette as Inspector Cowan reached his table. He pulled over a chair and sat down.

Cowan stared brusquely at the accordion player. "Your story the same as his?" he asked, pointing at the zither player who was placing his instrument in a scuffed leather case.

"Yes sir."

"Then give your name and address to one of the detectives and you can go."

The accordionist got up and left without a word.

Cowan sighed and knuckled his fists in his eyes. "Unless the old woman was a contortionist and shot herself then hid the weapon, we have another shooting," he said tiredly. He looked first at Susan, then Cal. "Now, let's try again; what are you two doing here?"

Cal took a long puff on his cigarette and dropped it in the ashtray, saying, "As I said, by chance."

The inspector had thick eyebrows. They lifted slightly. "Try again," he said.

"If he were here on a story, do you think he'd have me with him?" Susan asked, coolly. "After all, I'm only a researcher."

Cowan groaned.

"She's levelling, Charles," Cal said, poker faced.

Cowan's eyes bored into Cal's. "What are you afraid of? I know you didn't kill anybody."

"Nothing."

"Then, once more: Why are you here?"

Cal took a big breath and suppressed a desire to shiver. "Let's call it a follow-up. After the Hagen story, it just seemed natural to check out the United German Club and see what turned up," he lied, easily.

"And what turned up?" The inspector's eyebrows inched

upward and for a second Cal was sure they would disappear into his hairline.

"Another killing," Cal said.

Inspector Cowan grunted, unhappily. "Well, you and your lady might just as well be on your way," he said.

Cal rose from his chair as Susan did. "I'll call you later, Charles."

The inspector remained seated. "Do that," he said. "And in the meantime, see if you can't think of anything you should be telling me."

Cal had a mental picture of the note asking him to be at the club. Briefly, he toyed with the idea of telling the inspector, then decided against it. They had reached the landing before he remembered his raincoat. "Hold it a minute," he said. "My coat."

It was the only one among the rows of empty hangers. And Inspector Cowan watched him through half-closed eyes as he put it on, walked over to the stairs, took Susan's elbow and steered her up the steps and through the door.

18-5-66   2210 hrs GMT

File: AH 1945

For prime ministerial and presidential

eyes only; to be hand delivered on

receipt.

TO: MI 5, CIA, RCMP (Operation Alois

Sibling desks)

Getz fatal agitates Keepers.

Conditions red, white or blue?

                              Control.

CHAPTER 5

✱

THE RAIN HAD stopped. But the sidewalks and roadway glistened in the glow from the street lamps. A few lights shimmered through curtains in the three-storey brick homes huddled shoulder to shoulder in the gloom. Above them, tiny stars peeked down between the clouds scudding silently across the night sky.

They were in the car before Susan spoke. "I really think I had control of myself in that horrible little club," she began, a thin tinge of terror in her small voice, "but I'm right on the edge, like my mind is going to blow away!"

"Steady, girl."

"And don't 'girl' me!" She sucked in an audibly big breath. "But what in God's name is happening? Murder's what's happening . . . and nobody's talking! I've spent my time with crazies, but they didn't know they were crazy! This isn't crazy, it's madness. And *somebody* knows what's happening."

Cal swung the Merc out onto Dundas. "You wanted to come along . . . " He never completed the sentence. The powerful four-bulb beams from a car behind them reflected off the rearview mirror and, momentarily flooding the interior of the Merc, blinded him. He blinked rapidly and threw his right hand across the mirror, blocking the glare, and swerved right, north on Broadview.

"Damn!" he swore.

"That dead woman sent you that note, didn't she?" gasped Susan after the sudden turn almost rolled her into Cal's lap.

"I don't know that."

"That doesn't matter," she snapped, evenly. "You should have told inspector what's-his-name. Two people are dead and you don't want to talk to the police."

Cal drove between the streetcar tracks, the vast, empty blackness of the Don Valley and the river flats on his left. Heavy droplets of rain fell out of the shade trees and off overhead streetcar lines, splattering on the windshield. He started the wipers, cleared the glass then turned them off. The brilliant light from a car behind them again exploded inside the Merc.

"That nut is still behind us," he grated.

The traffic lights at Broadview and Danforth were red. Cal braked to a stop. The car with its brights on halted behind them. He rolled down the window to shout at the driver, but before he could, the lights changed. He shook his fist, then with an angry headshake gunned through the intersection and left-turned west, beating a string of three southbound cars. As they crossed the viaduct bridge, where Bloor Street began, he realized there was virtually no westbound traffic and the car with the upbeams had also left-turned and was still behind them, though further back. He must have been held up by the southbound cars, Cal thought, absently. Soon, it was closing the gap and its up-lights catching the rearview mirror.

"I got the feeling we're being followed!" Cal grunted.

A sudden chill made Susan shiver.

The Merc's tires made a buzzing, squishing noise. Cal's right foot depressed the accelerator pedal and the speedometer needle climbed to 55.

The valley fell away into a grey-black nothing on either side of the bridge's shoulder-high stone railings, the overhead lights spun by in a blur; ahead, a lighted streetcar, its glimmering reflection racing alongside it on the wet asphalt, swayed gently on steel rails. The tram's stop lights glowed a brighter red when the motorman braked for the turn before the Castle Frank traffic signals.

Cal swung the steering wheel slightly right, his foot still hard on the gas pedal. They zipped between the curb and safety island at Parliament Street. He glanced up. In the rearview mirror he could see the car fifty yards back.

He eased off to about forty-five and it began gaining.

"We do have company," he grated.

Susan said nothing, simply sat upright, her hands clutching her purse in her lap.

The lights at Sherbourne and Bloor were green. Cal looked up in the mirror to see if they hadn't changed and halted their pursuers. He began to hope he would see a standing cruiser, its lights low. No luck. They were approaching Church Street. Cal didn't brake, but eased up on the gas, letting the car's weight and compression slow it. "Hold on girl!" he rasped, "while I make like Sterling Moss!"

Spinning the steering wheel through his hands, he swung the big car hard right a full ninety degrees. For a split second, he thought he'd lose it. There was a sickening lurch. The tires spun on the abandoned car tracks, bit into the inlaid bricks and the Merc straightened away.

Susan's face was white. Her hands were no longer in her lap. She was using them to hang on to the arm rest on the inside of the car door. Open-mouthed, she gasped, "Cal! Cal! Be careful!"

He gunned the motor.

"Can't help it!" he sang out. "Our friends also made the turn. And I don't think they're cops!"

Asquith Avenue flashed by as the street veered left.

Susan almost shouted through clenched teeth: "How do you know?"

"No antenna, no markings. Had a good look in the mirror when they were under the intersection lights making the turn onto Church." He twisted the steering wheel hard right. "Here we go again!"

Susan only had time to stare through her window to see the black-lettered sign on white: PARK ROAD. She grabbed frantically for the armrest again. The swinging force of the turn tried to rip her fingers loose and roll her into Cal. She hung on with all her strength. Her purse slid across her lap and overturned on the carpeted floor. She could feel the Merc shudder and slither. Then they were racing into the night.

It was almost all downhill, a narrow ribbon of road between shadows and trees illuminated by small naked bulbs hanging high from wooden poles. She thought she recognized the general area—down in behind Rosedale, moving toward the Don Valley. She glanced back. With a sinking feeling, the car with its beams still up was only two bends in the road back. And moving quickly.

"They're still there," she said more to herself because she was afraid if she said it aloud Cal would know how frightened she was.

"I know," he replied, grimly.

"See if you can tell how many are in it!"

The grey-black night flashed by. The Merc shuddered violently as it thundered over a stretch of broken road.

"I can't!" she complained.

"Look when it moves through the arc of one of the overhead lights!" Cal snapped, impatiently, without turning his head.

Again she looked back. But the pursuing car was moving too fast and the lights too dim. "They're too far back," she gasped, unhappily. Then, "Two, I think. In the front seat. Oh, I can't see that far. And . . ."

A wall of water erupted over the car's windshield and the car slowed, then shot forward. Cal worked the wipers briefly. The fading white of a low, wood-planked fence loomed straight ahead. Cal wrenched the wheel this time, but the action was almost too late. The car was fully into its turn when it struck something that splintered with a screeching noise, slithered wildly then, fishtailing, straightened out.

"Whew!" he croaked.

Susan, flung against the padded dashboard, was bounced backward. The Merc picked up speed suddenly. She let out an involuntary scream.

They were on flat ground. Around them and above, small lights flickered in the darkness. The rim of night closed over the deep, broad valley, broken only by the string of lighted lampposts on the high ground.

Their pursuers were gaining. Cal didn't have to use the rearview mirror to know that. The growing strength of their lights told him. He wondered what kind of a high-powered car they were driving. Fifty yards. Thirty. Twenty. He was perspiring.

The first shot surprised him. The sound of the explosion was muffled, almost lost in the roar of the two cars' engines. But the pinging noise the bullet made when it screamed off the Merc's rear bumper wasn't. He glanced at Susan. There were hard lines on either side of her mouth. Funny, he thought idiotically, I never noticed them before.

Rows of weeping willows, their heavy boles whitewashed, appeared in the widening flare of the Merc's headlights. And the black-topped road disintegrated into a washboard track of water-filled potholes and ruts. The car's frame bucked crazily, the shock absorbers thumped in protest. The car slewed wildly. Cal fought the wheel. His wrists and arms ached.

Abruptly, there was nothing but trees all around him, ghostly grey and green and shadowy in the yellow-white light.

Susan jammed one fist into her mouth until she could feel her teeth sinking into her knuckles.

The Merc began to skid, its wheels spinning furiously in midair as each jarring bump lifted them clear of the muddy road. Not more than twenty-five feet separated the two cars and the willows were everywhere.

"Now!" yelled Cal at the top of his voice. His shoulders worked convulsively. He wrenched the steering wheel through both hands, swinging it to his left.

The gloom exploded. It was night and day all at once. Columns of blurred trees rushed swiftly through the Merc's headlight beams. Something black and oily reflected patches of light. The Don River, Susan realized, dimly. God! we're going into the river! The Merc lurched. She had the paralyzing sensation that it was going to roll over. Then, miraculously, it righted, trembled wildly and, yawing crazily, tires singing, biting into the muddy slop, it rocketed between the trees, straight ahead onto a black-topped road.

"Watch for 'em! See if they make it!" Cal bellowed. His face was bathed in rivulets of sweat.

Despite her terror, she swung around, holding herself so flat against the back of the seat her breasts ached. Her eyes focused just in time to see the pursuing car go into a skid as if at the last second the driver realized there was nowhere to go.

For a split second, as its engine roared, she thought it would pull out. The car, a dark sedan, blacker than the night, stayed on the road. But the driver had turned too tightly. Time stopped, but what happened seemed to be in sickening slow motion. The car straightened out and, without losing its momentum, plunged headlong into the screen of trees. Over the revs of the Merc's engine, there was one almost continuous screech of tortured metal when it struck the first tree, then the second. There was a violent boom when it slammed into a third.

Cal heard the explosion. Susan cried: "They've crashed!"

He stiffened, braking the Merc to a stop. Dropping the stick into reverse, he backed the car until they reached the broken road. The glow from the back-up lights picked out the shadowy puddles, the tires squished through them. He stopped and stared at the wreck. Susan sat bolt upright, her eyes on the road ahead.

The shattered sedan was on its side, dim broken lines in the gloom beneath a towering willow. The top front wheel was missing, exposing a jagged stump of an axle. The top front door was gone. The ripped-off hood, shredded into a meaningless mass of metal, lay between two trees fifty feet from the engine. A rounded fender protruded grotesquely above the naked engine, looking like a gnarled arthritic finger. Not a window was intact.

Nothing moved except wisps of steam which spiraled upward among the gently shifting, hanging boughs.

With a sudden movement, Cal opened the Merc's door and climbed out.

"Be careful!" Susan whispered.

"You stay put, in the car," Cal ordered.

"Not a chance," she said to herself. "Where you go, I go."

The smell of gasoline was overpowering. He cautiously approached the wreck. There was a snapping sound and he stopped in his tracks, head cocked, listening. "It's only me," Susan whispered, sliding her hand into one of his.

The car was a mash of twisted metal, streaked with gouges where it had careened off the first two trees. A man's heavy black oxford lay on the soggy ground. Cal disengaged his hand from Susan's and, working his way to the front, peered over the exposed frame and into the car. Two men were crumpled together like broken sacks of potatoes in the driver's seat, wedged one on top of the other between the dashboard and the lower front of the seat. They were packed against the groundside door that was bent inward as if hammered by a cyclonic fist.

With an inarticulate grunt, Cal recognized the topmost man. It was the chunky, very bald man he had seen at the United German Club. His eyes were glassy. A thin trickle of blood oozed from his mouth and ears. It was dropping on the discolored, pallid face of the man beneath him, matting his blond hair. Sickened, Cal remembered him as the second man in the party. Then he saw that his right shoulder and arm were caught between the car's post and the ground. His face was screwed up, his eyes closed tightly.

Where was the third man? And the woman? he wondered, suddenly.

In the silence of the night, Cal could hear the Merc's big engine idling. He worked his way along the frame and peered into the back seat. There was the older man, bunched on his hands and knees as if he'd been praying when the car slammed into the final tree. Cal pulled himself higher, reached in and worked one of the man's arms loose. He yanked hard and his face came into view. It was pink. His grimacing mouth was open, revealing jagged teeth. He dropped the hand and the body fell heavily.

"Is anyone alive?" Susan called.

Cal didn't reply. He took another look at the other two men. He raised the topmost man's hand clear. There was a scar on the blond's face. He was wondering where the revolver or pistol was when he realized it had to be somewhere under the car, maybe still in the blond's trapped fist.

Susan called again. "Cal," she said, "I think someone's coming!"

He turned and stared up into the high black wall of the Park Road's downhill length. Sure enough, twin pinpoints from a car's headlights poked moving holes in the night.

Police? Lovers? Cal didn't know and couldn't make up his mind. It didn't matter. He couldn't stick around although he desperately wanted to go through the men's pockets. And somewhere in the vicinity, if not under the car, was a weapon which had been fired at him. Maybe it had been fired at others. Like von Hagen or Frau Getz.

The lights were drawing closer. Quickly, he crossed the soft, damp ground to the roadway, plucked at Susan's hand and together they ran to the Merc.

"Who was in that car, Cal?" she gasped.

"Not now," he said.

Once behind the wheel, he extinguished the headlights, jamming the switch tight against the dash. Susan sat in silence. They drove blacked out at a turtle's pace, then more quickly as Cal's eyes became accustomed to the gloomy greys and blacks and picked out the solid white line on the road. One hundred yards, two hundred, then he asked, "Are they still coming?"

Startled, she asked, "Who?"

"Whoever you saw!"

Her "Oh!" was very small. She looked back. After a few seconds she said in a low voice; "No, Cal. They've stopped. By the wreck, I guess. But they've stopped."

"You're sure?"

"I'm sure."

He drove quickly now, braking when he came to a stop sign.

He recognized Mount Pleasant and brought the Merc to a halt. A small sports car, its muffler throbbing, hurtled northward. When its bright tail lights had disappeared from sight, he switched the Merc's lights on and eased out into the empty street.

"I heard the shots," Susan said quietly.

He ignored her.

"They were shooting at me, too, Cal." She paused. "Were they all dead? Both of them?"

"There were three. Another in the back seat."

"Did you recognize them?"

"Never saw them before in my life," he lied. And it surprised him how easily he could. Suddenly shaking and tired, he added, "I need some coffee. I'm going home."

"And I'm going with you."

He didn't argue.

The coffee was strong. And hot. Briefly, Cal considered adding a shot of brandy. But his stomach was in knots so he decided against it. He took a large breath and exhaled slowly, trying to make some sense out of the images and thoughts colliding inside his head. He unconsciously winced when he recalled the bullet ringing off the Merc's bumper. Funny, he mused, I hadn't heard those U-boat shells whistle through the rain the night the German skipper decided to fight it out with us on the surface.

"I'm getting old," he said aloud.

No, he rationalized, there's a difference. Those shells were impersonal. That bullet wasn't. It was meant for me. Cal Sanders. But why me?

The rush of water in the shower interrupted his thoughts.

Why me? he asked himself again. And who-in-hell was doing the shooting? What did I have they wanted bad enough to kill me? He sipped his coffee, inhaling the pungent fumes. And Frau Getz? Vaguely (because he couldn't logically explain his feeling) he *knew* the men in the shattered car on the Park Road had killed the middle-aged German woman. Why? He shuddered.

Susan turned off the shower and, still dripping, came into the bedroom, a skimpy hand towel wrapped around her narrow hips, her bare small-nippled breasts almost upright. He had asked her once how she kept them so firm and she replied simply: "I exercise. Want to watch?" He had declined. Carolyn Anne had never walked around with her breasts bare, he thought moodily. She was always in a housecoat or white (always white) bra and panties when she emerged from the bathroom.

Well, he reflected, Freud may have been right when he claimed sex was the motivating factor in our behavior. At least his theory applied to Susan Kimberly. But what was it that had motivated middle-aged Frau Getz straight into a morgue? Idly, he offered ten years off his lengthening life to be able to link the deaths of von Hagen and Getz. It's there, the link, he told himself, but where?

"Dig, Sanders, dig, that's what you do best," he said aloud.

Susan Kimberly glanced at him oddly. "Come to bed," she said.

Now, he allowed as he kicked off his shoes, there are two dead Germans. In my city. And another one alive, Carl Heindemann. Briefly, he thought of phoning the oberleutnant but rejected the idea just as quickly. "It's late," he said.

"That's why I said come to bed."

Hagen and Heindemann I can tie together. But where in hell does Frau Getz fit? Cal asked himself. He shook his head and yanked the sheet up to his chest, then closed his eyes.

"Are you going to sleep?" she asked.

"Where does Frau Getz fit?" he murmured. Then sat up and reached for his smokes.

"She must fit, or those three dead men wouldn't have been so interested." He lit up and stared at the ceiling. "Then she's linked to Heindemann and von Hagen." He butted it without puffing. Susan reached over and took his hand. "I'll dig tomorrow," he said.

19-5-66   0830 hrs GMT

File: AH 1945

For prime ministerial and presidential eyes only; to be hand delivered on receipt.

To: MI 5, CIA, RCMP (Operation Alois Sibling desks)

Third Party subs lose three in dust up.

Keepers ack Printer backgrounder.

                               Control.

CHAPTER 6

✷

THERE WAS NO answer at Carl Heindemann's residence. And his office secretary curtly told him she did not know where he was or when he would return.

The International Airport limousine despatcher had a cold. And a fondness for ten-dollar bills. He grinned, tucking two of them into his shirt pocket. "Between eleven in the ayem and noon? Two days ago, you say? Now, lemme see." He flipped the lined sheets like a card shark dealing off the bottom. "Here it is. Yep. The right date. And time."

A warm sun streamed through the open window.

"I got no names, y'know. But I can give you the runs. That enough?" the despatcher said.

Cal said, "Yes. Just tell me where some of them took their passengers. I can figure the rest out."

"Okay. We got one here at right on eleven. Took a couple of ladies to Streetsville. Limo 12. Nope?" His finger slid to the next line. "Scarborough? Three people?"

"I think the run I'm looking for would be with a solo passenger," Cal said.

The despatcher blew his nose and flipped the kleenex into a wastebasket. "I think I got it for you," he announced. "A single. To Dundas an' Broadview. That's out in the east end, y'know. At 11:14. Yep, Limo 32 at 11:14." He coughed. "Now, lemme see if there's any more."

"No need, buddy, you've made my day."

The despatcher sniffled.

Limey Lewis sat behind his office desk, blank-faced behind thick glasses. "So," he said sarcastically, "you were at the Heinie club last night when the old lady was shot to death. And you didn't write it. We had to go with a police desk yarn. And now you tell me it was you those three Czechs were chasing when they died in that so-called 'accident' on the Park Road. And you didn't write that, either. What-in-hell were you doing at the club in the first place?"

"I was invited."

Limey shook his head sorrowfully.

"How'd you find out those three fatals were Czechs?" asked Cal.

"Metro cops. Mounties told 'em. Members of a trade mission."

"Did the cops also say what kind of weapons they found at the wreck? Because they may have been with a trade mission, but they were trading in bullets."

Limey picked up his phone. He dialed the police desk. "Doug, did your sources indicate any guns were found at the site of that Park Road crash?" He paused, his eyes fixed on the doorway. "Yea, you do that. Thanks."

Cal's stomach rumbled.

"You aren't going to tell me why you didn't write about any of those . . . ah, accidents . . . you got into?" Limey asked, at last.

"Nope. I have no intention of hammering out a speculative yarn and incriminating either me or *The Express*."

"We got lawyers, you know," Lewis cracked.

Doug Henderson, a stringbean redhead, stood in the doorway. "Two guns. Both Makarovs. And they had been fired," he said. "Anything else?"

"No thanks. You can go. Okay?"

Cal waited for the police reporter to leave. "It was a Makarov that was used to kill von Hagen," he said.

"So?"

"Well, I checked with the limo people. And their runsheets insist he was dropped off at the German Club. Before he went to the Royal York. That's the Getz' place. First von Hagen is murdered, and Getz is killed. And a Makarov was used. Both times. Then they take pot shots at me. With Makarovs."

Lewis coughed. "I should've quit smoking earlier," he said.

"Let's go back a bit. You're sure you saw the three Czechs at the club? Before or after the shooting?"

"Before. And later in that wreck. I didn't know they were Czechs. But they were sure as hell the threesome I noticed at the club . . . with an older woman. And, no, I don't know what happened to her."

"But why would they shoot at you? Unless you had something they wanted. Badly enough to kill for . . ." Lewis peered quizzically at Cal. "You said you were invited to that Heinie club. By whom?"

Cal jumped to his feet and right-turned into the hall where staff coats hung in rows on cheap wire hangers. The piece of paper in his rightside pocket was folded. On it in an obvious European scrawl was: Calle San Roman 77, Marbella; El Perro Negro.

Limey held it in his hand. "It must've been stashed there by the old lady. And the Czechs wanted it. But why?" he asked, slowly.

Cal watched the editor carefully, stifling an urge to tell him about Carl Heindemann and his story. And the link to von Hagen. But he understood he couldn't. He had checked out the Huelva incident. It had been true. And Heindemann's background—a business consultant with a respectable firm— passed. And here was a connection between Frau Getz and von Hagen. "I don't know," he said, aloud.

"I know enough Spanish to translate that," said Lewis. "It means street San Ramon, 77, Marbella, The Black Dog."

"Where'd you pick up the lingo?"

"Before I had enough of the land of unions and strikes, I often holidayed in Spain," he replied. "Marbella is Spain's plot of plenty . . . plenty of Brits, Germans, Americans and rich Madrileños."

"Madrileños? Oh, yeah, from Madrid."

Lewis arched one eyebrow. "Sanders, there's hope for you yet." He frowned. "But why the hell would people kill for this address?"

Cal wanted a smoke. But he knew Limey was trying to quit. "Let's suppose that von Hagen brought that message, and dropped it off to Frau Getz."

"Espionage?" Limey swore. "Spies don't kill each other. Only in bloody books. They deal in cash."

Cal persisted. "Five people are dead. Suddenly. All of them foreigners. Doesn't that insist there's a story? Somewhere?"

"We're all foreigners. Some more, some less."

"Ah, hell, Limey, don't get philosophical on me. You sound like you should quit this business and make a lot of cash . . . selling ethnicity . . . or whatever they call it."

"If I was to take that advice, I could charge you with a racial slur. For calling me Limey."

Cal realized his city editor was putting him on while he made up his mind. Stalling to a decision. "Nobody'd listen," he said, at last. "You're British. And that makes you a non-minority."

Lewis handed Cal the piece of paper. "Have you really got a good reason why I should send you to Spain to check out this address? 'Cause that's what you're leading up to."

The banks of teleprinters were clacking out in the city room. Copy boys stripped them, walking the carefully sliced stories to the row of desks, centers for the international, North American, sports, and business editors. The men and women on the rim were cutting and pasting as staff geared up for the final edition.

"If someone needs this info bad enough to kill, I should check it out," Cal said firmly.

Lewis grinned faintly. It was more of a sneer. "Just so you can enjoy a loverly all-expenses paid trip to the Costa del Sol in May? When all of Andalucia is in bright bloom and the German frauleins are parading bare-breasted and bare-assed along the beaches beyond the overhead iron-ore buckets that feed the ore-carriers docked at the mole to the east of Marbella?"

THE LAST HUNTER

"There's a story there, Limey. And you know it," Cal replied, stubbornly.

Lewis looked through Cal and the door into the city room. His city room. "I'm going to go along with you."

"Thanks, Limey."

"You need an advance?"

Cal nodded.

"Go get it. Make it two grand. I'll sign it. And my secretary will make the air and hotel arrangements. Try the Los Monteros. It's about three miles east of Marbella. On the coast road. You'll like it. Don't try the Marbella Club; it's snotty and very pricey."

Cal grunted.

"You leaving tonight?" asked Limey.

"If I can get a flight."

"Alone?"

"Yep."

"Good thinking. And good hunting."

Cal collected two thousand dollars in U.S. travellers checks and cash, checked his wallet for his American Express card and reported to Miss Browning, Limey's sturdy old-maid secretary. She was so efficient, she was nicknamed the guillotine. Behind her back, of course. Heavy-breasted with carefully rinsed light brown hair cut short, no one knew her age. But guessed at fiftyish. She and Limey were part of the rumors for years, but Limey had always insisted he had slept in his office when appearing too early.

He stared down at her, trying to picture them thrashing around in bed. Thrashing? he thought to himself, vaguely, no way. Probably doing it by numbers. Like in an exercise.

"You'll leave out of New York at eight. Your flight, Iberia, departs for Madrid at 11:45," she said evenly. "I left your return tickets blank. You'll have to arrange them yourself. If our travel agent is on the ball, there'll be a car for you at Malaga and a booking in Los Monteros. It's about three miles *before* you reach Marbella. Oh, and just follow the main highway out of Malaga. Have a good trip." She smiled. "You know something Sanders? I wish I was going with you. I really do."

His mental vision of her copulating with Limey Lewis by numbers disintegrated.

"You got holidays, Miss Browning?"

Her smile broadened. "Unfortunately, no."

Cal made two phone calls from his apartment. The first was to Carl Heindemann. Still no answer.

"Susan, how the hell are you?" he asked. "You weren't in today?"

"You didn't ask me how I got home," she said, her voice brittle. "You didn't even check the schedule. I had a day off."

"How did you get home?"

"I walked."

"Very wise; it's called physical fitness."

"Too bad you aren't into that," she came back, airily. "And except for a story about an accident and three dead Czechs, there's nothing on the news about what really happened. To you and me."

"I'm going away for a few days," he said.

"Just like that, you change the pace." She was silent for a few seconds. "Where?"

"Spain."

"Oh."

He could hear her kitchen clock ticking off the seconds. "Did you hear me?"

"Can I go?"

"Sorry." Then: "Why?"

"Because I want to."

"That's not a reason."

"Can you think of a better one?" she asked.

"No."

"Well?"

He said it again: "No."

"Then that's it?"

"Yes. And I've got to go. You take care of yourself." He hung up before she could reply.

At the airport, he made one last phone call. To the night desk.

20-5-66   0955 hrs GMT

File: AH 1945

For prime ministerial and presidential eyes

only; to be hand delivered on receipt.

To: MI 5, CIA, RCMP (Operation Alois

Sibling desks)

Society Leader lost.

                                        Control.

CHAPTER 7

✷

IBERIA FLIGHT 70, economy class, was sold out. Which explained why Miss Browning had booked Cal first class. He stowed his briefcase and single piece of luggage and dropped in his seat next to a black-haired girl. He guessed she was a teenager. They sat side by side in silence during take-off. It was after a snack and glass of wine, and when the lights had dimmed, that she spoke.

"Can't sleep, either?" she asked, offhandedly.

He couldn't and said so.

"My name is Pamela. Pam." Her eyes were brown and bright, set apart over a sharp nose in a gently tanned face. Her mouth was broad and full. And she was dressed in a black pinafore and high-collared white blouse.

"I'm Cal Sanders."

"Businessman?"

"Why'd you ask?"

"You're travelling first class, that's why," she said.

"Newspaper reporter," he said. "And you're travelling first class and obviously not a businessman." He emphasized the "man."

She laughed. "I'm a student. And my daddy is a businessman. A big one."

Pamela Strong was on her way to school in Spain. A convent. "And I'm not even Roman Catholic," she snickered.

Her wealthy parents had shipped her to a good Catholic girls' school outside Malaga to ensure she received a sound education; not one served up in a liberal society.

"I didn't know school started in May," he said, taking his turn at small talk.

"It doesn't. But I went home for Semana Santa."

Cal grunted.

"Of course," she said. "You wouldn't know what *that* is. If this is your first time to Spain. And it is . . . isn't it?" When he nodded, she went on. "It's Holy Week. Leading up to Easter Sunday." She half turned and looked boldly into his face, revealing high cheekbones. "During my first year at school, I stayed in Malaga for Semana Santa. And, perhaps because I'm not a Catholic, I found it both weird and oddly moving. On Good Friday, the men march through the streets, robed and hooded, carrying beamed floats on their shoulders. And there are purple-draped statues of the Virgin Mary and Christ on the floats."

Pamela Strong had a very animated face.

"They reminded me of Ku Klux Klansmen. Except they were in purple. Not bedsheets. And the silence was eerie. Even with the children lining the streets. The songs people sang from balconies and doorways everytime the procession halted . . . they were spooky. Like laments with high sad notes."

The stewardess offered Cal a split of wine. Pamela Strong signalled for one. She poured both glasses half full of the ruby red liquid.

Pam sipped hers. "Anyway," she continued, "I don't stay in Spain for Semana Santa anymore. I call it winter break. And go home. I should've been back weeks ago. But I came down with mono. You know, the kissing disease." She laughed. "Now, I'm on my way back, trying to catch up."

"How many years have you been going to school there?" Cal asked.

"This is my fourth. I'm a senior now. With privileges."

Cal rested against the back of the seat.

She swung her head of hair around and stared at him quizzically. "Where are you going?" she asked. "In Spain, I mean."

"On to Malaga. Then Marbella." He said Marbella the way Limey said it.

She giggled. "It's not like that. It's Mar-bey-ya. All double L's are Y's in Spanish."

Smart-ass kid, he thought. He drank wine.

"Holidays? Or a story?"

He wanted to ask: What's it to you? Instead he said: "I hope there's a story." He shrugged. "But if not, then some holidays."

"Are you an American?"

Cal closed his eyes.

"Now you're sleepy. I'm sorry."

"Don't be sorry," he murmured.

"Good night, Mr. Sanders," she said softly.

The heavily travelled coastal highway south and west out of ancient Malaga ran straight through Torremolinos. In the morning light, he could have sworn he was in Baja. Smokey Joe's. California Breakfast.

The Ritz. Tacos. Burgers. Hot Dogs. Bacon and Eggs. The signs shrieked at his tired eyes. But the sky was high and bright blue, curving in from the towering shoulders of the mountains to the deep green of the heaving Mediterranean Sea. And the buses reminded him of the cannibalized wrecks he had seen standing forlornly in a hundred North American scrapyards. Only they didn't spew thick exhaust fumes anymore. Or move between white-faced towers—hotels, apartamentos and thick palm trees. They just squatted, shabby and deserted.

He drove the sharp switchback curves between Torremolinos and Fuengirola cautiously, caught behind a slow-moving van, even though one of its three tail lights was often flashing green. It was the rocks above him and the rocks below him against which the sea pounded relentlessly that slowed his speed. Yet, it was breathtaking. And he imagined the sweating laborers who had dynamited and hacked the roadway out of the uneven face of the hard cliffs.

It was a sharp ess curve that brought the road out of the mountains' humpback spurs and into Fuengirola. And a steady drive through pink and white-walled shops and bars studded with hotels and the inevitable high-rises took him to the farther outskirts and dark green stands of pines. The Hotel Los Monteros stood behind a bank of the cone-shaped trees peculiar to the semi-tropical climate.

Cal checked in and was told politely Marbella was "just beyond the golf course, across the small bridge, and the overhead cables which carry iron ore out of the mountains to the waiting sea-going carriers." The hotel clerk didn't mention anything about bare-breasted or naked frauleins, he thought dryly.

The sky over the heaving Mediterranean was darkening when he awoke. Groggy, he lurched into the bathroom and showered himself wide awake. He walked to the balcony window and stared out into the starry night. Jet lag, he said to himself. His stomach churned. He dressed slowly and walked down four flights of steps to the lobby. The clock over the long front desk had no numbers. Just two hands. One short, the other long. It read eight-twenty.

"The dining room," the bellhop said in the almost deserted lobby, "is to your right, sir. But dinner isn't served until nine-thirty."

Two couples, seated deep in black leather chairs, surrounded a drink-crowded heavy table, chattering in muted tones. A heavy-set man occupied a stool at the bar, staring into a glass he rotated slowly in one hand. A cigarette dangled from his mouth.

Cal climbed onto a bar stool. "I'll have a beer," Cal said to the red-jacketed bartender, deciding a scotch and water was too strong for his stomach.

"Spanish or imported?"

Limey had said the Spanish made excellent beer. "Spanish, please."

The heavy-set man was on his second cigarette since Cal had sat down when he said, hoarsely: "First day in Iberia?" His English had a slight German accent.

"Arrived this morning."

"You're quite pale."

Cal nodded slightly. Covertly, he watched the man order a double Bols Genevers and water. About forty or fifty, he gauged. With slender hands and wrists that didn't go with his heavy shoulders and barrel chest that fitted snugly inside an obviously expensive suit.

The bartender placed the glass in front of the man, then brought a fresh beer to Cal. "The gentleman at the bar ordered it, sir," he said, placing the bottle on a new coaster.

The man peered into his glass. "On holidays?" he asked, softly.

"You asking me?" Cal said, finally.

"I don't carry on conversations with bartenders." The man laughed. But it was more of a hiss. Like air escaping from a bicycle tire. He did it openmouthed, exposing enough gold in his teeth to pay off a small nation's national debt. "Only Americans talk to bartenders. Are you an American?"

"Something like that."

"Then you are a Canadian."

"And I'm on holidays."

"Alone?"

"Is there anything else you would like to know before I drink your beer?" Cal asked, suddenly irritated.

Again the man hissed. It flowed from his lips like small waves. "I apologize. I did not mean to offend you." He reached inside his suitcoat, removed a large wallet and, extracting a card, leaned across and offered it. "I am Dieter Rheinhardt." The embossed card said he was a planning and sales representative for BMW, based out of Hamburg.

"Well, Mr. Rheinhardt, I'm Cal Sanders."

Dieter Rheinhardt extended his hand. Its softness belied strength.

"You are holidaying alone?"

"Yes."

"Ah, you are single."

"Divorced." Cal was getting a quick glow from the beer, making him light-headed.

The two couples got up, left a handful of money atop the check and walked slowly out of the bar. Still chattering.

"Why don't we move to a table, Mr. Sanders?" Rheinhardt said, amiably. "It is never comfortable sitting on bar stools for too long." He glanced at his wristwatch. "And if you also are waiting for the dining room to open, we have another hour."

The faint scent of cologne drifted across the small table after they sat down. Frenchmen use cologne, he mused idly, but Germans don't. Cal stifled a sneeze. He raised his glass of beer to his lips and all he could smell was hops.

Dieter Rheinhardt was in Spain to meet with a group of Spanish industrialists interested in opening a BMW subsidiary in or around Malaga.

Cal listened politely.

"They are difficult to deal with, these Spaniards," Rheinhardt was saying between gulps of his Bols. "There is always a deal within a deal."

Cal stared at the man's face. Once hard, it had been ravaged by time. And too much Genevers, he thought, or cigarettes. The German lit a fresh Winston off a butt.

"You like American cigarettes?" Cal said.

"I like all things American!"

The flush from the first two beers had ebbed when Cal tackled his fourth.

"It's easy for North Americans to get divorces, is it not?" Rheinhardt asked, abruptly.

The question made Cal think of Carolyn Anne. "Divorce is never easy."

"I am married. But I should be divorced."

Cal shifted his weight uneasily. He didn't like the conversation. It left him with the feeling he was being measured. But for what? He shrugged.

Rheinhardt had strange eyes. They weren't blue. Or grey. Or brown. In the soft light of the waiter's shadow when he was bringing the drinks and beer, they seemed to change.

"In my business, divorce is unthinkable. It would ruin my career," Rheinhardt said. "What is your business, Mr. Sanders?"

"I'm a writer."

"Ah. Novels?"

"No. I'm a reporter."

"Journalists, we call them."

Cal said nothing.

"What do you write about, Mr. Sanders?"

"Anything or everything. I do what I'm told."

Rheinhardt smiled thinly. "We all do. But then, that is only small talk." He signalled the waiter. "I understand a man being alone on a business trip," he went on, "but when on a holiday?"

Cal pursed his lips. The waiter brought another beer and double Bols. "What's that supposed to mean?" he asked at last.

Rheinhardt's glass was halfway to his open mouth. He stayed it. His eyes flickered around the room. "Nothing, Mr. Sanders, nothing at all," he said blandly. "Again, I trust I didn't offend you. Perhaps I ask too many questions. But I am only making, as I said, conversation. And you are not an easy man to exchange words with." He ran the flat of his small hand across his black-grey hair.

And you're a man who is used to getting answers, easily, thought Cal. Professionals don't make small talk unless they have something in mind, something they want to know. "Is there something you want to know, ah, Mr. Rheinhardt? About me in particular?" The words slid out of Cal's mouth before he could stifle them and he faked a cough behind his fist to hide his own surprise.

Rheinhardt's eyes shifted through three colors before he replied. "I? What would I wish to know about a complete stranger?" He hissed mirthlessly. "Come, Mr. Sanders. What would a BMW planner and a journalist have in common?"

Cal allowed himself a smile. "Nothing, I suppose. Unless I drove a BMW. Which I don't."

"Or we knew the same woman."

"That's hardly likely."

Rheinhardt raised his glass and finished his drink, then nodded at the waiter before he put it down. He licked his lips. "You flew in from New York? Arriving early this morning?" he asked hoarsely.

Cal had made up his mind to have another beer, but the heavy-set man's sudden query cancelled the thought. "Perhaps, but I don't know if it's any of your business!" He stood up.

The German made no attempt to hide the amusement in his face.

Cal jammed his hands in his pockets. "I'm tired. I think I'll eat in my room."

Rheinhardt waved him off. "It was my treat. And I am genuinely sorry we won't have dinner together."

They shook hands. Rheinhardt did not get to his feet.

Cal had filet mignon, cauliflower and mashed potatoes. The milk was warm so he left it. Carrying the tray to the door, he set it on the floor in the corridor. He lifted the napkin. Under it was a card—Rheinhardt's card. Printed on the back in a quick, cramped hand was: "Perhaps we shall meet again." Bending it between his fingers, he closed and locked the door. He compared it with the card the German had offered him in the bar.

"Why another one?" he wondered aloud. "With a note?"

Cal cruised around Marbella's mid-town Alameda endlessly, until the white-helmeted traffic police must have thought he was merely another Americano looking for an easy pickup. Then he beat two other drivers to a single parking spot with his Fiat.

"Calle San Ramon?" the waiter asked, his tongue flicking rapidly between a mouthful of white-white teeth. "Habla Español?"

Cal shook his head.

"A minute, por favor," he said and was gone.

The grey-haired man had a bigger belly than Cal's. He smiled. "You are American?"

"Uh-uh."

"And you want to find the Calle San Ramon?"

"Right."

He took Cal's arm and moved him outside the cafe. The sign over the awning shading the sidewalk tables and chairs said: La Sportiva. "You see that street? With the barber shop? Yes? Well, you go up there to the Plaza Naranjas. Excuse me, the Plaza of Oranges. Turn right.

And the first way is the Calle San Ramon. It is steep, hombre, all uphill," he said.

"You speak pretty good English."

"I should. I lived in your country for eleven years," he said.

It was steep. And twisting. Every upper-storey window was glowing with flowers in hanging pots or bedded on sills. The balconies also erupted in color. Bright white washing hung from lines strung between the casas, even across the cobbled road.

He stood in front of No. 77 and hesitated. Ever since he had said an indifferent goodbye to Pamela Strong, and picked up the Fiat, he had been trying to think out what would happen after he reached Calle San Ramon 77. Or what he would say. Hell's damned bells, I don't even speak the lingo, he said to himself. But, it had to be a German. Male or female. It didn't matter. For some vague reason, he was certain whoever it was would speak English. He shifted from one foot to the other, stepping aside for a crowd of shrieking children scrambling full-tilt up the narrow roadway. And I was so goddamned sure of myself when I talked Limey into this trip, he thought morosely.

It was the strident wow-wow-wow of a Spanish police siren that snapped his indecision. A blue-grey edition of a Jeep swung through the plaza he had crossed and halted at the foot of the calle. All down the street, doors and balcony windows were flung open. Young women and old ones in black shawls peered cautiously in the direction of the wowing, flashing blue light atop the police vehicle. Even after it had ceased to wail and blink. Three green-uniformed policemen in shiny patent-leather hats, leaped out and hurried inside the house nearest the plaza. The children who had raced up the hill came pelting back, still yelling, to surround the police car and casa doorway.

The doorway into No. 77 hadn't opened. Cal reached out, took the iron knocker and rapped it solidly. He did it again before the heavy door swung open a few inches, revealing an ancient, lined woman's face. "Si?" the face asked. The mouth had no teeth. "Si?" the face repeated.

"Does anyone . . . ah . . ." he fumbled for words. "Ah, do you live here?"

"No comprendo, Señor." She shook her head. "Habla Español?"

It was Cal's turn to shake his head. For a moment she stared at him, then said, "Buenas tardes, Señor," and closed the door softly.

He grunted. Well, they're polite, he said to himself, and started down the narrow calle. "I'll get the guy from the cafe," he said, aloud. "He can do the talking for me."

The ambulance attendants carrying a rolled up stretcher (he hadn't noticed the ambulance arrive) loped into the house. A policeman led them through the crowd, shooing kids out of the way as he did. Cal stood and watched until they emerged one at either end of the stretcher. They were carrying what was obviously a body shrouded under a white sheet. Women blessed themselves repeatedly. The police held the curious back while the stretcher and its cargo were stuffed roughly inside the van.

"Did you find the Calle San Ramon, hombre?" It was the big-bellied Spaniard at La Sportiva.

Cal sat down. "Yeah. But not what I was looking for."

The Spaniard clucked his tongue, sympathetically. "You'd like a beer?"

"Si. Cold, please."

"Beer's always cold in Andalucia." He shouted in rapid-fire Spanish at a waiter. Again Cal was startled by the way the man's tongue flicked against his teeth. As though he was lisping. He took out his cigarettes and offered one to him. He lit both.

"Where can I get an interpreter?" Cal asked.

"Perhaps, hombre, I can help." He sat down. "But first, what are you looking for? That would help."

Cal took a chance. "A German."

The Spaniard spread his hands, his cigarette dangling from his lips. "We have many Germans in Marbella. In all of Spain. Touristas."

"One who lives here."

"Ah. And perhaps in the Calle San Ramon?"

"Number 77."

The Spaniard stared out onto the street where a cop was holding up traffic to enable horse-drawn two- and four-wheeled carts through the intersection. "Gypsies," he said. "Spain is cursed with gypsies." His eyes switched to Cal. "El número 77, you said." He scooped a fly off his thick, hairy forearm, squashed it and casually let it fall to the pavement, "Not in 77. But in 11. The legless one. He goes by the name of Don Juan Ricardo. Yet, he can walk. Not like you or me. But enough. A strange man who drinks only brandy. Fundador. Always Fundador. Every night, except Friday. Here. After he dines at the Place Vendome, a little French cafe beyond the Alameda. He must think it's French cuisine because he eats there." He made a face. "Even the name is a laugh. Place Vendome. That's expensive, but only in Paris."

"You're sure it's number 11?"

The Spaniard nodded. Taking a piece of paper from his pocket he drew the number 11. It looked like 77 to Cal. Then Cal remembered. Continental Europeans write sevens and ones with the same stroke. But they differentiate by crossing the stems if they mean sevens. He had gone to the wrong address.

"How old is he, Señor?" he asked, finally.

"Old? Perhaps fifty. More or less. Quien sabe?" He shrugged.

That expression I know, Cal thought, as an ex-Lone Ranger fan. But the age fits. He could've been an ex-German officer. "You said he was always alone . . ."

"Every night. Except Friday, about ten o'clock."

"Does he have company on Friday evening?"

The burly Spaniard laughed. "I don't know if he is alone then."

Cal frowned. "Does he live alone?"

"Except for the muchacha who makes his breakfast and cleans his house. Yes, alone."

Cal swung around. The sidewalk cafe was virtually deserted. He glanced at his watch. It was only 2:30.

"Siesta," the Spaniard explained. "Everything closes. Everyone goes home and tries to sleep. Even in Madrid. Too hot. Sometimes when it isn't . . ." He stubbed his cigarette and promptly offered one.

"No thanks. When's siesta over?"

"Sometimes about five."

Cal didn't know whether he meant sometimes it's over

at five or sometimes it's not over at all. "Thank you very much. Señor, you've been a big help. I'll see you tonight at ten."

"Hasta luego, hombre!"

"What did you say?" Cal asked.

"See you later." The burly Spaniard grinned. "It's the same thing."

Cal turned back. "Where's El Perro Negro?"

"The Black Dog?"

"Yes. Is it the name of a hotel? Or a bar?"

"Why do you ask, Señor?"

Cal shuffled his feet. "Is there one with that name in this town?"

Scratching himself, the Spaniard looked up and down the street. "Impossible. Because I know every hotel and bar in all of Marbella." He chuckled. "And most of them in Spanish Harlem."

Yeah, you would, thought Cal. "Well, thanks. See you tonight."

"Hasta luego!"

Dismissing the idea of visiting No. 11 Calle San Ramon before returning to the Los Monteros, Cal swore to himself. "Stupid!" he said aloud, "just plain stupid!"

Pamela Strong was waiting for him in the lobby when he got out of the elevator after changing to slacks and a loose Hawaiian-style red shirt to mask his stomach.

She was taller than he remembered. Over five-seven in flat sandals, dressed in an open skirted, tightly belted floppy frock that revealed one long, slender leg right up to a full thigh when she walked.

"I've skipped a class tour of Granada. I thought I would visit," she said simply.

Cal frowned.

"Is there something the matter?" she asked.

Abruptly and for no apparent reason he remembered Dieter Rheinhardt. He wondered why.

"Is there something the matter?" she repeated.

"You are one too many damned coincidences, that's all!" he snapped, suddenly upset.

Pamela Strong's eyes widened. "I'm a coincidence?"

He wanted to ask her: Who sent you? Instead, he controlled himself and, taking her arm, steered her toward the glass lobby doors. "If you are," he said softly, "you're a good-looking one. Why don't we go for a walk?"

It was her turn to frown. "You don't sound too happy to see me."

They were outside. He managed a grin. Looked her up and down. "Nothing wrong with me," he said, "and you look like we should go to the beach. Or pool. There's one here . . ."

Her eyes searched his. "You have a car?"

"I do."

"Good. I have a beach in mind. But we'll have to drive there."

They drove westward a few hundred yards east of Marbella. "Stop here, Mr. Sanders. There's a secluded strip of beautiful beach. Or *playa* as they call it, where we can sunbathe."

After a few minutes walk, she led him inland among weedy, high, rolling sand dunes. Extracting a brightly colored, king-sized beach towel from her tote bag, she arranged it against a dune. Another dune was between it and the Mediterranean.

"There," she said, "that's it," as she unhooked her belt and stepped out of her frock. Pamela Strong sure as hell didn't look like the rumpled convent school girl in the pinafore he had talked with on the plane. Not in a bikini.

She lay back, shielding her eyes from the sun with her left hand. Baby, he thought, conscious of his belly as he lay down beside her, no damned wonder you got mono, you've been around. And how often have you stretched out with some guy in this godforsaken little sandy hideaway?

The sun was hot, the air dry. "How'd you get away from the nuns?" he asked at last.

"Not too difficult. There aren't enough of them to go around anymore. So, they've brought in lay teachers. Good Catholics, every one of them. They teach most of our final year classes. But they can be had. Not like the old nuns. So, I made an arrangement."

Cal grunted. "How old are you?" he asked.

"Twenty. Going on twenty-one."

THE LAST HUNTER

They're always "going on" to a higher number when they are growing up, Cal mused. "I'm forty-one. Just in case you should know. Going on forty-two." He lit a cigarette. "Like one?" he asked as an afterthought.

"No thanks. You wouldn't have any grass, would you?"

"You like pot?"

"I've tried it. It's better than tobacco."

That's a matter of opinion, Cal reflected. Or depends on what you want. Like to escape reality.

"Are you really on a story?" she asked after a long silence.

"You asked me that on the plane."

"And you have a good memory."

Cal exhaled smoke.

"Does it involve murder? The one in Toronto?" she persisted.

Cal started. "What do you know about that?"

"Front-page headlines on the newspaper you had tucked under your arm," she replied, blithely.

"Mebbe," he said at last. But he couldn't remember carrying a paper when he boarded Iberia flight 70.

"That's a silly answer."

He found the conversation unsettling. And he couldn't see her eyes. They were still behind her left hand.

"Let's just say I'm interested in finding out why some people have died. Suddenly," he said.

"I only mentioned one murder," she murmured.

"That's right. You did." He closed his eyes.

She was quiet.

Lulled by the sounds of the sea rolling rhythmically against the packed sand, his mind drifted in neutral behind eyes slitted against the sun's glare.

Almost against his will, Cal glanced at Pamela Strong. She was on her tummy, facing him. Casually, she opened one brown eye. "Are you married, Mr. Sanders?"

"Why?"

"You act like it. Really, really uptight."

Cal rolled over. "So?"

She closed her eye and turned her face away. "Nothing, I guess. I'm going to sleep. Okay?"

The quick-setting Mediterranean sun was slipping into

the sea, etching distant Gibraltar like a sturdy dog sleeping on its back against the evening sky when he drove into the parking lot.

"Just leave me here," Pamela said in a child-like voice. "I'll get a taxi to Malaga."

"Tell me, young lady, how did you know I was staying at this hotel?" he asked.

She winked. "They have telephones in Spain, too," she murmured. "and I did know your name. Okay?"

Cal was seated at an outdoor table at La Sportiva by 9:30. He enjoyed a beer, followed by a bowl of chilled gazpacho soup and a tortilla that covered the plate. "Dónde está el hombre grande?" he asked the waiter. Pamela had taught him the phrase and he used it because he didn't know the large Spaniard's name.

The waiter cocked his head. "El Grande? Si! Paco Rivera!" He stared through the crowded tables. His face was animated. "Ahora, Señor! He comes now!"

Paco Rivera was in a summer suit, complete with shirt and tie. Cal introduced himself. They shook hands. "All day, I am boss," he said, expansively. "But at night, I am a patron. Just like you."

"Will you sit down, Señor Rivera?"

"Of course I will."

Cal ordered scotch and soda, twice. It was Spanish-brewed Dyck, more than passable.

"The water is shipped in from the Scottish lochs, enabling us to produce our own fine whiskey without paying British prices," he said, matter-of-factly.

It was almost ten o'clock. The palm trees in the Alameda were lit with strings of bright lights. Tourists straggled along the crowded sidewalk in front of the cafe, craning their necks to spot an empty table. Even a chair. Two policemen in their medieval, polished leather hats watched curiously from between two parked cars, their carbines slung carelessly over their shoulders.

Paco read Cal's mind. "The carbines? They are only for show," he said. "They don't even have bullets for them. Out in the countryside, or on the playas searching for smugglers, maybe."

"Señor Ricardo is always here at ten?" Cal asked.

"Usually. You would like another scotch?" Paco picked up Cal's empty glass.

"A small one, por favor."

"Ah, you are picking up some of the language!"

"A little. But I'm here to meet Señor Ricardo."

The Spaniard insisted on paying. He looked steadily at Cal. "I am afraid, Señor Sanders, you will have a very long wait . . ." his words trailed off.

"Has he checked out of town? Left Marbella?" Cal started to get to his feet.

Paco Rivera reached across the table and took his arm. "Please, Señor, sit down. Don Ricardo, I'm afraid is dead. A knife in his heart. It is sad. First because we are a *tourista* town and that is bad news. It frightens the patrons. And second, because he was a good man. Always, he paid his bills."

"Good Christ!"

The Spaniard blessed himself, then glanced nervously around the tables. "I am not what you would call a good Catholic. Not like the women." He smiled apologetically. "But I bless myself just in case. It's what you would call insurance. Si?"

"When?" Cal held his breath because he knew what Paco Rivera was going to say for he suddenly and vividly pictured the police and ambulance and body under the sheet on the stretcher in the Calle San Ramon.

The Spaniard's blue jowls trembled. "It must have been during the night. Or early morning. No one saw anything. Or heard a cry." He spread his hands. "His muchacha had the morning off. He had told her he was expecting an important visitor. But she still must go to the mercado—ah, market—for fresh food, especially chanquetes—anchovies. Don Ricardo always had them with chilled gin early each afternoon. She found him just before siesta when she arrived at the casa."

And the ambulance attendants had carried him out with his artificial limbs still attached to his hips, Cal thought, idiotically.

"I've got to talk to the police. Will you come with me?"

"Not tonight. The brigata—the commandante, what you in America call the 'chief'—is the only one who could tell you anything. That's the way it is here. And he was called *muy presto* to Malaga. Perhaps even Madrid." He peered curiously at Cal. "This Señor Ricardo, was he a very important man?"

Cal stared at a fat matron, talking too loudly in English to her table companion. "I don't know," he replied. To himself: And I don't even know where he fits in this goddamn "hunt," as Heindemann calls it. Except, if he's suddenly dead, he must have been a player.

"Do you know when the chief will be back?"

Paco shrugged. "Perhaps tomorrow. He has never been called away so fast before. Yes, perhaps tomorrow." The makings of a small smile in the Spaniard's face began to broaden. "Tonight, we will have a few drinks. I have some fine Spanish brandy."

Cal got to his feet. "I can't, Señor Rivera. I can't. It's probably fine brandy, but my stomach won't handle it. So, thank you. Muchas gracias, but no. I am sorry. Besides, I am very tired. Perhaps tomorrow. After we speak with the chief, we can drink some beer."

The hefty lady was yelling at one of her neighbors when he reached the roadside. And two couples were arguing over who had first rights to his table.

Cal's mind tumbled free, end over end. He drove slowly through the east end of Marbella, keeping to the right to avoid the turn-off to Coin. A low, full moon paved a shimmering silver highway across the Mediterranean before bathing the exclusive villas between the road and sea. They glowed a ghostly white. Rows of pale cauliflower lined the low-ground plots on either side of him while far to his left, the shoulders of high mountains butted against the night sky.

The headlights of the oncoming car told him the driver was riding the center of the coastal road. He eased up on the accelerator, repeatedly blinked his high beams and edged his Fiat over as far as he could on the gravel shoulder. "Damned drunk!" he muttered. But the twin lights, growing holes in the night, kept coming. They grew as the gap narrowed until he suddenly realized they were both in the right-hand lane. Despite the glare, with startling clarity Cal understood that if he had to veer farther to his right to avoid a head-on, he wouldn't be able to see where he was going.

With the onrushing lights blinding him, Cal swung the Fiat's wheel hard to his right. For a split second in the sudden darkness, he sensed the Fiat was airborne. It landed with a sickening jar that lifted his stomach almost up into his lungs. It bounced. Automatically, he shifted into neutral and jammed the brake pedal to the rubber mat. The Fiat fish-tailed to a halt.

Cal took a large breath, his head jerking back and forth. His heart was pounding against his ribcage. He waited for it to slow while his eyes grew accustomed to the darkness. In the silence, he cautiously opened the car door and stepped out into ankle-deep muck. In the beams of his own lights, he could see where, twenty yards directly ahead, the muck and loam ended and the field plunged straight downward to meet the sea.

"Holy Christ!" He heard the words explode from his mouth. "Holy Christ!"

Lighting a cigarette, he sat sideways in the car, his feet in the dirt and stared at the moon. "I got to come four thousand miles to get chased off a highway by a damned drunk!" he said aloud. "And I thought it could only happen in America!"

It took two Spanish farmers and their three sons (who showed up out of mere curiosity) and five hundred pesetas to help him back the Fiat onto the road.

Cal parked under the hotel pines and stared moodily across the lot at the row of expensive German and British cars, every one of them showroom bright, reflecting the overhead lighting. From behind the hotel, he heard music and occasionally voices when the night wind carried them gently through the trees.

Okay, Sanders, he reflected, forcing his mind to dismiss the drunk driver, now what? Your man in the Calle San Ramon is *kaput*. Like the others. Only this time with a knife. Six dead. And that big fat Spaniard has never heard of El Perro Negro. He cursed silently. And who else knew about the house in the San Ramon? Heindemann? He cursed again. If that chief—or whatever they call him—can't tell me anything, I'm fresh out of leads. Goddamn. He sighed. I'm tired, he thought. Too much sun.

The desk clerk in his white jacket smiled. If he saw the muck on Cal's trousers, he ignored it. "Good evening, Señor Sanders!" he greeted. "I have an urgent telephone message for you." He plucked a piece of paper out of a desk. "Ah, here it is. A Mr. Lewis. He asks that you call him the moment you come in and . . ."

"I'll call. From my room."

The clerk demurred. His smile remained intact. "It would be better Señor Sanders, if you allowed the hotel switchboard to make it straight through. Long-distance calls can take some time in Spain, if you don't know what you are doing. And I'm sure . . ."

Cal looked at the paper. It wasn't *The Express* number. It had to be Limey's home phone. He looked up. "Okay. Where do I go?"

"If you will step inside the resident's booth, across the lobby, it will only take a minute or so. Could I have a drink sent to you?"

"No, thank you."

Limey Lewis' words were clear and strong. "All right. What have you got?"

"Another dead man. With a Spanish name. At that address the old lady provided. But I think he was probably a German."

"Did you get to him before he was . . . killed?"

Lewis never liked the word "murder."

"Nope. Just missed him. But I've got a man who'll let me speak to the local cops' head honcho tomorrow. Then I'll see whether I've got anything," Cal replied, then explained what Paco Rivera had said. "But I don't think you asked me to call you up at home just to report in. Right?"

"Exactly. I wanted to tell you I had a long chat with your Inspector Cowan." Limey chuckled. "He's the epitome of a brooding Buddha. But he opened up a little when I reminded him we have invested a lot of good American dollars, sending you to Spain. By the way, doesn't he ever laugh?"

"No," Cal said. "What'd he say?"

Lewis was serious. "He said to tell you the Feds think something big's coming down. And you should get your ass out of the way. Before it's too late. If it isn't already. Those last words were his, not mine. Also, they've closed their books on the case. It belongs to the Mounties now."

Six people dead, Cal repeated to himself, soberly. "Ah, Limey, you talked like that when I was running down that Mafia-labor story in Montreal and New York. Nothing happened."

"That was different. The Mafia doesn't kill newsmen. It's bad for their image. International thugs don't care if you're Whistler's Mother."

"Okay. I hear you. Did you call my friend Heindemann?"

"Who?"

"Heindemann. I rang the night desk from the airport before I left and asked them to message you. To call Heindemann. H-E-I-N—"

"I hear you. Yeah. We phoned half a dozen times. But he's away. Out of town on business, his wife said. Who is he? Is he important?"

"Someone I know. And I don't know if he's important. But ask the desk to keep trying. If they get him, call me. I need that guy."

"What's he got to do with this?"

"I don't know."

Lewis' sigh was audible. "You don't know a lot of things, do you. But I hope to hell you at least know what you're doing."

He knew someone was in the bathroom when he stepped through the door. He glanced around. His casual shirt and trousers were hanging in the open closet. Not where he had thrown them. His passport, instead of inside his briefcase, was atop the dresser. And someone had finished off a tray of food, leaving the linen napkin bunched inside the coffee cup.

Pamela Strong's tote bag lay on his bed. He flung open the bathroom door. She stood there, flossing her teeth in front of the mirror. She turned to look straight at him, the string of white floss taut between the fingers of her left hand. She said, brightly: "Hi there!"

"What the hell are you doing here?"

"Temper, temper, Mr. Sanders," she replied, switching to a little girl voice. "I'll be finished in a sec." She resumed flossing.

He backed out. Goddamn her, he thought, goddamn her. Shrugging off his jacket, he started to fling it across a chair, changed his mind and hung it up.

She called from the bathroom. "I'm here with my class; you don't think I'd stay in the convent, do you? Just for tonight. Any objections?" She emerged and sat on the edge of the bed, in the same frock she had worn earlier, her legs crossed. Showing the same yard of leg and thigh.

"Any objections?" she repeated.

There are twenty-year-olds and there are twenty-year-olds, he thought shrugging.

"You're upset," Pamela said. "Why?" She cocked her head. "And you're a mess. Look at your trousers, they're filthy."

He glanced down at them. "I had an accident."

"Are you all right?"

"Certainly. Some drunk tried to run me off the coastal road just outside of Marbella. That's all."

Pamela was abruptly very quiet.

Cal sat back in the chair his chin on his chest, watching her curiously through half-closed eyes.

"You must be very careful when driving in Spain," she said slowly.

"Why Spain?"

She shrugged and her unbuttoned frock opened, exposing the deep cleft between her breasts. She seemed absolutely unaware of it. Running the fingers of one hand through her thick hair, she almost spoke to the ceiling: "They say that if you're in an accident in Spain—and you injure a Spaniard—you will spend the rest of your life paying for his real or imagined medical bills," she said.

He sensed she was being evasive. "That's a dumb reason," he said.

She leapt to her feet and bent over him. "Get your legs

up, Mr. Sanders!" she said, suddenly blithe. "And I'll de-pants you so the valet will have them cleaned overnight."

Without thinking, Cal extended his legs.

Jamming them into a paper bag, she placed it outside the room door. "And your shoes," she said, briskly. "They must be shined."

"You going to leave 'em outside? Just like that? Hell, somebody'll steal them!"

She closed the door. "Not in Spain, they won't," she said, returning to the bed. "You've got good legs. Strong legs," she said, hugging her frock closed. "Are you still upset?"

"No."

"How did your meeting go?" she asked.

God almighty, he thought, she's crazy. "It didn't."

She stood up, swung her tote bag over her shoulder and walked back to the bathroom. "I'm going to have a shower."

Cal heard her through the closed door: "Don't worry, Mr. Sanders, I've brought a nightie. I won't embarrass your Victorian principles by coming out in the nude-oh."

So, he reflected, relaxing. That's the way it is. He smiled, remembering another girl like Pamela. Only she had been shorter, sturdier. Her name was Marilyn. And she had been a private school girl. Was it Graydon? He couldn't remember. But she had been just as strong-willed. He chuckled silently at the pun. My ex was wrong, he said to himself. The world hasn't turned upside down. It's always been like it is today. Only, there weren't so many players. Or were there? He couldn't make up his mind. And unaccountably, it made him uneasy.

"You're not married," she said, standing beside the window leading to the balcony, drying her hair.

"You checked my passport."

"That wasn't nice, was it."

"What else do you know?"

"That we're going to sleep together."

He was barely conscious of the dawn's faint orange and purple light filtering into the room. She was shaking him gently, her large, firm breasts swaying as she tugged at his hand. "Come, Cal," she said, softly, "come to the balcony windows. And I will show you the most beautiful sunrise you will ever see."

He followed her sleepily. Almost in a spell. Until they stood together, gazing through the sheer curtains. On the eastern rim of the Mediterranean, the sun was a fiery orange-red ball, pushing upward out of the sea toward the pink-and-grey streaked heavens. And he could see the sweep of the coast, jagged and grimly outlined against the still sky. In the dawn's haze, they marched straight into the deep-colored waters. He swayed imperceptibly while the sun slowly rose till it cleared the sea and, as if suspended by invisible threads, brightened the water and land and mountains. Two small Spanish fishing boats—their unblinking "eyes" peering sightlessly from their prows—chugged slowly eastward.

Pamela sighed. And the spell spilled over into their bed.

Cal finished his coffee, wiped his lips, folded the napkin, set it on the small table and lit a cigarette. Through the smoke, he squinted at Pamela. "Where do you come from?" he asked at last.

Her eyes widened. "I've already told you—the States—and the Santa Maria convent in Malaga." She smiled. "I'm playing hooky."

"I mean, what's with you?"

She wrinkled her brows. "Do you think I'm mysterious?"

He stretched his legs, accidentally kicking her under the small table. "Excuse me."

Pamela smiled her little smile again. She could turn it on and off like a neon sign.

"Frankly, young lady . . . ah, Miss Strong . . . the only thing I really know is that you're here. And that's what bothers me."

"Why should that bother you?"

"Why me?" he persisted.

"Why not? You're a rather handsome specimen, in a dishevelled sort of way. With a certain kind of promise."

He puffed on his cigarette. "Do you often pick up strangers whenever the fancy strikes you?"

Cal had expected a hurt expression combined with an

angry riposte. Instead, Pamela's full mouth framed a patient smile. "Would it upset you if I said I did?" she asked, softly.

Answer a question with a question, he thought, that's what my ex always did. "I don't owe you," he said.

"That's true."

Standing up, Cal butted his cigarette. "I've got to meet somebody. In Marbella." He walked to the bathroom doorway, turned and looked back at her, still seated at the table, her coffee cup halfway to her mouth.

"I'll be around all day," she said, reading his mind. "That's if you don't have any objections."

Her faint smile annoyed him while he shaved.

21-5-66 0955 hrs GMT

File: AH 1945

For prime ministerial and presidential eyes

only; to be hand delivered on receipt.

To: MI 5, CIA, RCMP (Operation Alois

Sibling desks)

Third Party escort collects Printer.

Field insists Society Leader

Spain bound.

                                      Control.

CHAPTER 8

✸

"You've had breakfast, Señor Sanders?" Paco Rivera asked. It was only a mid-morning sun but sweat stains were already building up under his arms.

"Si, amigo. At the hotel."

"Pity. I serve good breakfast, too. Churros and coffee."

"Churros?"

"Like your donuts. But without the holes. A beer, perhaps?"

"No, gracias. How about your coffee?"

Cal felt better than he had in days. He should have been tired. He sipped the hot black coffee. Too strong for his stomach, he mused, setting it aside.

"Ah, then we'll bring you Nescafé and water and sugar and you can mix your own," Paco announced.

"What about the brigata? When do I get to see him?"

Paco shrugged, expressively. *"Lo siento.* I am sorry. But he has not returned." His eyebrows shot up. "Perhaps tonight? Don't look so sad, Señor. There is someone who wishes to see you. He is watching you now."

Cal's eyes followed Paco Rivera's. Seated several tables

across from him, smiling enigmatically, was Carl Heindemann, pink-faced and immaculate in a white summer suit.

"So," Cal said, with exaggerated politeness after brief hellos, "there's a small businessman who needs his finances audited—for his own good—here in sunny Marbella?"

"You have an excellent memory for details, Mr. Sanders."

"But we aren't here to discuss memories, are we Mr. Heindemann. Or should I say Oberleutnant Heindemann?"

Heindemann smiled faintly. "Are you working your diesels up for a fast surface run, my friend, Cal?"

Touché, thought Cal. "Okay, Carl. Let's only go back to Paco Rivera. He said you wanted to see me. That's on the square. Another is: What-in-hell's going on?"

"How many squares do you wish to go back?"

"Like to Frau Getz. She's dead. You knew that, didn't you?"

"I did. But before we go too far back, may I ask you why you are in Marbella? When did you arrive?"

"What if I said I was on holidays. Would you believe that?"

Heindemann's eyes glittered in the sun. "You followed me. Yes. That's it. Someone at my office gave it away."

"Why was Frau Getz murdered?"

A vein in Carl Heindemann's jaw twitched. "Tragic," he said. "And so unnecessary. She could tell them nothing."

"Who's them?"

"Czech agents. The same three who died in the car crash later during that night, such stupid tactics. Even after that, they should not have pursued you. You could tell them nothing, either. But you could lead them into a row of trees. Couldn't you?" He uncrossed his legs and looked away. "But the Czechs are incompetent. Or appear to be. Perhaps because their hearts aren't in this business. They don't like the KGB. You knew that, didn't you?"

"Then why send them at all?"

Heindemann flicked two fingers across his jacket lapel. "Because the KGB had no one else available at the moment. Ach!" He shook his head in disgust. "They do what they are ordered to do. When the KGB talks, Iron Curtain agents listen. And obey."

"If the Getz woman had nothing to say, then where did she fit?" Cal asked.

"Her husband, an ex-U-boat unteroffizier, I suspect was a key player in the 'hunt.' Unhappily, he died a month before. Heart attack, his physician said."

Cal watched a Ford wagon with a New York State license plate move slowly along the avenida. The rear seats were down, jammed with kids. So, he thought, staring out into the roadway, there's the link. And he doesn't know I picked up a message the night she was murdered. Maybe, he thought ironically, he does, but it's not worth a tinker's damn anymore with the occupant of 11 Calle San Ramon dead.

"Would you like a cerveza? Beer?" Heindemann asked. He ordered two and paid. "Something is bothering you, my friend."

"Where do you fit in this society, or 'hunt,' as you call it?" he asked.

Carl Heindemann tightened his lips into a single line, then sighed. "At this point, it could be fatal to admit more than what you already know—I am involved."

Cal lit a cigarette, offering the package.

"No. No thank you." He slipped one hand inside his jacket and removed a Dutch cigar. "But I shall enjoy one of these."

"What was Don Juan Ricardo's real name?" Cal asked. "The legless man."

Heindemann's narrow eyes flickered in surprise for a split-second before he said: "Freiherr Joachim Heinrichs. He lost his legs when his U-boat was accidentally rammed by a training ship while on maneuvers in the Baltic. A good man. And yes, he was a key player in the 'hunt.'"

"A personal friend?"

"Some said he was an ardent Nazi. I never believed that. He was too intelligent. He was a friend." The German blew a slim stream of cigar smoke into the sunlight. Cal realized he didn't inhale. "You know, of course, that he is dead?"

"I stood outside when they carried him out of the casa on the Calle San Ramon."

Heindemann stared at him for almost a minute, a cryptic smile tugging at his thin lips. He took two short puffs on his cigar before he said: "Of course. Frau Getz passed his address on to you." He nodded as if he was pleased with himself. "There was no other way you could obtain his address. What else did she tell you?"

"I never really talked with the lady, except when I checked my coat."

"Ah. Then she placed the address in your coat pocket. I never knew her, but obviously she was clever." Carl Heindemann chuckled. "And so you hurried off to Marbella."

"Correct."

"What else have you discovered? Did you expect to meet me?"

"Nothing. And no."

The sun was strong. Almost directly overhead.

Heindemann leaned forward. "And you are here because you sense a good story. Or should I say 'feature'?"

The German's evenly spaced words irritated Cal. "Even if I wasn't a reporter who smells a good story, you should remember I have been shot at. Not to mention the drunk who tried to run me off the road last night just east of this town."

The former U-boater's pale eyebrows lifted. His face tightened. "Are you positive it was a drunk?"

"All I could see in the darkness was the lights from his car. When I hit the field, he was gone in a flash."

"Hmmm."

"What's that supposed to indicate?"

"Have you considered returning home? After all, your only contact—if you exclude me—is dead." He smiled thinly. "Unless, of course, you have some other information. Do you have something, ah, special?"

Cal shook his head. "My editor asked me the same question."

"And what did you tell him?"

"Exactly what I'm telling you. Nothing."

Carl Heindemann's facial muscles relaxed slowly. "You

cannot want revenge. The Czechs who tried to take your life are dead," he said. "Strange. But then, most North Americans are strange . . ."

Perhaps because we're not as bloody minded, Cal thought. Nor as cunning.

"Perhaps because your ethics are clear-cut: good versus evil. A kind of eternal competition between the two feeds your drive. With Europeans, it has never been that clear-cut. Always there were real or mythical wrongs to be righted."

Carl's lips framed a hollow smirk.

"That is not becoming, my friend. Did you know that?" The lines on either side of Heindemann's thin mouth were deep. He straightened his shoulders.

"Even if I concede what you're saying," Cal interrupted, "I'm only saying . . ."

Heindemann interrupted: "Patience, my friend. Allow me to finish. Nazism *was* real. And our code, as onetime German officers, insists the bill for *their* conduct be stamped *paid in full*."

"I'm not into codes of conduct, yours or mine," grated Cal, impatiently. "Now let me ask you a question: Why did you tell me—a casual acquaintance—as much as you did a couple of nights ago in your home? First, my friend, you set the table at the so-called reunion, then you served the entree. Why?" Absently, he rubbed his stomach, as if attempting to untangle the knots he felt were forming. "Why?"

The German placed his small cigar precisely in the ashtray and watched the smoke curl upwards until it disappeared. "Because, as I have said and say again, I instinctively trusted you," he said.

Cal grunted. He needs me, he thought. And he clucked his tongue against the roof of his suddenly dry mouth. But he still hasn't said why.

Carl Heindemann stood up. "Come, my friend. We shall take a walk."

They stood in the municipal market, surrounded by stalls piled high with oranges, rice, eggs and the largest cabbages and cauliflowers Cal had ever seen. The babble from the buyers and sellers was unceasing.

All under the eyes of two policemen whose duty was to bring to a successful compromise any complaints of cheating or price gouging, Heindemann explained. They watched people buying ham by the slice or a chicken by the wing or leg; or the biggest jackrabbits he had ever seen still encased in their fur. One thing was familiar: the smell.

Siesta began. The market stalls were closing. The crowds in the narrow calles and avenidas thinned until they were virtually alone—two *touristas* who didn't know enough to go back to their hotels.

"We were discussing trust. And instincts. Nein?"

Cal nodded. They climbed the steepening road up toward the ruins of an old Moorish castle.

"Well, first, let us discuss instincts, instincts honed under the grueling rules of war. They tell me we are reaching a critical point in our game. Not simply because there is a very wildschwein at bay, if I may use my hunting analogy."

"Wild boar?" Cal interrupted.

"A former Nazi who was the epitome of villainy."

"Such as a Martin Bormann?" Cal scoffed: "Hell, he's been reported in every city between Buenos Aires and Moscow! Once my editor wanted me to fly to Uruguay . . . on spec!"

"Bormann was a pig," Heindemann responded, gently. "But not dangerous. And never at bay. He would flee. No, a great wildschwein. And we believe we know where this boar can be found."

"Then bag him and your problems are over. And I've got my story."

The ex-oberleutnant smiled faintly. It was a sailor's smile, reflecting the secret union with the watery universe every mariner feels. "Patience, my friend. Your story will come in good time. Our immediate problem is more pressing: I fear we have a mole in the game."

"A mole? You mean a Judas?"

"Exactly. And I shall tell you why. Two months ago, an undercurrent of conflicting reports began circulating throughout our society. Too often they were quite contradictory. What they insisted is not important. But what they did was confuse the network. We concluded—because we

THE LAST HUNTER

sensed we were closing in on the wildschwein—that someone was attempting to steer us in another direction."

Heindemann looked back over his shoulder, down the deserted red-clay path leading to Marbella.

"If that conclusion was correct, there was a traitor who had violated a sacred German officer's oath. Which, in turn, made the game even more dangerous than I suggested it was when you visited my home." Heindemann's voice was almost a whisper.

Cal lit a cigarette and puffed raggedly. If he's telling me this much, he's going to deal me into this goddamned hunt, he thought. His stomach churned. And I don't know half the rules. *"Now,"* he said, "you are not suggesting I go home . . ."

The ex-U-boater's eyes were fixed on the horizon. Slowly, he swung his head and stared at Cal. "I leave that to you, my friend. But consider the facts. Frau Getz passed you a message. I believe I know why. Knowing nothing about her late husband's activities, she reached out to you: the journalist who wrote the story on von Hagen's killing."

"I figured that out," said Cal.

"I, too. It is the only explanation."

"So?"

"But why was Freiherr Joachim Heinrichs' address in the Calle San Ramon so important?"

Cal dropped his cigarette and squashed it with his shoe. "I have no idea. Was he the mole?"

Heindemann shook his head. "Hardly, if he was murdered by, shall we say, the KGB. Yet, he must have known who that mole was. It is the only conclusion I can reach," he said.

"Are you inviting me to join your group?" Cal asked.

Heindemann smiled. "In the light of the shooting in Toronto—the 'drunk' on the coastal road—that is no longer under discussion, nein?"

Cal grunted.

The German looked up at the ruins of the castle. "The Moors were Arabs," he said. "And they were very tolerant conquerors. They didn't exterminate either Christians or Jews. They built magnificent palaces. You should visit Granada before you return home. Pause to admire the

Alhambra. It is a splendid example of Moorish architecture at its peak. Do you know why these ancient descendants of the men of the desert surrounded themselves with splashing fountains? The sound constantly reminded them of the dry world they came from, making them more determined to hold onto what they had created."

The Alameda parking lot was almost empty when they returned.

"Have you ever heard of El Perro Negro?" Cal broke the silence.

Heindemann laughed. "Oh yes; it's what people today—the tourists anyway—call an English pub. It's up the coast a piece. In Fuengirola. On the street nearest the sea. Today's generation of young Germans, in particular, like to sing and drink British ale of a night. Why?"

"Because Paco Rivera said he didn't know where it was, I guess."

"Did Señor Rivera say that?" The German continued to laugh. "He knows where it is. He probably said that because he didn't want to lose your business. Cafe owners everywhere are like that." He tapped Cal's shoulder lightly. "Would you like to go there?"

"I just might," Cal answered.

"Tonight?" Cal nodded. Heindemann said, "I shall meet you there. Shall we say nine-thirty? Good. Now, if you would kindly drive me to the Marbella Club, I shall be most grateful, for hill-climbing was never my choice of exercise." He looked up at the cloudless sky. "Ideal weather," he noted. "But it is also spring in Paris."

"What can we expect to find at El Perro Negro?" asked Cal.

"I understand Joachim Heinrichs often went there. To meet a friend."

They drove to the Marbella Club in silence.

"Would you like to come in and have a drink?" Heindemann asked after Cal had braked the Fiat to a stop.

"No thanks."

The German glanced at the low facade of the club, then at his hands. "You have acquired a travelling companion, my friend?"

THE LAST HUNTER

The gently worded question startled Cal. "Christ!" he said, "isn't there anything you don't know about?"

Heindemann's hand was on the Fiat's open door. "Do you know who she is?"

"An American."

"Living in Spain?"

"Travelling," Cal lied, glibly.

The ex-U-boater officer's pale eyes searched Cal's face. He closed the car door. "Be careful, my friend," he said. "Always be careful."

Cal watched Heindemann enter the club.

Pamela wasn't at the hotel. But she was among the sand dunes, stretched out, dozing on the beach towel. She heard him laboring through the fine sand.

"It's you, isn't it?" she asked, sleepily.

"Who else did you expect?"

"Don't be snide, Cal. It's not becoming. Kiss me, old man." She stood up and they embraced. "Now I can strip."

Cal got down to his undershorts (he hadn't been certain she would be there so he hadn't worn trunks), and declined to make love in public.

"But there's no one watching, my dear old Victorian prince. Well," she laughed, brushing grains of sand off her breasts, "then let's talk."

"I'm tired. Very tired. I'm going to sleep a while."

"I don't know why you're tired now. You certainly weren't last night. Or early this morning." She shook him, gently. "Are you going to sleep with a naked young lovely beside you? Yes, I believe you are."

Pamela was sitting up in her bikini when he awoke in a puddle of perspiration.

"Some people came by so I put it on," she said.

Cal sat up. "Where are they?"

She giggled. "I think the size of you—looking like a beached whale—discouraged them. They sat one dune over, talking, then left."

"Men?"

"Women don't frighten me."

She made a wry face. "So, tell me about your meeting."

He scooped up two hands full of sand and let it trickle slowly through his thick fingers. "Nothing much to tell," he replied, suddenly remembering Heindemann's words: Be careful. Always be careful. He peered at her obliquely. She was almost up on her tiptoes, staring out over the dune at the sea. It was as if she had simply forgotten she had even asked him a question. Or didn't expect an answer.

Sticky with sweat, he sighed wearily. What the hell am I doing here, stinking like an old dog who had rolled around in a carcass, becoming paranoid about answering a leggy American woman's casual question?

"I ought to be back on my beat," he said.

Pamela swung around. "What brought that on?"

He wanted to grin. But he couldn't shake the German's words out of his mind. He said, "Nothing. I'm going to El Perro Negro tonight."

"Good, I'll go with you."

Cal rubbed his nose. "Maybe. What about this excursion bus you're supposed to catch up with?"

She slowly stroked her thighs. It made him think of a cat. "Now, don't get upset Cal. There is no excursion bus. But there is a convent. And I am a student."

Suddenly, he grabbed her tote bag, shook it open and pulled out her passport. "I was brought up never to do this, but there's got to be a first time," he said, grimly.

She yanked it out of his hand, opened it and passed it back. "There. I am Pamela Strong. Single. Twenty. And I have a Spanish student's visa. Satisfied?"

He returned it.

She said: "After we landed at Madrid, I phoned the school and pretended I was an American state official. I told the night house mother—an old nun—that Pamela Strong was still recovering from mono; that she would be delayed a few more days. The poor dear didn't understand much English, but she got the point."

"What on earth for?" Cal asked.

"I had my reasons. I'll tell you sometime. Probably. Now, may I go to El Perro Negro with you?"

Cal leaned back on his elbows. "Not dressed like that, you can't. Not in your slit dress."

When Pamela bent over, her breasts almost escaped

from her skimpy top. She hugged him. "I knew you'd say yes, but I didn't know you'd be jealous." She pressed him onto his back.

"I'm too old to get jealous," he murmured, stirred by the feel of her bare skin.

"Nonsense! Only older men get jealous anymore. Most of the younger ones haven't the time. There's too much sex waiting for them at the next taxi stand."

Cal gently but firmly pushed her away. "Let's go back to the hotel."

"I knew you wouldn't make love in the sand," she gasped. "I just knew you wouldn't."

At the hotel, he sent a wire to Limey Lewis: "Found a friend."

El Perro Negro backed onto the beach, behind a line of tall, high-topped palm trees. And except for a two-storey section just beneath a clump of pines, it was long, low and lit up brightly by a bank of lights perched atop a pair of tall poles which flooded the hard-packed-sand front-side parking lot. Between the lot and road stood a row of pines. The neon outline of a dog, up on his hind paws, hung from a black, wrought-iron bar over the double doors. And a persistent, but soft, wind blew in off the Mediterranean, stirring the palm fronds and pine needles. All under a solemn moon.

Pamela took Cal's arm and hugged it. "That's the *poniente*, darling. And it blows in from North Africa, bringing madness. Some say old pirates come alive, walking the playas, searching for buried treasure and lost loves."

"They say that, do they?"

"But only blondes. *Las rubias.*"

Someone was thumping out "Roll Out The Barrel" on a piano and Cal began to hum. The ragged chorus of men's and women's voices sang lustily. With German accents. Low-beamed and walled-in pine had been brought to a high polish with varathane. And the globular lights glowed. Picnic-style heavy wooden benches, every one of them occupied, separated the leather-backed, leather-cushioned cubicles and a small planked dance floor. In the far corner on a raised platform sat the piano player, a derby on his head, his sleeves rolled up, exposing skinny arms.

"My gawd," Cal yelled in Pam's ear, "they couldn't make it any noisier in here if they had a rock group!"

She took his hand and led him across the floor to a two-seat space against the far wall. He stared through the smoke and lights at the bar. A wide-faced woman in her forties stood behind it, her elbows on the shiny top. A toothy smile plastered her mouth. Next to her was an older man, lean and slightly stooped. He had a cadaverous look. And his eyes continually swept the room, taking in the faces of his too scrubbed, too tanned, mobiled-faced youthful customers. Cal caught his eye for only an instant and a waiter appeared.

"Cerveza?" he asked Pam.

She nodded, her mouth slightly open, her lips moist.

They clinked glasses. "Well, at least the waiters are Spanish."

There was a break in the piano playing.

"Ah," Cal said, gratefully. "Tell me something, my sweet young thing, are the Spaniards a race of lispers? Or am I hearing them wrong?"

She drank half her glass of beer chug-a-lug. "It's an affectation. Want to know why?"

"Sure."

"Well, back in the late fifteenth century, when Ferdinand of Aragon married Isabella of Castile, they decided the twin kingdoms would drive the Moors out of all of Spain. They did. By 1497. But that's not the story, is it?"

"I don't know, you're doing the talking."

"So I am. Anyway, Ferdinand was a mighty warrior. But he lisped. Now it wasn't a very slick idea to mimic such a man, and to avoid any kind of faux pas that could cost one one's head, all the courtiers began to imitate his speech impediment." Pam picked up her beer and finished it. "We need another."

Cal lifted the empty glasses. The gaunt man noticed. The waiter brought two more.

Pam continued: "Over the years, the affectation seeped down to the average peasant. Until they all talked like Ferdinand. Even after he had died."

"Do you expect me to believe that?" Cal asked.

She laughed, tossing her head. "That's what they say. And that's also why the New World Spanish don't lisp. Unless of course they're wealthy and were educated in Spain."

Cal frowned.

"Oh," she said, "you obviously weren't educated in a Spanish nunnery. Think about it. By the time the Castillian lisp, as it is called, trickled down from the court, the Conquistadores and their followers were long gone. So, they couldn't take it with them to Mexico!"

Cal was going to say "I see" but the piano player was thumping again: "Lili Marlene." He began in march time, but gradually slowed the tempo. The drinkers stopped talking, watching him or staring into their steins. First one voice, then another, until a dozen had picked up the words. In German.

Vor der Kaserne, vor dem grossen Tor
Stand eine Laterne und Steht sie noch davor.

They aren't shouting the words, Cal thought, his eyes scanning their faces while they sang the melody. Their blond heads swung in slow motion as if someone was directing them.

So woll'n wir uns da wiederseh'n
Bei der Lanterne woll'n wir steh'n

They belong to the new generation, he reflected, bringing his beer to his mouth. And he added to himself: I wonder if I killed any of their fathers when we were up against the wolfpacks?

Wie einst Lili Marlene, wie einst Lili Marlene . . .

He joined them when they sang the line again: *Wie einst Lili Marlene, wie einst Lili Marlene . . .*

The piano player tipped his derby when he got a sustained hand.

Pamela put her hand on his and looked into his face. Her eyes were damp. "That was very melancholy," she said, softly. "Bittersweet."

"It was originally a love song about a soldier going off to war who wanted one more night with his love," Cal said. "But pop versions turned it into a goose-stepping march because that's what we thought a German song should be." He kissed her gently and struggled with an urgent desire to hug her. Instead, he stroked her cheek. She closed her eyes.

The woman behind the bar even smiled when she served beer. And so did the young German who asked Pam to dance during an impromptu polka that clogged the small floor with exuberant, whirling couples. No thank you, she told him, firmly. She glanced at Cal after he had left. "And you don't have to sit there and shrug. He wasn't asking you to dance!" she said, then softened and traced the outline of his mouth with her fingertips. "You don't have many wrinkles."

"And I don't have many polkas left in me, either," he replied, grinning. I'm getting tight, he thought, trying to remember how many beers he'd had. It didn't matter. Again he glanced around the room. There was no sign of Heindemann.

The piano player swung into "Elmer's Tune."

"Surely you jitterbug!" said Pam.

He was going to say "Nobody would be safe on that little dance floor if I did" when he heard what sounded like two firecrackers going off outside the windows facing the parking lot. They were followed by peremptory shouts. He froze. The milling dancers froze. A car door was opened and slammed shut. Another. Cal felt Pam's long fingers close tight on his left arm. "What was that?" she hissed.

Two more firecrackers went off. Louder. Distinctly spaced. Someone revved up a car motor until it began to whine. There was a staccato burst of gunfire. A voice cried, "Los Basques! Terroristas!" The lights went out.

Cal shook off Pam's hand and, bent low, almost on his hands and knees scuttled across the floor in the direction of the entrance. He sensed Pam was right behind him. Two car doors slammed shut in quick succession. Funny, he thought, I didn't hear them open. The engine was screeching now. Tires squealed. He felt for the brass knob, turned it and pushed one of the double-doors open. The parking lot was silvery white in the glow of the floodlights. And the rear red lights of a fishtailing, quick-moving, black sedan lurched out onto the coastal road. It turned east and, bucking as the driver changed gears, raced into the black night toward Torremolinos.

Cal straightened up. Behind him, a man yelled, "Silencio!" He barked it again, louder, over the scream of the whining engine in the black limousine at the far side of the parking lot. A thin layer of grey-blue smoke eddied from an open rear door.

"Stay where you are!" Cal snapped at Pamela, loping over to the limo. The smell of gunpowder was still strong. Whoever had pulled the trigger on the submachine gun had sprayed the back seat. He checked for the driver. Two shots had struck him in the face, flinging him across the seat. His hatless head was tilted grotesquely over the arm rest, exposing a long, thin neck. His right leg was extended, his foot jammed against the accelerator. Cal opened the door, reached across and pulled the leg free. The engine sighed, then coughed and was silent when he turned the ignition off.

"My God!" It was Pamela.

"God had nothing to do with it!" growled Cal. "I thought I told you to stay back?"

"Terrorists? Why?"

Cal closed the limo door. On it, neatly stenciled in grey letters: Marbella Club. He grunted.

The lights inside El Perro Negro flared. Excited men and women scrambled through the double doors, onto the hard packed sand. Wide-eyed, they moved hurriedly toward their cars. Half a dozen motors jangled into life before the wow-wow-wow and flashing lights of two Civil Guard vehicles barred the only exit to the highway.

Cal peered again into the empty rear of the limo. The gunpowder odor was fainter. Clusters of empty bullet casings littered the sand. He picked one up and dropped it into his trouser pocket. Swinging around, he found Pamela's hand. "C'mon, let's get back inside. The police are going to ask questions. Remember, only answer what you're asked. Nothing more."

She nodded, gripping his fingers tightly.

They stood inside the English bar. What had been a party of high, happy drinkers was a ragtag collection of sober, pale—despite their tans—witnesses, seated at the wooden tables.

The gaunt man stood behind the bar. "That was quick thinking," he said to the woman, "pulling the switch. It's not as easy to break the place up when you're not sure where you can run."

The police were polite, but laconic. They demanded passports. "I brought ours," Pamela said. "I knew you wouldn't have yours." They waited their turn.

"You are a journalist? On holidays?"

"That's right. Staying at the Los Monteros. Been there three days." Cal got his passport back.

"The officer touched his patent leather hat. "And you, Señorita—ah, Strong?" He coughed behind a hand too small for a man so tall.

The cheekbones in Pamela Strong's tanned face worked gently. "I *was* a student, as my visa says, but I have left school. I'm getting engaged."

"A most fortunate man, Señorita. Is he here?"

She slipped her left arm inside Cal's. "Señor Sanders. You just spoke to him."

The Spaniard's face was bland, but his eyes glistened. "Then both of you are registered at the Los Monteros?"

"We are."

"Be kind enough to remain there for a day or two. Por favor? We may wish to interview you later." He handed Pam her passport.

"Gracias, hidalgo!" she replied.

"What the hell did you tell him we were both registered for?" Cal asked as they drove out of Fuengirola. "They'll check that and find out . . ."

She laughed. "Would you like to lay some good Yankee money on that, darling? Spanish hotelmen aren't stupid. But they are discreet. And tactful. The minute they knew I was staying with you, I was registered. I'll guarantee that."

It made him feel uncomfortable.

"That bothers you, doesn't it? Yet you didn't bat an eye when I said we were getting engaged."

"I never gave it a thought."

Pamela slid across the seat and rested her head on his shoulder. "I'll just bet you didn't," she said.

"Christ!" he blurted aloud. "How did they know he was supposed to meet me at El Perro Negro?"

Pamela's voice was muted and small. "Who darling?"

Cal wheeled the Fiat along the coastal road. "Nothing," he said. "I'm only thinking out loud."

"About what?"

"The shooting."

"You heard the policemen. It was Basque terrorists."

No it wasn't, he said to himself. No it wasn't. One of the beer drinkers—or waiters—yelled that. After the shooting began.

Cal brought the car to a halt on the Los Monteros lot. But his mind was still moving.

In the darkness, Pamela asked: "Then who was it?"

Cal shook his head. "Let's get out of here. And go to our room. I've got a phone call to make."

The night clerk at the Marbella Club was certain. Señor Heindemann was in his room. But he was not accepting calls. Or visitors. Cal hung up.

"Who was that, darling?" Pam called from the bathroom.

"Just a friend," he replied. "I'm going to have a drink. Or two. I think I need it. Want one? There's only scotch." He splashed two fingers into the tumbler, adding soda. "Are you old enough to drink?"

"If I'm old enough to bed, I'm old enough to drink scotch," she said, sitting on his lap.

"How do you like it?"

"I'll sip from yours. Ugh, it's warm. And with soda." She made a face.

Pamela Strong had beautiful twenty-year-old skin. Clear. Almost translucent. It distracted him. And why the hell isn't she sitting on a twenty-five-year-old's lap, he wondered.

"I really feel you have something to tell me," she said, "now that we're engaged."

Cal shook his head and began to smile. It turned into soft laughter. He opened his knees and she sank slowly to the broadloomed floor without saying a word. She stayed there, looking up at him. "Very funny. Speak, old man," she said and reached for his glass. He lifted it beyond her outstretched hand.

For a full minute he stared up at the ceiling. Then as if the words had been yanked out of him, he said: "Who in hell can you trust anymore?"

"What's that supposed to mean?"

He gulped down a mouthful of the tepid scotch and soda. "On the basis that it was *not* a Basque shootout, why was a Marbella Club limo shot up?"

"I don't know what you are getting at, my darling."

Cal's stomach rumbled. He blamed it on the warm soda. "*Who* knew that particular limo was going to arrive at El Perro Negro?"

"The Basques."

"Well, someone *knew*. That's for damned sure!"

Pamela averted her face. "I knew *you* were going to the club," she said almost absently. "Does that help?

With his free hand, he stroked her thick hair. "I don't think so. But I certainly wish I knew what the hell's coming down around me."

"Why bother?" Pamela's words sounded far away.

"Good point. But if the killings continue, someone's going to mess up and I'm liable to be a mistaken target. I'll guarantee that nameless little Spaniard in that limo didn't leave home today expecting to get shot to death."

"Not you, my love, not you! Not if I have anything to do with it!" She spit her words out so vehemently he was startled.

"That's reassuring," he said.

She climbed to her feet, kissed him lightly on the cheek. "Perhaps more than you'll ever know."

He poured another scotch, skipping the soda, and drank. This time, his stomach heaved. He listened to her in the bathroom, humming to herself until the sounds of running water cut it off. She emerged in her nightgown, holding a bright red dress.

"What is Cal short for?" she asked.

He blinked. "Calvin."

"Wasn't he a preacher?"

"That was John Calvin. Why do you ask?"

She tilted her head. "Well, we *are* engaged. And I really should know something about the man I'm going to marry. Isn't that so?"

Christ! he thought. We're thousands of miles from home. We've just escaped a shoot-up. And she wants to know where I'm coming from. He grunted. "You're the second person in two days who has wanted to know what I'm all about."

"Oh?" she asked. It was a very muted "oh."

Almost buried in his psyche a small bell began to ring.

"That's right."

"Who was he?" she asked, bending over and tipping his chin upward with her free hand, kissing him. It was a moist kiss. And their mouths were together for a long time. The bell stopped ringing. Finally, they parted. She sighed. "My God, what you do to me, my old darling!" she whispered softly.

She straightened up, slowly.

Cal sat there, fighting an urge to climb to his feet and begin unbuttoning her nightdress.

Pamela decided for him. "I'm tired, and I'm going to bed. Don't you sit there all night, trying to solve the problems of the world. Or what's happening around you. It never changes anything. Just remember that whatever you're into will pass."

Cal hiccuped. "Don't you think you should be getting back to your convent?"

She shook her head. "Too late, darling. I've already handled the problem. As I told that Spanish policeman, I'm not going back." Crossing the room, she hung the dress on a hanger in the closet. He watched her retreat to the bed and, in one quick motion, slide between the turned-back sheets.

"When did you get that dress?" he asked.

"While you were snoozing. Before we went to El Perro

Negro. Are you telling me you didn't even notice I had it on?"

Later, Cal undressed and climbed into bed behind Pamela. She muttered something in her sleep that he didn't understand. He slipped into a troubled reverie. Dreams punctuated with gunfire laced his mind. Once he awoke with a start, lathered in sweat. He sat up and stared down at her on her side, his eyes following the curve of her hip, the outline of one long leg drawn up almost to her chest. God, he thought, remorsefully, it must be great to be young.

22-5-66   1459 hrs GMT

File: AH 1945

For prime ministerial and presidential eyes
only; to be hand delivered on receipt.

To: MI 5, CIA, RCMP (Operation Alois
Sibling desks)

Third Party involved in Society Member
fatal Marbella. Society Leader flushed.
Shoot-out suggests Prize available.
Suggest Keepers go to condition Blue.

Control.

CHAPTER 9

✳

CARL HEINDEMANN GLANCED at Cal cursorily. "You are getting sunburned, my friend."

"I'm red. But that's the way I tan. I'm not sore, if that's what you mean," Cal replied.

La Sportiva had a high-noon crowd. The Britons drank gin and tonic. The Germans and Americans enjoyed beer and the Spanish sipped scotch. A dirt-streaked little gypsy girl with a round, doll-like face, her tiny baby brother (or cousin?) hitched over one hip like a young mother, was begging: "Peseta! Peseta!" She repeated the words in a litany. Cal watched her collect a handful of coins before she came up against Paco Rivera. He dropped a bill into her tiny hand and shooed her away.

"Hah!" Cal called to the burly Spaniard. "I thought you said gypsies were the curse of Spain. And there you go handing out money!."

Paco shrugged. "They are a curse. But someone has to look after them. Si?"

Cal held the spent casing he had picked up outside El Perro Negro. He dropped it into Heindemann's hand.

"Probably fired from a Kalashnikov, the Soviet's duty

THE LAST HUNTER

submachine gun," the German said. "I was told there was heavy firing, briefly."

"Did you send the driver in the Marbella Club limo?"

"Why do you ask?"

"Did you send him to see me?"

"The reports indicate it was just another incident involving Los Basques," he said, obliquely.

"I happen to know you don't have a car. So, perhaps, you were sending a message to me." Cal didn't smile. "Because *someone* was waiting for *someone*. That limo wasn't shot up just for the hell of it."

"It was clumsy, was it not?"

Cal couldn't decide whether Heindemann meant he had been clumsy, sending the limo; or those waiting for it had been clumsy.

"You were there, of course," Heindemann went on smoothly, "with your companion."

"Yes." Cal lit a cigarette. "And it had nothing to do with any Basques."

Heindemann nodded, almost affably.

Annoyed, Cal said: "I believe they were waiting for *you*!" He inhaled, watching the German. "And what bothers me is how in hell did *they* know *you* and *I* were going to meet at El Perro Negro?"

"If we agree that someone knew—and informed Soviet agents—then what do we have to go on? Any names? Suspects?"

Cal opened his mouth to speak, but Heindemann silenced him with a hard stare. "Cal, my friend, one would only dig one's grave and waste time, sitting around trying to logically come to a winning conclusion. That is for students in sidewalk cafes, not men involved in a struggle to survive. We must act."

Cal swallowed hard. It's "we" now, he thought.

"They cremated the good Joachim Heinrichs late yesterday," Heindemann said, switching the conversation so suddenly, Cal swallowed again. "The Spanish do not inter their own Catholics that quickly. But Joachim was a Lutheran. If he was anything. Thus, I did not have the opportunity to pay my last respects."

"Sorry."

The German's shoulders twitched inside his summer suit. "I did not get to attend many of my U-boat colleagues' final passing, either. Often there were no survivors. As the history books will tell you," Heindemann said almost wistfully, then leaned forward. "Cal," he said, lowering his voice, "I must ask you to do something."

Cal searched the sharp face and mentally counted: one, two, three, four. The German's blue eyes didn't waver. "Name it," Cal said, finally.

"There may be some danger . . ."

Six people dead, not counting a limo driver, Cal thought.

"But if all goes well, it should be minimal." He paused. "I would like you and your companion to leave the country. Either tonight or, at the latest, tomorrow." Heindemann's words were barely audible across the table.

"Why the girl?"

"Trust me. She must go with you."

"Christ!"

"The Deity has nothing to do with it."

"But why the girl?" Cal repeated.

Heindemann glanced briefly into the Alameda. "It is, I believe, better that she go with you. I apologize, my friend, but that is the way it has to be."

"So be it," Cal said. "But there could be a small problem. I don't know if the Spanish will like it if we leave for . . .?"

"Gibraltar. Why?"

"Last night, the police suggested rather strongly we stay around for a few days."

The German's grey eyebrows came together. "You didn't get into any involved questions and answers with the police?"

"I knew better than that. I played *tourista*."

"Good. Then they formally asked you to remain. For a time. That is routine and can be fixed."

Cal blew acrid smoke out of his lungs and inhaled clean Costa del Sol air. "Will the okay come to the hotel?"

"It will." Heindemann stood up. They shook hands. "I shall get word to you on the precise time," he said. "By the way, do you have a pistol, my friend?"

"No."

THE LAST HUNTER

• • •

The call came from the Civil Guard. Cal Sanders and Pamela Strong were free to leave.

"What does that mean?" she asked, standing on one leg, trying to slip her other foot into a high-heeled pump. "I like being with you. You're tall. And I can wear spikes if I want."

Pamela had an infuriating way of asking a question, Cal reflected. "It means we're free to leave. That's all."

"Are *we* leaving?"

"I will. You're going back to school."

She pouted. "Let's not get into that again. And stop being obtuse." She half-turned away. "Look, why don't you have a shower, then we'll dine here at the hotel. The cuisine is excellent. Hmmmm?"

Cal was rinsing when she stepped into the tub-shower. He felt her hands circle his waist and her nipples against his back. She pulled him firmly to her body and ran her fingers over his groin. "Now!" she whispered. The water hissed warmly to the climax.

The string ensemble's chamber music gently flowed and eddied through the darkened dining room. Pamela had asked for a martini; he, Black Label on the rocks.

"This kind of music gets to me," he said absently, surveying the tables, half of them empty, each guarded by a silent waiter in his short, red jacket.

"That's composer Georg Telemann," she said.

"Whoever he is. Or was."

"He was a contemporary of Wolfgang Amadeus Mozart."

"Never heard of him. Telemann, I mean."

She sipped her martini. "It's soothing; unobtrusive. Why don't you like it?"

Cal lit a cigarette. "When I was a kid, there were a lot of period movies. With the ladies in hooped dresses, painted moles on their cheeks, the men in elegant velvet coats and powdered wigs. All pre-French Revolution. The rich and titled lived it up while the peasants were hungry; do you understand what I'm trying to say?"

She nodded.

"It smelled of death and decay. I'm always reminded of that when I hear this kind of music."

"Do you think times have changed much?"

A waiter moved to Cal's shoulder. "I think we should order," he said. He glanced over the embossed menu in its imitation velvet cover. The descriptions of dishes like squid and spicy paella made his stomach twinge.

Pamela ordered shrimp cocktail and Catalonian-style *butifara con judia*— pork sausage and beans—followed by a flan—custard. He opted for filet mignon, skipping the shrimp and custard. They accepted the waiter's advice and a ruby-red bottle of Valdepenas.

Cal spread his napkin in his lap. "Do I think times have changed? Yes. Now *we're* the peasants. At least I'm one. But we're a hell of a lot better off than they were when chamber music was served up in the royal courts."

"That's not what some of my friends say."

"Who are your friends?"

"Oh, just people I know. Not schoolgirls, either."

"And what do they know that I don't know?"

She finished her martini. "Teachers. Ah, some professors I've met . . ."

The waiter served the shrimp cocktail. She prodded the pink crustaceans in their skimpy lettuce bed, selected one and forked it to her mouth. "You know, professors. They teach at . . ."

"Yes, I know. Universities. What do they *know*?"

"The poor simply get poorer. The rich get richer and more powerful." She bit into another shrimp. "That democracy is dead. It has no future as it exists."

Cal shook his head slowly. "It's funny, you know that? When I was at university—a long time ago, I'll admit—"

"Not so long ago, my dear old man."

"Well, in our freshman year, we thought our professors were very smart. Clever. By the third year, we weren't sure anymore. By our fourth, we *knew* most of them were out of touch with the real world. Oh yes, there were good ones. Hell, excellent ones. But too many of 'em reminded us of lab mice: Throw 'em out in a field and the owls and snakes would get every one on the first night."

Pamela had stopped chewing. "Meaning?"

"Meaning only that impressionable, raw students, governments, newspapers and TV commentators take them too seriously. Most self-thinking students who graduated into the working world remember them fondly, and recall that they lived in a kind of sterile, lab-type world where everything is controlled by immutable laws."

She bit off half a shrimp. "You mean the world isn't what it's supposed to be according to what we're taught, but is what it is?"

"Something like that."

The entrees appeared when she finished the shrimp. And the wine. In the soft, muted light, they ate in silence.

It was while sipping Manzanilla sherry that Pamela returned to the conversation. "I don't think you're being fair to professors when you make statements like those."

Cal had forgotten. "Such as?"

"That they're nothing more than lab mice. Out of touch with the real world."

Ah, he thought, lighting a cigarette. She's going to tell me they have excellent minds so it follows they are intelligent.

She frowned. "You're not listening."

"Yes I am."

"Then?"

She can form faint lines across her forehead when she frowns, he noted. But when the frown fades, so do the lines. "Pamela," he said at last, "I've met people with fine minds, but it was no guarantee they were practical. And it's practical people who make this world go, regardless of whether they work with their hands or brains."

She ran her tongue across her lower lip. "Still, there are too many inequalities. Even in America. Socialism could change much of it—if given the chance."

"If the voters go for it. Which they won't."

"Well, they don't because they are brainwashed by mindless politicians and big business," she returned.

Cal smiled. "I agree it *looks* like the guys on the street are fed a lot of pap about how good they've got it. But that's not why they won't buy the socialists' song from the high-brow top. It was a young guy, a member of the *lumpen proletariat*, as the left refers to them, who explained it: 'We're all capitalists,' he said over a beer and hamburger in a place I frequent back home. 'We want to own cars, houses, cottages. Not right quick, but some day. That's why I ain't ever gonna buy socialism.' "

"Quaint, if true."

He leaned across the table. "Some day, woman, we'll meet in good old Toronto and I'll take you there to meet the real people who drive the trucks, repair highways, deliver the mail."

Abruptly, she smiled. "You will?"

"Yes, and I'll introduce you as my daughter."

"And I'll tell them I'm your mistress. That should start some gossip!" She placed two fingers against his lips. "Do the *lumpen proletariat* gossip, my darling?"

Christ, he reflected as they stood up, she can change moods like a chameleon switches colors.

The same burning sun that had shone on the ancient Carthaginians and Romans when they fought over the Iberian Peninsula two thousand years earlier, punished the hordes of tourists who spent their deutsche marks, pounds sterling and American dollars in search of sex, peace and bargains. And the descendants of the original Celts and later Vandals still fished the sea, harvested the pockets of loam in the mountainous land and served the new conquerors. Only this time, the conquerors with money had turned sleepy, sun-splashed villages like Marbella, San Pedro di Alicante and Estapona into groves of high, white-walled hotels and apartamentos, and clogged the narrow highway and streets with expensive cars.

And the twentieth-century Spaniard, a complex combination of the serious and happy sides of life, retained his inbred fatalism and watched without prejudice. I am here, he would say to himself. I am sure of that. But who are the others if both life and death are jokes?

Paco Rivera was a twentieth-century Spaniard. "Look at them, *los touristas*," he said, "always in a hurry. Don't they understand there are only twenty-four hours in a day; that even during a hundred lifetimes, this . . . all this," he waved his thick arms around him, "'is only a mirage? At best an excellent illusion?'"

He laughed darkly. "It is only eleven o'clock. I know that. But you look too serious. Have a beer, eh?"

Cal couldn't help himself. He laughed.

"I said something funny?" Paco asked.

"Nothing. Let's both have a beer."

Paco raised his black brows almost to his hairline, then lowered them. "Tonight. When I am a patron. Not now. I am the owner."

Cal's stomach didn't like early-morning beer. But he finished it, then stood up. He was halfway down the street when he heard Paco's shout.

"Señor! Señor! You forgot your package!" The burly Spaniard weaved through the tables, carrying a flat package above his head. "Your cigars, hombre. You must not forget your cigars!"

It contained a very small Baretta packed in tissue and wrapped in a single sheet of white paper. Cal smoothed it out. He read: "You will proceed to your sunbathing as you have. Take only the woman's bag and beach towel, the clothes you are wearing, your passports and money. Do not check out. Everything will be seen to. Gibraltar. Montarik. You will prefer the Casino." It was unsigned.

Cal tore up the note, scattering the pieces along the highway. He could feel the Baretta in his hip pocket when they drove to the beach. "Don't get down to the buff today, eh," he said to Pam while she spread the towel.

"Don't be silly, darling," she murmured, slipping off the bra and rolling the panties over her hips. "I enjoy sun bathing." She glanced at him, grinning. "Especially when I'm with you." She lay on her stomach.

The sun was beginning to parboil Cal. He sat up, examined the redness glowing on his chest and thighs and sighed. "I gotta get a shirt on," he said.

He was a sad-eyed Spaniard under a panama-style hat. And he spoke softly when he poked his head over the dune. "Perdone, Señorita," he said, "but Señor Sanders, eet is time to go." Even the sight of Pamela's bare back and bottom didn't change the melancholy expression on his pale face. He disappeared.

She rolled over and sat up. Her eyes narrowed. She struggled frantically to yank her beach towel from under her hips. Once. Twice. Then it came free. She wrapped it around her breasts and midriff.

"Who the hell was that?" she hissed.

"It doesn't matter," he said. "We have to go."

It was an old black sedan, with high rounded fenders and running boards. It made Cal think of Chicago mobsters.

"Well," Cal said, "yesterday you said 'we' would be leaving together. And here 'we' go."

She nodded.

"It's kind of late to have second thoughts . . ." he said, tentatively.

"Where *are* we going? And what about . . ."

"The car? Our clothes?"

"And who's he?" Pam nodded toward the driver.

Cal shrugged. "Forget 'em," he said. She snuggled against his bulk and was silent.

The Spaniard drove carefully, taking the partially paved road that climbed into the mountains to Coin. Staring at the stony-faced casas, the inevitable cathedral and treed plaza flanked by shops, Pam murmured: "Quaint and charming." Three men were herding a dozen pigs across the main road, yelling and smacking them with long rods to keep them in line. Patiently, their driver waited until the road was clear. Then, he took the route through the sierra to ageless, almost medieval Ronda.

"It was in the bull ring here that Manolete died on the horns of a black Miura bull," she said.

Cal was startled. He thought she had gone to sleep. "Who?"

Her face was quiet. "Manolete was a famous matador. Or so said Ernest Hemingway. Surely you've read Hemingway? Manolete was killed in this town. Or city. Whichever." She paused. "No, it was in the ring at Linares."

"If he was so good, how come he died?"

"The old-timers—the real aficionados—say his manager cheated, allowed him to fight bulls which had had their horns blunted. Or were too young. But when Franco took over, he restored the ancient bullfighting rules." She shrugged. "I guess when Manolete came up against a Miura that hadn't been tampered with—was too mature—he lost."

THE LAST HUNTER

They were riding through the mountains again.

"How do you know so much about bullfighting? Have you ever watched?" Cal asked.

"A few times. I saw El Cordobes once in Marbella. He's very quick. But a butcher at the kill. I would go with some of my Spanish classmates. And they would get very excited. Sexually turned on, I guess. Frantic."

"And you?"

"I don't think bullfighting is sexy."

Ninety minutes later, silent as he had been when they climbed inside the sedan, the Spaniard braked to a stop on the ferry dock at Algeciras.

Across the bay, Gibraltar rose out of the whitecapped black waters in the eastern reaches of the Atlantic Ocean. Up close, it reminded Cal of a primitive man's giant, sharp flintstone, flaked to a slope on the side facing Spain and steep (streaked with cement catch basins to save precious rain water) on the side facing Morocco.

Cal left Pamela at the stubby ferry's lower-deck door marked: *Señors, Señoritas, Herren, Damen*. He climbed the steel rungs to the upper deck of the Spanish ship, listening to the steady thunk-thunk of its diesel engine and bent over the railing. A sharp wind blew steadily. He eased the snub-nosed Baretta out of his hip pocket. It was almost hidden in his big hand. Staring down at the rushing water flecked with foam, he dropped it. Barely making a splash, it disappeared. He felt better.

The British Customs officer offered a skeptical welcome in the one-storey, windowed building separated by a single, wooden signal arm from the runway that served incoming and out-going commercial and RAF planes.

Glancing at them in their casual wear—and Pamela Strong's tote bag—he offered: "I trust you're staying with friends, tonight, for unless you turn right 'round, that's the last ferry to the Spanish mainland tonight." He motioned at the squat boat, tugging on its lines, rolling slightly in the swells.

"We have friends," said Cal. "It was just a sudden whim . . . to come here, I mean. We'll go back tomorrow."

The official returned their passports. "Enjoy yourselves."

"Where's the Montarik?"

"The hotel? So, that's where you're going! You can walk easily. Cross the runway, go 'round the meat market and just follow the main street. It'll only take a jiff. Mind, it's steep. All our streets are steep." He removed his hat and scratched his head. "Or you can get a taxi. Right outside the door."

The lobby of the Montarik was as compact as a country doctor's waiting room. And their double room, antiseptically clean in pastels, merely functional.

"I almost died laughing when that little man behind the desk suggested twin beds!" Pamela laughed, plumping both pillows and stretching out on the counterpane. "You acted like a husband, just standing there until I said double if you please." She stretched. "I think he thought I was your daughter."

Cal winced. "I've got a daughter damned near your age."

She jumped to her feet, crossed the carpet and kissed him tenderly. "I'm sorry, darling. I will never say anything like that again. Promise." He gently disengaged her arms. Goddamn, he thought. He kissed her.

"That's better," she said. "Now, tell me—what did all that word play between you and the manager mean?"

Cal told her about the note from Heindemann.

"So, your name must have been all that funny little man needed. That's why he asked if you preferred the casino. And why you agreed." She paused. "Are we going there, darling? It won't be Monte Carlo, but it'll be a nice place to lose some money."

Cal needed a drink. "I'm going downstairs for a whiskey."

"And leave me alone?"

"I won't be long."

"That little man on the desk said a tailor would be by with some suits and dresses. So, don't be, my darling."

Cal heard the lock turn in the door as he headed for the stairs.

The deskman remembered names. "Ah, Mr. Sanders," he greeted. "Can I help you?"

"Is your bar open?"

"No sir. Closed for alterations."

THE LAST HUNTER

Cal wondered vaguely if there was enough space in the entire building for a bar, let alone alterations.

"But just up the street, to your right, is the Mariners Pub. It's quite comfortable, sir."

There was a chill in the air, riding the breeze off the Atlantic Ocean. Cal looked up the narrow, steep street until his eyes became accustomed to the gloom. A car, parked slightly up the hill, was the only vehicle in sight. As he passed it, walking slowly, he wondered idly if everyone on the Rock went to bed early in the evening. The front door was flung open and a squat man leaped out. Cal strode to his right to avoid him, but not far enough. Iron fingers closed around his left forearm. A gun was jammed into his ribs. He gasped. In a quick move, the gunman had jostled so close to Cal, his mouth was almost in his left ear. "Don't move!" he grated hoarsely in unmistakable American. Swiftly, his free hand brushed against Cal's underarms, the small of his back and his thighs. "Now!" he added, "Get into the car!" The rear door opened and Cal was shoved sideways. Instinctively he ducked his head and hunched his shoulders.

Cal landed on the rear seat in a half-sitting position. Even before he tried to glance quickly around the sedan's dark interior, he knew he wasn't alone. Another man, hunched over the back of the front seat, stared at him from under thick eyebrows. He held a pistol in one bunched fist. It was pointed directly at Cal's head.

The man who had hurled him into the car climbed in behind the wheel. He said something in a soft language that wasn't German. The car began to move up the hill. Cal began to turn his head. The man with the gun motioned him to keep his eyes on the pistol. Abruptly, the sedan stopped. Cal realized he was perspiring.

"Mr. Sanders," a soft voice hissed, "we meet again. And so soon . . ."

The distinct smell of cologne pervaded the sedan.

Cal froze. Droplets of sweat began to trickle down from under his armpits.

"We are just beyond the governor's palace," the voice intoned. "And if you turn your head toward me, even in the darkness you will make out tombstones, Mr. Sanders."

The fist holding the pistol waved the weapon.

Cal realized he had been holding his breath when he exploded: "You! Rhinelander!"

"Rheinhardt, please. But what is a name? Merely a passing identity."

The beads of perspiration were rolling down Cal's ribs now. He peered at the German, slowly turning his head to get a full view. Only the outlines of Rheinhardt's bulk came into focus. His face and chin were pale, his eyes in shadows.

"For Chrissakes!" he managed, "what's this all about?" Cal opened and closed his hands. "Can't we have some light?"

"No lights, Mr. Sanders," Rheinhardt said pleasantly.

The pistol was pointed at Cal's chest.

"What the hell do you want? I can't help BMW make any deals with the Spaniards," he said, tautly.

Rheinhardt lit a cigarette. In the light from the lighter's flame, Cal recognized the ravaged features. He extended the pack of Winstons. "I am sorry, Mr. Sanders. Would you like one?"

Rheinhardt lit it. In the brief glare, the gold in his teeth glittered. He nodded carelessly toward the window. "Most of the men buried in that tiny graveyard died at Trafalgar, Mr. Sanders. Officers, of course. Where your Admiral Nelson defeated the combined French and Spanish navies. In 1805, I believe?"

Cal took a long drag on the cigarette, heaved his shoulders high, then slowly lowered them, exhaling smoke. "I'm damned certain we aren't here to discuss an ancient sea battle, Mr. Rheinhardt. We could've done that in any pub down the street."

"No, I suppose we are not."

Cal squinted at his glowing wristwatch. He had been gone from the Montarik less than five minutes. Christ! he wheezed, inwardly.

"Then what?"

"I have noticed you're an impatient man."

"What's that supposed to mean?"

"Two days ago, you were alone on your holidays." He

motioned with his cigarette. "Now you have company. And you are here in Gibraltar."

Pamela Strong, Cal thought. He was afraid his hand, holding the cigarette would shake. He stared at it. "So? What's your point?"

"As you can see, in my own way I'm not alone either." His small laugh gushed from his mouth.

In the gloom, Cal waited.

"I too am looking for a friend. You know him as Carl Heindemann."

"I know a man who claims he is Carl Heindemann," Cal replied, slowly. "I also know a man who claims he is Dieter Rheinhardt . . ."

Rheinhardt coughed.

"Who are *you*, really?" Cal asked.

"Believe what you will." Rheinhardt coughed again. "What would you say if I said I am with West German security forces?"

"I wouldn't believe you."

"Ah, Mr. Sanders, you are smarter than I first believed."

Cal sensed Rheinhardt was enjoying himself. "Thanks for the compliment," he said, dryly.

"Why are you involved in this business?"

"What business?"

"Please! Don't suddenly play the fool."

"I can't be a fool and smart—all at the same time," Cal blurted, stubbornly.

In the darkness, Rheinhardt sighed. His words were abruptly crisp. "In the beginning, Mr. Sanders, you were a puzzle. But you continue to turn up—like a bad penny— and that changes your status. You are becoming a problem."

Cal could almost hear someone's heart beating. It was his own. "What's your interest in this 'business,' as you call it?" he asked.

"Let's agree that I am on the other side."

"Whatever that means."

"Precisely, Mr. Sanders."

A hand tapped Cal's knee. He understood it was Rheinhardt's.

"I can make it worth your while, Mr. Sanders, if you

can tell me where I can locate this Carl Heindemann, no matter what he calls himself."

Cal peered at the fist holding the gun. "We're talking money?"

"Not necessarily."

"My life?"

"I didn't say that, Mr. Sanders."

Cal made a production out of butting his cigarette in the armrest ashtray.

"I'm waiting, Mr. Sanders." Rheinhardt didn't sound amused anymore.

"And I'm thinking."

"Mr. Sanders, I can also be an impatient man."

Cal, despite his will, shrank back until his shoulders were against the door and window. He said slowly: "I don't know where Carl Heindemann is." He paused. "Last time I saw him, he was in Spain."

The thick-set man in the front passenger's seat lifted his free hand out of his pocket. It held a silencer. He spoke tersely in a soft language.

Rheinhardt shook his head. "May I see your passport, please?" he asked.

Cal handed it to him. He rifled through it. "Ah, I see you are still Sanders."

Cal nodded.

Rheinhardt snapped the covers shut before returning it. "Mr. Sanders, may I give you some advice? Why don't you go home? Or visit Yugoslavia. It's much more conducive to good health. And the Dalmatian beaches can be most inviting. I am certain your lady friend would enjoy them."

"And why don't you get a divorce?" Cal shot back.

Rheinhardt's smirk was more of a gasp. "A clever riposte!" he said. He tapped Cal's knee again. "Well, if you won't take my advice, perhaps, just perhaps, if you should meet our mutual acquaintance in the next day or so, would you be kind enough to pass along a message? Tell him, we know the wildschwein is at bay."

"If I meet him."

"Thank you."

The man with the gun abruptly reached in front of Cal

THE LAST HUNTER

and opened the door. Cal half fell out before he got his balance.

"Just walk downhill," Rheinhardt called hoarsely from inside the car, "and beyond the Lipton's store and you will come to your hotel. Good night, Mr. Sanders."

Cal held the door open. "Before we part, Mr. Rheinhardt," he said, "a drunk tried to run me off the coastal road the other night. Know anything about that?"

In the dark interior of the sedan, Rheinhardt replied: "Perhaps it could have been a suggestion that you should stay out of business that doesn't concern you."

Cal inhaled the faint fragrance of cologne. "Ever been to Toronto?"

"Why would you ask that?"

"No reason. Just thinking if you ever are, I will return your hospitality."

The door was yanked shut and the sedan drove quietly uphill. Only its parking lights were on.

"Goddamn!" Cal blurted, standing on the pavement watching it.

He began walking, slowly at first, past the two sentries in front of the Governor's Palace, hugging the facades of the Main Street shops to take advantage of their shadows, the echoes of his footsteps following him on the deserted sidewalk. And his bewildered mind admitted what it wouldn't tell him in the sedan: Dieter Rheinhardt wasn't a German with BMW and he wasn't a member of Carl Heindemann's "society." He was a KGB agent, it said, over and over again. He began to sweat again. "Christ!" he breathed aloud. Then he thought of Pamela and broke into a ragged trot.

Standing in front of their room door, he forced himself to rap softly. But he couldn't control his heaving chest.

"Is that you, Cal?" he heard her ask.

"Open the door!"

He almost stumbled into the room and, panting, dropped into the only chair.

"My God!" she gasped. "What's wrong with you?" She kicked the door shut.

Pamela crossed the small floor. "Are you ill?" she

asked softly, bending over him, her troubled eyes searching his face.

He shook his head, deliberately avoiding her gaze. "I bumped into some people . . . people who can't be classified as friends," he said at last.

"In the hotel bar?"

"There is no bar."

"Then where?"

"It doesn't matter."

"Certainly, it matters," she said, impatiently. "You come in here, all shaken up, and you say 'it doesn't matter.' What the hell kind of talk is that?"

It was the first time he had seen her angry.

"Are we going to have a fight?" he asked.

"You take me out of Spain, abruptly and almost secretively. We park in this little hotel like twenty-dollar-a-day tourists. You barge back into the room, looking like a man who has seen ghosts, and you tell me it doesn't matter."

He blinked. Christ! he thought, I don't really even know who you are. In fact, I don't know who anybody is anymore.

"Am I going to get the icy silent treatment?" she demanded.

"Settle down," he said softly. "And sit down. Here please." He motioned to the arm of his chair.

She did. And began to stroke his shoulder, then his forehead. "Now, tell me, old man," she said, suddenly sweet, "what happened?"

He removed her hand and looked up at her. The anger that had risen in her eyes had gone. "You aren't getting involved," he said.

"Involved in what?"

He remembered the sedan and it left him with a sense of déjà vu. "It doesn't matter. You aren't getting involved."

"That certainly sounds final."

"It was meant to be."

"When are we going to the Casino?" she asked.

"I'm going alone. To meet a friend."

Pamela stood up. He realized she was in her bare feet. "Not alone, my darling, not alone," she said, brightly but firmly. "I'm going wherever you go. Whether you like it or not. And that's final too."

He couldn't help himself. He laughed.

"Laugh, my love. Have a ball. Who's your friend?"

The knock on the door startled him. He could feel his blood speed up and his heart thump. "Who is it?" he asked hoarsely, wishing he hadn't flung the Baretta overboard on the crossing from Spain. *"Who is it?"*

It was the tailor. He had four suits. The brown cotton-rayon fit him. He refused the vest and opted for white shirts, brown socks and a pair of brogues. Pamela stared at the shoes. "They are *not* very stylish, darling," she murmured.

"And neither am I."

She selected two dresses: a simple knee-length black frock and a blue skirt with blouse and jacket. And two pairs of shoes. "One for walking, the other for parties," she said, blithely. Plus a silver-grey purse.

The tailor declined payment.

Cal squinted at Pamela from under his brows while he tied the laces in his brogues. Christ! he thought. We're on the run. We don't know whom we're running from. Or where we're going. And she picked dresses as though she was shopping in downtown Paris. He groaned. He didn't know whether it was from exasperation or exertion.

They took the stairs to the basement, avoiding the dozing night desk clerk, emerging from a rear door leading into a small, fenced yard. She held his hand tightly. In the gloom, he located a wooden fence. The latch opened easily.

"Why are we going this damned way?" she whispered. "And where does it lead?"

He tugged her hand. "Ssh!"

Over twenty years earlier, he had picked his way along this same route which led to the meat market. Only then he had smuggled a nurse inside the Montarik, avoiding the Shore Patrol stationed in front of the hotel. He could still remember her name. Diana. Buck-toothed and British. But it had been good while his frigate had been in Gibraltar for fuel and supplies.

The cabbie was Maltese. "The Casino, sir? Right!"

The Casino huddled just below the spine of the Rock, snuggled against the hard granite. And despite the number of people at the tables, it was quieter than anything Cal had ever experienced in Las Vegas. There the noise had left him with the feeling he was spending his time and money in a boiler factory powered by one-armed bandits.

A tuxedoed attendant steered them to the cage. Cal bought $100 worth of white ten-shilling chips. Pamela opted for red, at a pound per. Told the crap tables were closed because there weren't enough Americans, they drifted to the roulette tables. There were three, sited like the spokes of a wheel with the double-zeroes at the axle.

Cal studied the small crowd. Round faces. Long faces. Broad faces. All under different haircuts and hairdos. And they were all ages. But none added up to Carl Heindemann. Or Dieter Rheinhardt. Or his friends. The croupiers had bland expressions pasted on their faces. It was too quiet. He hunched his shoulders. For a moment, he focused on a short, dapper Frenchman with two neat rolls of blue chips cupped in his small, well-manicured hands. He was betting intermittently, sometimes on all three tables at once. Casually, he placed chips on number five. It came up. Silently, he raked in a pile of chips, leaving two for each croupier. He hit again with the same number. This time, he stacked his winnings.

Six Brits sat together at the far end of a table. One played ten-shilling chips while the others hastily recorded the numbers on a pad as they came up.

The Frenchman won again. With double-zero. He had bet all three tables. The losing players stared at him politely for an instant, traces of icy smiles on their lips.

Pamela stood across the table from him. She looked up and winked. Cal left to find the slots. He picked up some change at the cage. The one-armed bandits were in a long hall outside the gaming room. He hit a fifty-pound jackpot with his second coin. Bells didn't ring. Lights didn't flash. And he didn't have a plastic bucket, so he loaded both suitcoat pockets and went to collect Pamela and cash in.

"The Frenchman was playing with five-pound chips, darling!"

Cal watched two tall men in grey suits walk through the foyer. They went straight to the chips cage.

"Do you know them?" she asked.

"Nope."

"Then why were you staring at them so intently?"

Cal half turned slowly. "Did you win?" he asked.

She opened her purse. It was jammed with red chips. "Of course."

He patted his pockets. "So did I. Let's turn this stuff into real money."

The cashier pushed a wad of notes at Pamela, then a neat stack of new ones toward Cal. He counted his.

"One hundred quid," he said.

She stuffed hers in her purse.

"Aren't you going to count it?"

"It's only money." She paused. "And it's past midnight. Where's this friend of yours?"

Again his eyes swept the gaming room. The Frenchman was still playing the three tables. "Unless he's disguised, he sure as hell isn't here. Or anybody like him." He took Pamela's elbow. "Let's go outside."

She shivered in the night. He draped his jacket over her shoulders while she peered into the mass of dark shadows blanketing a row of parked cars.

"See something?" he asked.

"Cal," she said, touching his arm, "I think someone is trying to get our attention. Look. Over there. A pinpoint of light in that large sedan."

"You stay right here, in the light. I'll check it," Cal rasped. Hunched slightly, he crossed the asphalt until he neared the limousine. The rear door opened. Cal dropped into a crouch.

"Mr. Sanders!" a voice whispered. "Come in. Quickly!"

Cal inched closer until he could see Carl Heindemann. "What about my friend?"

"Bring her, too. But quickly!" It was almost an order.

In the inky darkness behind the glassed-off driver, Carl Heindemann's face was a blur.

"I am sorry, Fraulein," he nodded toward Pamela, "but there is not enough time for any proprieties." He handed Cal two passports. "Tomorrow you will fly to

Paris. British European Airways. The early flight time is noted. Pick up your tickets at the Montarik desk. You will need photographs. But that will be no trouble. There are many shops where they can be processed in minutes." He paused, then went on: "But you must use these passports. That is important. For your own safety. And you will surrender them when you check into the Hotel Bristol. It is on the Rue de Rivoli. Just before it enters the Place de la Concorde. What you do with your own passports is your concern. But I would retain them."

Cal grunted. "Carl, I . . . we . . . came here to Gibraltar on your say-so. Now you are *telling* us to go to Paris. Don't you think . . .?"

"I *have* asked you to *trust* me."

Cal looked from Pamela to Heindemann. He nodded.

"Do you?"

"At this point, yes."

"Do you understand clearly what I have said? Yes? Good. Now, behind the Bristol is the Rue Saint Honore. Just beyond the Rue Cambon is a little restaurant, Chez Pyramides. I shall be delighted to dine with both of you at nine o'clock, the evening after next." There was an unnerving urgency in the one-time oberleutnant's voice. "For now, I must go."

"Hold it for a minute," Cal snapped. "I've got some news for you." He glanced at Pamela, then shrugged. "Earlier this evening, I was almost mugged in a car where a man who claims he is Dieter Rheinhardt . . ."

Heindemann interrupted. "Does he speak in sibilant tones? Use English with a faint German accent?"

"Yes."

"Did he wish to know where I was?"

"Yes."

"Ah, so they know I have left Spain."

Cal swallowed hard. "You mean they—whoever they are—*knew* you were in Spain?"

"Certainly, my friend. They are the KGB. And they had me under surveillance for the last two days. At least."

Cal suddenly knew why Carl Heindemann had coldbloodedly sent the Marbella Club limo to El Perro Negro. It made him shiver.

THE LAST HUNTER

The ex-U-boater stared through the rear window of the limousine. No one was visible in the darkened parking lot or in the glare of the Casino lights. "How did you get here? By taxi from the Montarik?" he asked abruptly.

"Hell no. I took a backyard over-the-fence route I knew to the big meat market south of the air strip and caught one there."

"Did the night clerk see you leave?"

"At the Montarik? No. I don't trust him anymore. But that's not the news. This Dieter Rheinhardt said to tell you—and I quote—we know the wildschwein is at bay."

Pamela's almond-shaped eyes were large in her face.

Heindemann glanced from Pamela to Cal. "You are certain that he said that? Not 'where' the wildschwein is at bay?"

"I'm positive."

"Good." Carl Heindemann smiled grimly. "I warned you there would be danger, my friend. Are you having second thoughts?"

"That's the second time tonight someone suggested I go home, or at least clear my hide out of the area," said Cal.

"And you, Fraulein?"

"Where Cal goes, I go," she said, quietly.

Heindemann shook his head slightly. "So. Then I must insist you change your departure times and buy your own air tickets. Do you have sufficient funds?"

Cal nodded.

"I strongly suggest you go for a walk and casually leave the hotel early. Visit some shops. Spend an hour or two. Keep moving. Don't take your baggage. I shall have it collected and moved to the airport terminal." He sighed. "Now, I must go. Remember, be careful."

"Who's Dieter Rheinhardt?" asked Cal, getting out of the car behind Pamela.

"He is not Dieter Rheinhardt. And he is very dangerous," Heindemann whispered.

The limousine's tail lights faded as it rolled silently down the steep roadway leading into the town that clung to the rock.

Pamela Strong handed Cal his suitcoat.

"Aren't you chilly anymore?" he asked.

"Chilly?" she giggled nervously. "I'm warm. All over. I can feel my blood rushing through my veins. In fact, my God, I'm perspiring. Here, feel my arms."

Her skin was warm and clammy.

"Let's go back inside and get someone to call a taxi," he said.

"Good. And I can go to the ladies' room, to avoid a most unlady-like accident." She giggled again.

Pamela lay atop the bed, her back against bunched pillows. She was still in her red dress. "So that's what it was all about," she said moodily.

Cal stood in the middle of the room, holding the passports. He lifted his eyebrows. Now he understood why she had been so quiet in the taxi to the hotel. "I knew you'd get around to that."

"Were you afraid?" she asked.

"I'm always afraid."

"It's not supposed to happen like that," she said, almost absently.

"What's not?"

"Only in movies. And that's make-believe."

"This isn't."

"Who is Carl Heindemann?"

"A friend."

She frowned. "What does he mean to you?"

"Just a friend. A contact, if you like."

"I'm not sure I like him."

Cal tossed her new passport to her. "He won't lose any sleep over that," he said. "Here, find out who you are." The conversation unsettled him. Just as it had that first afternoon they had gone to the sand dunes together.

Pamela opened the document. "I'm Lucianna La Grassa, a student, born twenty years ago in New York City. Well, it's not a very good fake. That's all I can say. Even if they almost got my exact age."

"You wouldn't know a fake from the real thing," Cal snorted.

"Wouldn't I though," she taunted.

"Nope."

"Because any American passport office would know I'm from Kansas. Just by my accent."

Bullroar, he thought. Private school girls don't have regional accents. They all sound alike. Aloud he said: "But you're only using it to get into France."

She smirked. "And who are you?"

I'm me. Cal Sanders, but I'm still wondering who in hell you are. Pamela Strong? Lucianna La Grassa? Or any woman in the whole damned world, he thought in exasperation. Every one of them made of mercury.

"I wonder who dreams up these names?" she asked.

He opened his passport. "I'm Richard Todhunter. From upstate New York. An engineer."

"What's supposed to happen?"

"I don't know," he said gently. "Sorry now you missed that tour?"

She blinked her eyes rapidly. He thought for a moment she was going to cry. "I wouldn't have missed you for the whole damned world!" she said, huskily. She jumped off the bed to embrace him. "Oh my God, darling, how I love you!"

Cal lit a cigarette in front of the small window. Gibraltar's main street was deserted. Except for a taxi parked with its right-side wheels up on the sidewalk in front of the hotel. Idly, he wondered who was inside it. Was the occupant waiting for someone to come out? Me? He shrugged. Across the gap between the row-on-row shops, a hand-painted banner was strung from a series of balconies. "British We Are—British We Shall Remain" it read. He remembered the back-page stories in *The Express:* Spain wanted Gibraltar returned. London and the Gibraltarians wouldn't concede the point. He butted his cigarette and watched Pamela get into bed. His stomach was churning as he undressed.

"You should marry me. Soon," she said after he lay beside her.

He flattened his pillow into shape under his head, raised himself up on one elbow and looked into her eyes. She had been crying quietly in the bathroom.

"What brought that on?" he asked. "And what would

your good parents have to say about you marrying an old man?"

"They love me. They wouldn't do a thing to prevent it." She smiled. "And I have an awful lot of money."

I'm twenty-odd years older than you are, he thought.

"And I have so much love to give you."

Which is more important young lady? Money or love? he asked himself.

"I'm old enough to know that a lot of people insist money can't buy happiness. But they only say that because they will never have enough money to prove their theory."

I wonder, he mused, if you can buy happiness on credit, like twenty percent down and the rest over thirty years. He ran one finger across the bridge of her nose, her eyebrows.

Pamela's brown eyes were brimming with large tears. He pretended he didn't notice.

"Do you think I'm a tramp?" she asked. "Is that it?"

She can't see me twenty years from now, he thought. Perhaps a little bent. Wheezing when I try to run. "I think you are the most lovely woman I've ever met. With brains to match." She sighed against his cheek. And turning off the night light, he held her until she slept.

Out on the street a truck backfired, snapping him wide awake. Gently, he eased his arm from under her shoulders. Pamela stirred. And he wondered vaguely why she had stopped asking him what was coming down or where they were going. It troubled him because, God help them both, he liked her too much.

23-5-66   2210 hrs GMT

File: AH 1945

For prime ministerial and presidential

eyes only; to be hand delivered on

receipt.

To: MI 5, CIA, RCMP (Operation Alois

Sibling desks)

Flushed is lost again. Ditto for

Printer and Third Party Escort.

Field indicates Gib. Keepers

ack Condition Blue.

                                        Control.

CHAPTER 10

✱

A LATE-SPRING rain was falling when they landed at Orly airport. The taxi driver had flat boney hands, with knuckles that turned very white when he gripped the wheel of his Citröen.

"The Bristol. On the Rue de Rivoli. S'il vous plaît," Cal said.

"Oui monsieur, oui," he said cheerfully, although he looked depressed.

The auto route into the city Julius Caesar had once called Lutetia when it was occupied by Gallic tribesmen, that the driver referred to as the Parisii, was crowded and shiny with rain.

"Well, Mr. Todhunter. Let me introduce myself, since we are both going to the same hotel. I am Miss Lucianna La Grassa. Engaged." She spread the fingers of her left hand.

Cal whistled without realizing it. "Christ! How'd you get that by French customs?"

"I wore it."

He hadn't noticed.

"Didn't I act like a newly engaged young woman?"

Thinking back, he nodded. "But I thought you were just in one of your affectionate moods, nothing more. Where'd you get it?" he asked.

Pamela switched on the overhead light in the taxi. Rotating her hand slowly, the stone caught and held the rays, turning each into fiery silver. "In Gibraltar. While you were picking up our photos and buying that terrible luggage." She smiled. "Do you like it?"

He shook his head slowly, saying nothing.

"I am engaged, you know. It was made official in front of a Spanish Civil Guard officer."

He kissed her lightly on the cheek. "Congratulations."

Pamela took a last look at her ring, then switched off the light.

Cal stared through the window at the moving street scene. Taxis, buses, motorcycles, jammed together in an endless slow-moving parade. Caped gendarmes in their box-like hats, dark uniforms and red-striped trousers were everywhere, directing traffic, standing in pairs or walking. And traffic signals winked, triggering packs of pedestrians in one direction, assorted motor-driven vehicles in the other. Trees, dripping with the fine rain, stood like so many green sentinels as if waiting for some bemedalled general's inspection.

"I thought it would bring you out of your gloom," she said, finally. "Did I turn you off last night, when I talked about getting married?"

"No." *She's beginning to sound like my ex*, he thought, *always wondering why I'm quiet. Or asking what's up when I'm not.*

"Votre hôtel, monsieur," the driver said.

If their room in the Montarik had been compact, modern and antiseptic, the Bristol's looking down on the cobblestoned one-way Rue de Rivoli, was big enough to accommodate a handball court. Cal glanced at the Tuileries Garden across the road, then closed the window, shutting off the constant sounds of heavy traffic.

"It may be old-fashioned," said Pamela, "but Oh Lord! what a big brass bed!" She threw herself on it, bouncing up and down. "And the mattress was made for sleeping and loving, whichever comes first. Preferably the loving, darling." She looked at the diamond on her third finger left hand, watched it catch the light again, but said nothing.

"That was another front-desk bastard who thought you were my daughter," Cal said, laughing.

She glanced at him, shifted her eyes to the flowered wallpaper and smiled.

First thing in the morning, he planned, I'll call Limey and bring him up to date without too many details. His belly heaved when he thought of the editor's reaction after he told him he was in Paris. What kind of a goddamned holiday scam are you working, Sanders? he'd ask. I'll look up our Paris stringer, Rene Charters, and work out of his office, he decided. Just to be safe. Mentally, he counted his U.S. cash and traveller's checks. More than enough, he totalled. Hell, I haven't paid a hotel bill since I left. Only two airline tickets. He wondered who'd get his bills. Heindemann, he said to himself. His people would. And who'd audit these expenses? Being good Germans, he concluded even the society would have accountants.

"Did you play around when you were married?" Pam called from the bathroom. Flossing her teeth again, he thought.

"I would bet you did not," she continued.

"You'd win your bet."

She poked her head through the doorway. "I knew I would," she said.

"Get a move on, young lady," he countered. "I'm hungry."

"I shall be faithful, too," she continued. "I have been since we met."

Lights from thousands of motor vehicles, bulbs in iron lampposts, sidewalk cafes, shops and hotels tried to chase away the misty night. They stood in the Place de la Concorde. Almost squarely in the center towered the seventy-five-foot-high stele commemorating Egyptian Pharaoh Rameses II's victories over his enemies almost 1300 years before the birth of Christ.

"How did it get here? In Paris?" she asked.

"The gift of some Egyptian pasha. Over a century ago, I think," he replied. "Rameses was quite a man by anybody's times. He ruled the Twin Kingdoms for about eighty years, fought everybody, and still found time to sire about a hundred kids."

"He must have had many concubines."

Cal nodded. "To begin with, he married his sister, and then added the ladies to his harem."

"His sister? How disgusting!"

"Whoa. Don't judge our customs against theirs. There's a three-thousand-year gap, remember."

The spotlights highlighting the 250-ton obelisk turned the ancient pink granite almost white.

"I'm hungry now," she said, quickly losing interest. "And I recall a little bistro on the Rue Royale." Pamela pointed to their right. "Just along the street. They serve Italian food. I hope you like lasagna, because they have the best there is, outside of Italy."

She was almost running when they crossed the cobblestones and went into the restaurant, its sidewalk tables under a maroon-and-grey awning.

"Whoa, again, woman!" he chided, slowing her with his hand.

Glancing from diner to diner, then out on the street where a gendarme placidly eyed the evening crowds, she said, happily: "It hasn't changed one little bit."

They shared a bottle of Chianti Classico and lasagna, Neapolitana.

The rain had stopped. And the night air was warming. Two taxi drivers tried to occupy the same parking spot at the corner and fought verbally in angry French. A placid gendarme sorted it out, the loser giving both the policeman and winner the two-finger salute before he spat.

The big brass bed squealed when Cal dropped his bulk on it next to Pamela. If she had been emotional through the light dinner and the walk back to the Bristol, it had only been a beginning. Her love-making absorbed him. And, as he drifted out of the glow, he kissed her for a long time. It was a gentle coming-together of their lips.

"You do love me, don't you Cal Sanders," she said.

"Yes." And he understood he meant it.

"I knew you did. And I knew you would tell me tonight."

"And what do you have to tell me?"

"That I love you." She paused. "And much more . . . but it will have to wait. Until everything is right again."

He lay on his side, his eyes closed.

Out in the night on the Rue de Rivoli, the lights from a hundred street lamps reflected dully in the small puddles.

"What else do you have to tell me?" he repeated, lazily, conscious of her long fingers tracing odd designs on his chest.

"Like—like for the first time in my life I know what I have and where I'm going for the next million years!"

Cal chuckled.

"Laugh your low laugh, my darling old man, but you don't know where I've been. Or what I've done. Yet you give me your love, no questions asked."

He stretched one arm across her bare breasts and pulled her against his chest. "Go to sleep; tomorrow's going to be a long day." He listened to her steady breathing from behind closed eyes.

The noon skies were crowded with quick-moving, rolling grey clouds when Cal reached the sidewalk. Automatically, he looked up from under the arcade-cover of buildings and put his hand out. No droplets. I'll walk, he thought, and stepped out toward the Champs Élysées.

Rene Charters was a fat Frenchman. His office desk was stacked carelessly with newspapers and telephone books. And his typewriter sat on a mobile, sheet-metal trolley. "*The Express* desk didn't tell me you were coming," he said in faultless English. "But then, that's not unusual. What can I do for you?"

Cal explained he had to make some phone calls. "Privately, if you don't mind."

"Not at all, I'll attend a 'conference' at the cafe," he said, grinning, "and have a beer or two."

Limey Lewis didn't ask Cal if he was pulling a scam and enjoying a holiday at the paper's expense. And if he was surprised to hear him from Paris, his sarcastic voice masked it. "What can I do for our exotic, roving foreign reporter?" he asked. "Because I've heard nothing new from *him* since I got that screwy little wire about finding a friend. Unless, of course, he has something to add."

THE LAST HUNTER

"Limey, I've got nothing new. But you can do something. Get the desk—no ask Jim Emmerson, he's the best—to run a check on a Pamela Strong. Aged twenty. From Kansas City. No, I don't know whether it's Kansas or Missouri. And just mebbe, he's got some contacts with the federals so he can pull together a confidential backgrounder on Carl Heindemann."

"Your friend?"

"I'm not sure about anything anymore. But something's due, I can feel it."

Limey said: "Well, something better be due soon. Or I'm yanking you home. Better still—and because you're already over there—you could head for Barcelona. Back in Spain. We've got a story that a Montreal real estate dealer fleeced a helluva lot of local people out of a bundle of local moola on phony land deals. And he's ensconced in a villa somewhere near Barcelona. How about that?"

Cal waited.

"That's the way it is, Sanders. Call me inside forty-eight hours with something definite. Or it's Barcelona. If not, I'll tell the assignment editor you're on holidays."

The late-afternoon sun was struggling through the clouds, slanting pale rays across the tired rug in the hotel room. The brass bed seemed to mock Cal. So did the luggage Pamela had called "terrible" from where it sat on a low bench beside the walk-in closet. He picked the Paris edition of *The Tribune* off the bed for the third time in three hours and scanned the same front page. Elizabeth II, Queen of all Britons, had offended Charles De Gaulle, President of all Frenchmen, with her reference to German troops who had hurried to the aid of the Duke of Wellington, and helped crush Napoleon at Waterloo some 150 years earlier. He flung the tabloid on the bed, the pages scattering. Then he saw it: Pamela's ring. It was nestled, half-hidden, between the pillows.

What was it doing there? he asked himself, picking it up. He partially closed his fingers and, shaking the ring in his fist like a crapshooter getting ready to throw, asked himself: Was she trying to tell me something?

"That she left against her will!" He stifled a groan.

"And I should have realized the odds were that we were under surveillance. By Heindemann's people? Or the other side?" He didn't want to say KGB.

Cal slipped the diamond into his jacket pocket and paced the small room, stopping in front of the closet. Pamela had worn the blue skirt and jacket and blouse. He slammed the door shut. I'll try the Chez Pyramides, he thought. Now. Not tonight at nine. And lead any surveillance team right to the door? a tiny voice of reason asked. He shook his head. Go to the police? And tell them what? That a twenty-year-old girl had walked out on an older man? The Paris police have heard that one before. A million times. Rene Charters? He laughed at himself dryly. What the hell could a fat Frenchman know that he didn't know?

The concierge's eyes were slate grey. "Monsieur Todhunter, I can only tell you what I saw. It was about two o'clock." He clasped and unclasped his hands. "She walked through the lobby with two gentlemen. Americans, I believe."

"How do you know they were Americans?"

"A few minutes earlier, sir, they asked me for her room number. In American. Did I do something wrong?"

"No, no. What did they look like?"

"They had close-cropped hair. As I said, they spoke English like Americans." His face brightened. "And one of them was carrying one of the papers all Americans read. The *Times* or *Tribune*. I'm not sure . . ."

Goddamn! Cal thought. They "looked like Americans" and I walked out of here without even a thought about her safety. "I mean, were they tall? Heavy?"

The concierge tilted his head. "Heavy, I would think. And one had very large feet. Yes, very large."

"When they went out together, were they talking? Was anyone, ah, holding her arm?"

"Hmmm. No, they were not talking. Just staring straight ahead. You know, walking together. With the woman in the middle." Suddenly agitated, the concierge added: "They were very polite. One of them held the door for her before they went outside. To a car!"

Cal was silent. Damn, he thought, helplessly, damn! damn! and damn!

"Perhaps, Monsieur Todhunter, they are friends? Did anyone know you were here?"

Cal stared at the little man.

"They may be expatriates. Many Americans live in Paris. And they have gone shopping together? Perhaps?"

No goddamned way, Cal swore to himself.

The Frenchman studied Cal's grim face. He spread his hands. "American visitors to Paris always shop," he said gently.

"You're probably right," Cal said aloud. But his mind was wheeling and dealing. It returned to Carl Heindemann's people. They could've taken her. To get her out of the line of any possible fire, it said. It made him feel better. The ex-U-boater had made it plain that he didn't like her around. Right from the beginning, it added. He sighed. But a squeaky little voice nagged: KGB. "Christ!" he said aloud.

"I beg your pardon?" the concierge asked, startled.

Cal grunted. "Is your bar open?"

"But certainly." The concierge's grey eyes reflected bewilderment. He pointed down the hall to a door on the left.

"Thanks. I think I'll have a drink." He paused. "If Mademoiselle La Grassa returns, tell her where I am. Okay? But if those two Americans show up, say nothing. Just let me know. Got that?"

He placed twenty new francs in the Frenchman's hand. "What time do you go off duty?"

The concierge looked over his shoulder at the ancient wall clock. "At six o'clock, monsieur." He pocketed the money. "In an hour."

The bar was well-lit. He sat at a corner table, facing the small entrance. They didn't serve Black Label. He settled for Red. With water and ice. With his first, he deliberately forced his troubled brain to accept the fact Pamela was shopping. With friends. After two, it would not.

The first sip from the third upset his stomach as he turned off his brain and entertained his instincts. The police were out. The KGB were in. And that left Carl

Heindemann. But he would not be in Paris until later. At least that's what he had said. Getting to his feet, he paid his bill and went upstairs. For a moment, he stood, key in hand in front of the door. Quietly as possible, he fitted it into the lock, then turning it in one swift movement and pushing, flung the door open and jumped inside. The room was deserted. He was sweating like a damned fool.

Everything was as he had left it. Only the bed had been turned down.

Maybe, he thought, Heindemann is already at that little restaurant. Off the Rue St. Honore, he had said. Now his mind and instincts were in sync. Before leaving, he carefully tore the cover off a book of hotel matches and inserted it between the door and jamb. He closed the door and opened it. The scrap of cardboard fell out each time. But it was too visible on the hall floor. He made the scrap smaller, until it was only a sliver. Satisfied with his work, he took the stairs to the lobby and went through the door out onto the Rue de Rivoli.

The cobblestone roadway was thick with traffic, moving in bursts timed by the blinking traffic lights stretching beyond the Notre Dame. The broad, colonnaded sidewalk carried an endless stream of pedestrians—some striding out, others window-shopping. Many ignored the traffic lights and, daring the horn-honking drivers to hit them, shuffled mindlessly in all directions. Cal's restless eyes searched the passing faces uneasily.

He squinted at his wristwatch. Almost seven-thirty. Ninety minutes to his meeting with Carl Heindemann at the Chez Pyramides. Without Pamela Strong. And the thought made him feel quite alone. He shook her image out of his mind. Concentrate, he told himself, on how you're going to get there without leaving a trail. He walked slowly to his left. The small narrow side streets were lined with parked cars. He glanced at them nervously. Retracing his steps toward the Bristol, he halted in front of a large well-lit window. Huh, he said to himself, an American-style self-serve cafeteria. Right here in downtown Paris. It was just after eight. And if he remembered Carl Heindemann's instructions, the Rue St. Honore was somewhere behind it. He shouldered his way through one of two swinging doors.

THE LAST HUNTER

Joining a short lineup, Cal picked up a tray, collected a fork, ham sandwich, Coke and apple pie. Putting his elbows on a small table near the window, he chewed the sandwich out of his hands. His eyes roamed the room. It was half full. He felt everybody was watching him. Even the women. The dry sandwich finished, he lit a cigarette and sipped the coke, before forking the pie into his mouth between puffs. Casually, he stopped and, leaving his pack of cigarettes and half-eaten pie, went to the door signed: HOMMES.

The bathroom was too small for the size of the cafeteria. But it had a window large enough to squeeze through. Sweating, he dropped to the concrete in a narrow passageway. It had only one outlet. Cautiously in the gloom and stink of overripe food and fumes from an exhaust fan, he edged sideways, groping his way against a rough brick wall. It led to a tiny courtyard. Two doors broke the lines of the old walls. The first was locked. The second wasn't. Slowly, he eased it open. His stomach was churning. It was a storeroom, stacked with cardboard boxes. He stood quite still, listening. Nothing. He felt his way between the crates to another door. It opened easily. And he stared into a shop. Its shelves were loaded with figurines, brass bells, pots, plates, trays. Silently crossing the floor, he slid back the deadbolt and stepped out into the night. A young couple, hand-in-hand, glanced at him. He smiled and they nodded.

The sign on Chez Pyramides' glass door said: FERME. And the blinds were drawn. Cal stood there, wallowing in indecision. He twisted the door knob noisily. Then again. The door opened a few inches. Two black-brown eyes stared into his face for what seemed like a full minute.

"Monsieur Todhunter?" the mouth asked.

"Christ! Yes. Oui!"

"Come in." The door swung wide. "Mr. Heindemann is waiting for you."

Cal barely recognized Carl Heindemann. His face, slightly burned by the Spanish sun, was too young. And it was fuller. His tightly cropped grey hair was sandy brown, matching a walrus mustache. He was smoking a Dutch cigar.

"You are surprised, my friend? It was time for a change. New make-up. Excellent, do you not agree?" he said, smiling.

Cal leaned across the small table. "I really don't give a damn what you look like. She's gone!" His voice was brittle. "Do you know anything about it?"

The one-time oberleutnant's eyes never blinked. "I? Why should I remove your young lady?"

Cal slammed the flat of his hand down on the brown-white checkered table cloth. Knives, forks, spoons and a glass vase sprouting artificial roses shook. "Goddamn!" he exploded. "Then people working for that bastard Rheinhardt have picked her up! Where the hell does he fit?"

"Tell me about it, my friend," Heindemann soothed. "But first, please sit down." He motioned to a chair.

Cal sat. And lit a cigarette from a second pack in his suitcoat pocket. "It happened around two o'clock. This afternoon." Smoke escaped from his mouth and nostrils as he talked. "Two guys who sounded like Americans—according to the concierge—just walked away with her. No struggle. Nothing. Why?"

"First things first. Did you contact the French police?"

Cal shook his head.

"That was wise."

"But those two birds weren't Americans. I'm sure of that."

"Why," asked Heindemann, "are you so sure?"

"Because the night I was shoved into that limo in Gibraltar, with Rheinhardt, there were two heavy-set men with him. One did the talking. And he spoke like an American. When he spoke at all. The German did most of it."

The ex-U-boater smiled grimly. "Your Rheinhardt is not a German. Not if he hisses when he speaks. He is Anatoly Lebedev. KGB. He is directing operations against our group. And, as I told you, a most dangerous man. He practises a dozen ways to kill despite his proclivity for drink."

Cal remembered the quick succession of double Bols Genevers and water in the Los Monteros. He mashed his cigarette in the porcelain tray. "But why in hell would he pick up Pamela? To get at me?"

"Possibly."

"She doesn't know anything!"

"She knows you know me," Heindemann said, softly.

"So?"

Heindemann scratched his chin. "Think about it, my friend, from Lebedev's point of view. Should you be upset, you could become careless, then lead them directly to me. Did you?"

"No." Cal explained how he had slipped through the cafeteria's rear window. "I couldn't be sure I wasn't under surveillance, so I took precautions. Pamela's disappearance made me jumpy." He paused. "Christ, Carl, what's going to happen to her?"

"You are in love with this young lady?"

"Men my age don't fall in love."

"Then . . .?"

"I like her. Very much."

Heindemann sighed, studied Cal's face, then said gently: "It is difficult to predict what will happen to Miss Strong. Because Lebedev is unpredictable."

Cal waited impatiently. The ex-oberleutnant sometimes left him with the sense he was indulging him. It was irritating.

"Once Anatoly Lebedev was considered by the Kremlin to be an agent with a future. The KGB believed the same. He was crisp, dependable and, yes, he could be patient. A product of the turmoil of the Stalin era, and Stalin did not trust men who had enjoyed what we would term a liberal arts education. He had a peasant's narrow mind. Unimaginative," Heindemann intoned.

"And while that mind improved over time, his successes in the hurly-burly espionage activities of the early Cold War gave way to clumsy stalemates at best. Yet, it was his proclivity for drinking and womanizing that sealed his future.

"Still, he was too valuable to discard, for they trusted him implicitly. He was assigned to investigate the society.

Confirm their operations and where necessary eliminate any key players."

"What about Pamela?" Cal interrupted.

"I am coming to that. But first, there is Lebedev. He must complete the assignment satisfactorily. Or . . ."

Cal waited in silence.

"Aware of that, murdering Pamela Strong—no matter who she is—could be a critical error. Especially now that you have disappeared."

"Is that supposed to make me feel better?"

"She could lead the KGB to you . . ."

"Pamela wouldn't do that!"

Heindemann relit his Dutch cigar. "We do not know that . . . do we?"

Cal shook his head slowly.

"Are you hungry, my friend?" the ex-U-boater asked suddenly.

"I am."

"Good! But first, we shall have a good brandy. Not what the visitors drink. Or many Frenchmen, either." He half-turned in his chair. And for the first time, Cal had a good look at the man who had admitted him into the cafe; he was slender but wiry, with a narrow pale face under a receding hairline that led to thinning black hair shot with grey. "Marc," Heindemann said, "could we have two small snifters of your private stock? Annsback Uralt? Bitte?" He turned back to Cal. "It is a heady German brandy. Good for a man who is troubled."

"Who is he?"

"He goes by the name of Marc Fauberge. But in truth, he is Herbert Mueller. Once long ago, he deserted from the submarine service to occupied France. He went to ground until Paris was liberated. He waited two years, with his Lisette. Right here in the cellar under this very cafe. With her mother and father living and working in the building above him. She protected him. Fed him. Clothed him. And loved him."

The German coughed. "She is a remarkable woman. A mute, although she lip reads. She is also a fine cook. And a most skilled make-up artist, working with many of the little theater groups which thrive and die in the Montmartre, a district of Paris which is, incidentally, better known to more foreigners than Parisians." He smiled. "I am tonight what Lisette Fauberge created."

Heindemann sipped his brandy.

Cal made a face when the liquid churned in his stomach. "Damnit! Damnit! Damnit!" he said, helplessly.

"Anger and love are very similar," Heindemann said gently. "Both are very difficult to control. But one must. If one is to survive."

Cal knew the German was right. "I don't need any of your philosophy. She's gone! That's all I know."

Heindemann squared his shoulders and sat smoking.

Cal adjusted his tie, loosening it until his neck moved freely. "Got the shirt in Gibraltar. Courtesy of you," he said. "A little tight for my liking."

The German smiled. "Are you still in the hunt?" he asked.

Cal swished the brandy 'round the inside of the snifter. "Yes."

"Good. Then I will bring you completely into the picture as I understand it," he said. "But first, do you still have your real passport?"

"Yes."

"With you?"

Cal patted his inside jacket pocket. He nodded.

"Miss Strong's?"

"No. It'll be back at the hotel. Unless the KGB picked it up when they walked away with her."

Carl Heindemann rubbed his hands, then brought the fingertips together. "It is more than likely they did. After all, it is the correct procedure."

"Why?"

"Passports, particularly valid ones, are more important than hostages."

Cal didn't like the word "hostage" and winced inwardly.

"A few days ago," Heindemann began, "I told you I suspected there was a traitor, a mole, in the hunt. Frankly, I had felt it was Joachim Heinrichs. Juan Ricardo. Yet, I had to be sure. Before I could eliminate him. And I must tell you, his killers enjoyed their work, the police informed me. They shredded his face with his artificial limbs. After he was dead. I even considered Señor Rivera." He noted Cal's frown. "Oh, yes, he worked for us. But he engineered your move to Gibraltar. Still, the KGB *knew* I was expected at El Perro Negro."

"Whoa!" interrupted Cal.

Heindemann smiled.

"You're going too fast."

Heindemann's smile remained in place.

"It's you the Russian wants. Right?"

"I expect so."

Cal grunted. "And they knew you were in Spain. So why didn't they just pick you up?"

"I would never take a stroll on a deserted street. Not at noon, nor at night."

Touché, thought Cal. Aloud he said: "But whoever it was that night at El Perro Negro shot up the rear seat of the Marbella Club limo. If you'd been inside, you would have been very dead . . . which tells me you're wanted dead or alive."

Heindemann chuckled. "The gentlemen who did the shooting were, in all likelihood, Basque terrorists. Amateurs who would kill anyone for money or out of frustration. I am quite certain they had orders to take me alive. But in their frustration at my absence, they killed the driver. Sad, isn't it?"

Cal tacked. "Do you know where this wildschwein is at bay?"

"Perhaps."

"You could be made to reveal that info," said Cal. "Haven't you heard of truth serums? They work, I'm told."

"I would die first. And the KGB—especially Lebedev—knows that." Heindemann watched Cal's eyes widen. He knew he had proved his point. "Now, my friend, may I return to the subject?"

Cal nodded.

The former oberleutnant puffed on his cigar after a sip of brandy.

"That was when I had decided you and your friend must leave Marbella quickly," he recited. "And because I had to trust someone, I went to Rivera. As I said, that appeared to go smoothly. But your mugging—that is your term, not mine—was disturbing. Most disturbing. There were, in short, some loose ends."

Heindemann drummed the fingers of his left hand on the tablecloth. "I could reach only two conclusions: The faked passports were known as fakes to the KGB and you were both under surveillance. Or Rivera had sold out. I decided he had not despite the fact you were picked up and questioned. With that in mind, logically, I had two options: Warn you at once. Risk a wire. But what if I was in error? And made you so nervous you could lead the wrong people to the Chez Pyramides? I knew I had the KGB in my wake. I had to shake them before I met with you outside the casino. And, my friend, shaking a shadow in Gibraltar takes a lot of hiking, something as you know, I have never relished.

"I opted for my last card. I would call on my man in Estapona, a small village west of Marbella, and check his integrity in the matter of your passports. It took me until almost noon to reach his place of business, a photography shop. He was already dead. The Civil Guard, patrolling the playa, had fished him out of the swells that morning. He had been beaten, then shot. I felt, instinctively, it would have taken a stronger man than he to withhold any information."

"Why were the fake passports so important?" Cal asked.

"Do you not realize that when you turn in your passports at any French establishment, they are noted each night by the local police?"

"No."

Heindemann said: "Even if they had missed you leaving Gibraltar. Or at Orly. A few new francs to the right official would lead them straight to the Bristol."

"If you knew that, then why tell us to go through those elaborate precautions to shake any possible KGB people before we left?" demanded Cal.

"Because I had to buy time. Thus, your action was a diversion."

Christ! We were nothing but decoys, Cal thought. "Go on."

"I flew here straightaway. But it was too late. I can only apologize for what has happened."

Cal sat in silence. The Cezanne prints on the brown-papered walls whirled around him. Even the Frenchman, Marc, was blurred. "Why didn't you phone today?"

"I did, my friend. There was no answer."

While I was out, Cal thought, bitterly. Or while two "Americans" abducted Pamela. He looked at the German. "Are we under surveillance here . . . now?"

"In this restaurant? No. Of that I am certain."

"What about the 'Frenchman' here?" Cal nodded toward Marc.

"This is *my* safe house. Even my most confidential colleagues do not know of it."

"But what makes you so sure he hasn't been bought?"

The ex-U-boat officer sighed. "I knew his father. A pastor in my village. And Herbert Mueller, although younger, was one of my playmates. He had wanted to be a violinist. But war changes peoples' lives. He became a torpedo man and sailed off for the hard life in *frontboot*— a German expression for a submarine in frontline action. Later, I learned that his left hand had been horribly smashed in an accident. And when my staff duties took me to Paris, I visited him in hospital. Before he deserted. It was a reluctant friendship in the beginning. But time heals. And I understood."

Cal looked at Marc. Three of his fingers were withered and shorter than those on his right. "Now what?" he asked.

"Are you still in—as you said?" the German asked. "You can leave. I can make arrangements which will be quite satisfactory."

"I'm in!"

"But in anger."

Cal said: "Probably. But I have to tell you, there's one little item that bothers me, my friend. You said—it seems like years ago—that a society, a group of ex-German officers were in this hunt together. That sounds like a helluva lot of officers where I come from. Tell me, where are they now? When they're needed."

The poker-faced expression in Heindemann's face remained. "Because I do not know who the traitor is, I trust none of them."

"Yet I'm supposed to trust you. After what's happened?" Cal's voice rose an octave.

"You must." The German stubbed his unlit cigar.

"Now what?"

Heindemann allowed himself a grim smile. "We are now, as a theater devotee would note, approaching the final act. When the loose pieces are tied together in a satisfactory ending!"

"And where do I fit in?"

The German's blue eyes narrowed. "My friend. First the mole. The traitor. Then the wildschwein at bay. Remember?"

Cal nodded.

"You and I shall hunt him down."

"When?"

"Soon. In a week. Or less."

"Where?"

"I cannot answer that. Yet."

"And what do I do now? I can't go back to The Bristol. That's obvious."

Heindemann stood up. With his make-up and dyed hair and mustache, and rough tweed suit, he looked like an Englishman. He stretched. "I could do twenty-four consecutive hours on sea watch, when I was young," he said. He walked stiffly around the chair, like a loser at a card table trying to change his luck, and sat down. "You will stay here. Madam Fauberge will change your identity. Marc will provide a new passport. But keep your genuine one, as a safety precaution."

"They sounded like Americans," Cal said, more to himself.

"Who did?"

"The two men in the lobby of The Bristol. Before Pamela was . . ."

"The KGB carefully train some agents to talk like Americans. Britons. Frenchmen. Even Germans," Heindemann said. "All your necessities will be looked after while you are here, my friend, until we make *our* move."

"Don't you think I should know something about this 'move'? After all, I'm fifty percent of us."

"Not yet."

"Well, there's one thing that I need first. A gun. Something heavy. That will kill."

"Where is your Baretta?"

"In the Atlantic. Off Gibraltar."

"I am certain Marc can look after that." Heindemann straightened up. "Now, Marc, could we eat, please? Something light. With a bottle of your splendid Riesling. From a vineyard in Ockfen, if I remember correctly."

Marc Fauberge smiled faintly. "It has been ready for you since you arrived, Oberleutnant Heindemann."

The small room behind the false stone wall didn't have a window. In one corner was a cheap stand-up screen masking a toilet. The seat was almost too small for him. A basin, bolted to the brick wall, had running cold water. The single light glowed inside a pink lamp shade. There were books, all old, in German or French, stacked atop each other in a crude case. And because he couldn't even hear footsteps above the ceiling, he concluded his "cell" was totally soundproofed.

Slowly, he undressed and climbed between the sheets on the small iron cot. How in God's name, he thought, could that poor bastard upstairs have stood it for two years? He sighed. I guess he could. Because there's always something worth waiting for.

Cal woke often. Once he thought he could hear Pamela breathing beside him. He sat up, reaching to his left. Nothing. In the total darkness, a wave of loneliness almost smothered him until he was finally lost in a bone-weary sleep.

The false door slid open noiselessly. It was Marc Fauberge. "Allo!" he greeted. "An' 'ow are you theese morning?" He had a large mug of coffee in one hand.

Like some Brits, when the French speak English, they often drop their H's. Yet they don't particularly like each other. Cal vaguely wondered if there was a connection, then realized this Frenchman wasn't a Frenchie. He was a German.

"I bring you coffee in the morning," he laughed. "Would you prefer croissants? Or an omelette? Or both?"

Cal sipped the coffee. It was very hot. "I could use some sugar."

"Je regret, Monsieur Sanders. I am sorry. I shall be back at once."

The breakfast sawed off his hunger. Cal smacked his lips. "Police been nosing around?" he asked.

"Toujours. But not nosing. They lunch 'ere, the detectives, I know them all."

"What do they talk about?"

Marc Fauberge shrugged expressively. "What they always talk about. Wives. Children. Mistresses. Inflation. Politics. Rugby. France defeated the British in an International."

Not much German left in you, Cal observed. You even say "France" like a Frenchman, softening the word and sliding over the A.

Cal had eaten two breakfasts and walked off his room hundreds of times before Fauberge measured him for a set of clothes. "One suit will be formal," he explained. "The other? Eet will be casual. Like those American visitors wear. Perhaps with Adidas. Non?"

Cal wasn't listening. He had been thinking about Pamela. Twice he had asked Marc Fauberge about her. The Frenchman had merely shrugged. He had tried to picture her captors, but the images blurred. He was afraid. And lonely.

It was after his third omelette, croissants and black sugared coffee when Lisette Fauberge accompanied her husband. She carried what looked like an old-fashioned, squared-off train case. First, she indicated, Cal should remove his trousers. He looked at her husband, who laughed. Cal stepped out of his pants. Then she wrapped a long roll of tensor bandage around his right leg from calf to thigh.

"You mus' limp," explained Marc, "an' theese way guarantees you shall. You will 'ave pains in your buttocks for a while—because you will try to compensate—but eet ees necessary."

Moving his head with warm, insistent hands, Lisette Fauberge clipped his hairline back, shaved his upper forehead and patted it dry. Then came the rinse. It stung his scalp. A towel hard against his tingling forehead prevented the strong solution from dripping into his eyes.

He was convinced Madam Fauberge was going to literally shift his scalp when she dried his head.

They left together, Lisette smiling. "I'll be back. In a moment or so. 'Ave a cigarette, Monsieur Sanders. Eet will not seem so long, eef I am delayed," Marc said.

It was three hours, four cigarettes and a limping five hundred paces before the false door slid open. Marc was carrying a suitcase. He had a loose-knit brown suit over his arm. "S'il vous plaît, monsieur, you mus' change. Now." Cal wanted to ask what the hurry, but the wiry Fauberge cut him off. "The oberleutnant will be 'ere in only a few minutes. And you mus' discard the old clothes and be ready to meet 'im." He grinned. "Upstairs in the cafe." He paused, opened the case and removed a hand mirror. "Oui, I almost forgot. Look at yourself," he said, "before I take your picture for your new passport."

With his hairline shaved back and a smaller crop of graying hair, Cal barely recognized himself.

"Vite, vite, monsieur! Be queek! There ees not much time," Fauberge said, shoving the mirror inside his hip pocket. "Remember, you mus' shave the 'airline at least once a day. Or the stubble will give you away. An' remove the bandage eef you take a bath or shower. Eef you do not, eet will lose eets tension."

As he awkwardly climbed the steps from the cellar, he wondered: Who's going to phone Limey and tell him what's happened? To hell with him, he reconsidered, limping stiff-legged into the cafe restaurant kitchen.

"Those instructions are simple enough," said Heindemann. "Now repeat them, please."

Cal recalled: "Take the midnight cross-channel train from the Gare du Nord overnight to Victoria Station in London. Wait a few minutes at the W.H. Smith bookstore, then taxi to Covent Garden. From there, the tube. Follow the blue lights for the Piccadilly Line. Get aboard either the first or last car, because they aren't as crowded. Get off at Knightsbridge and walk to Kensington Road. To the Pavo Rojo.

"Then wait for a phone call. The caller will identify himself with the code word *Regenbogen*— rainbow. Act on his words."

"Yes, I have said it before, my friend; you have a good memory. One must suppose that goes without saying if one wishes to be a good newsman," said Heindemann. He lifted a compact pistol from inside his tweed jacket, handing it to Cal. "I know, you wanted something large. Perhaps an American Browning. And a shoulder holster." The German smiled. "They are unwieldy. They also take some getting used to. And you do not have the luxury of practice." He smiled as Cal began to object. "Believe me, my friend. This Walther P38 will do everything you ask of it. And wear it inside your belt. You are right-handed, nein? Then on your left side. You can reach it easily, even when your jacket is buttoned, as it should be. Or when you are hurried."

Cal lifted the clip-fed weapon. "No silencer?"

"Here is another clip. Should you require extra ammunition," Heindemann said. "Silencers are only really effective in the movies. Now for your newest passport."

Cal Sanders was now John Russell, school teacher from Toronto, Canada. Single. Aged 48. With a permanently disabled right knee. He thought of another passport he had received. In another place. "Did you bring a copy of *The Times?*" he asked suddenly.

"There was nothing in it of interest to you." Heindemann answered.

Cal slid the Walther inside his belt, stood up and buttoned his jacket.

"Marc will drive you to the station. At about eleven o'clock. It is not far. That will give you plenty of time."

Cal fingered Pamela's engagement ring in his pocket. "Tell me, Carl, where is the American Embassy?"

Heindemann frowned. "On the Place de la Concorde where the Avenue Gabriel enters." He shook his head.

"And it is next to the Hotel de Crillon? I seem to remember that from a previous trip."

"Yes."

"And some embassy staff would probably drink in the bar, or dine in the hotel?"

"Probably."

Cal placed the Walther on the table.

"You have not eaten," said Heindemann.

"I'm not hungry anymore." He stood up. "I'll be back in an hour. Or less. I need the walk," he said, "and I can test my new disguise. Take care of the pistol, Marc, until I return. I won't be late." He closed the door softly behind him when he stepped out onto the Rue St. Honore.

Heindemann glanced briefly at the pistol, then at Fauberge. "Why don't you bring us another bottle of your fine Riesling, bitte, and we shall both do justice to it."

"Where 'as 'e gone, Oberleutnant?"

"To ask discreet questions when there are no answers. Not there. And to think, Herbert," he added, slipping unconsciously back to Fauberge's boyhood name, "if the Gross-Admiral Donitz himself had told me that man was a romantic, I would not have believed him! *Ach, mein alter kamerad.*"

Marc Fauberge expertly half-filled two glasses with the pale yellow wine.

"Thank you," Heindemann said, automatically. He raised his glass toward the cafe door. "Prosit!"

"You have known 'im long?" Fauberge asked.

"Not so long in years, yet long enough." The ex-U-boater lit a small cigar, rolled the smoke around in his mouth and blew a small ring that rose quickly and slowly disintegrated.

"And 'e is not one of us."

Heindemann sipped wine, then wiped his thin lips. He shook his head. "No," he said, slowly, "no, he's not."

"That ees too bad."

"At this moment, Cal Sanders is troubled by a young woman's fate. Despite the possibility in his mind that she could have been on the other side."

"Because he cares for her?"

"Precisely. Yet she *was* on the other side, working for the KGB."

"Of course you are certain?"

Carl Heindemann puffed on his cigar. It was out. He

laid it in the ashtray. "Sadly, yes. For all the wrong reasons. At home, she ran with the chic radical left. Simply for what Americans term 'kicks.' It is a classical recruiting gambit with the Soviets: first the harmless thrills, then assignments. Pamela Strong was on that Iberia flight to maintain surveillance on Cal Sanders."

"But it went wrong?"

"Yes. Because too many North Americans believe in love at first sight." He smiled. "Or bedding." Lifting his glass, he added: "It was she who tipped off the KGB that I would be at the El Perro Negro."

"Yet you did not tell Monsieur Sanders so a few moments ago."

"Never pour benzine on a man's personal fire," Heindemann replied.

"Still, I do not understand. If she ees one of them, why would they pick 'er up, 'ere in Paris?"

"I have told you, mein kamerad. She was in love. That made her a liability."

Marc Fauberge ran his crippled fingers through his thinning hair, picked up his glass and drank in quick mouthfuls. "Then she ees *kaput?* Dead?"

Heindemann pushed his chair back and crossed his legs. "Not necessarily. If we escape their net, and make it to London, they just might turn her loose to lead them to our friend. For his sake, I almost hope so."

"Truly?"

"Not quite."

24-5-66   2300 hrs GMT

File: AH 1945

For prime ministerial and presidential eyes only; to be hand delivered on receipt.

To: MI 5, CIA, RCMP (Operation Alois Sibling desks)

Third Party flocking in Paris. Assume to meet Society Members. Leader still AWOL. Is Prize available? Printer disappears. Third Party Escort picked up by First-Stringers. Why? Suggest Keepers go to White.

                              Control.

CHAPTER 11

✴

"THE PAVO ROJO," the sallow-complexioned Spanish-born manager Julio Ruiz said, "is the Red Turkey." And no, he didn't own the hotel. But together with his wife, he was in charge. Nor did he know who the owners were, he added. "It's not important, sir. I have a good position here in London. My wife and both niños are with me. I can ask for nothing more. Who made the reservation?" Ruiz glanced through the guest ledger. He spread his pale hands. "I do not know. All I understand is that this is a family hotel and I never expect trouble."

It was like every other small hotel on Kensington Road, facing Kensington Gardens, a few acres of lush green English Maytime flowers, bushes and grass separated from Hyde Park by the Serpentine. The four stone steps leading to the heavy door flanked by stone columns held up an ornately carved small roof. Once they had been the homes of wealthy Londoners who bred fashionably large families and could afford enough servants to ensure that their wives had little to do but procreate and preside over teas.

But time and styles change for the rich, too. So they moved on, selling to the highest bidders—the upwardly scrambling middle class. They divided the labyrinths of rooms into multiple dwellings before they too departed. Finally it was the turn of the investors—Spaniards, Swiss, Germans, Lebanese. They converted the homes into hotels. Occasionally a restaurant, but mostly hotels.

Cal's ground-floor room faced a tiny garden. He tried the window. It opened easily. He left it that way and threw his suitcase in a chair. Shaving gear. Two full tubes of toothpaste. One toothbrush. A suit. Two white shirts. Another tie, this one with soft gold stripes running diagonally across it. A hairbrush and comb. (He hadn't seen that combination since he was a boy.) Four pairs of socks. And Adidas. He lit a cigarette and patted his forehead, touching the stubble where Lisette Fauberge had shaved him. Automatically, he thought: Better shave that before I go out. He shrugged off his jacket and removed the Walther from his belt, then lay down.

The twilight filtered through the window when the ringing phone woke him up. "Yes?" he asked.

"*Regenbogen.*"

"Yes?" Cal repeated.

"The Strand. Noon. By the sign of the ocarina." The line went dead. Cal thought he recognized Carl Heindemann's voice. He sat in darkness. His stomach growled. I'm hungry, he said to himself. He was sliding one arm into the sleeve of his jacket when he remembered his hairline. And the Walther. He shaved.

Standing on the broad sidewalk, he wondered which way to go. Two bright red double-decker buses followed each other toward Knightsbridge and beyond to Hyde Park corner, their lights bright in the early evening. He remembered the war years when they ran almost dark. At the same breakneck speed. He also remembered The Bunch of Grapes, on Brompton Road near the Knightsbridge station. Then it had been a gathering place for pro and amateur prostitutes and horny, half-drunk servicemen.

The pub was still filled with young men and women. And noisy. But the women were uncommonly good looking as a crowd. Flashing good-teeth smiles, they laughed too much. Modishly dressed in short skirts, open-necked blouses that showed off their breasts, their eyes were bright with eye liner. They didn't seem to be with anyone in particular, but knew every young and middle-aged man in the saloon bar.

One quite tall woman caught his eye. Her thick hair shimmering in the bright brassy light, framed a high-cheekboned face. Her mouth was full. She was talking animatedly to a young man with a sombre, pale face. For a few seconds, he watched her, until she began to look like Pamela Strong. He jerked his eyes away. Limping, he worked his way to the bar and ordered a pint of mild and bitter.

"Where you been luv?" asked the barmaid. "People only order bitter nowadays."

Cal nodded toward two women with what he thought were wine glasses in their hands.

"Oooh, that? That's Babycham. The lovelies are all into that now. Still mild an' is it?"

"Mild an'."

The Bunch of Grapes had been renovated, but the Victorian form remained. So did the oak panelling. He paid. Money's been renovated as well, he thought. It used to cost about one bob a pint. Now it's almost three times higher.

"Them?" asked the barmaid. "They're all starlets. At least they think they is. Works TV an' back-street theater. An' the men? They're directors. Producers. You know luv, they who makes everythin' go 'round." She looked at him. "Been 'ere before, 'ave you?"

Cal smiled. "During the war."

She laughed shrilly. "Not changed much," she said, "but the game's the same! Can I get you a refill?"

"Yes, please. And I'll have one of those cold pork pies. Make it two, will you?"

Old and young, they marched like army ants through the misty rain along the length of The Strand's sidewalks. In and out of shops and restaurants, around each other, men and women spilled into Trafalgar Square or Fleet Street or headed for the Law Courts, Waterloo Bridge or secret lovers' lunches. All under a bobbing, weaving canopy of umbrellas. Between them, swerving through honking London taxis and small British cars, big buses advertising Player's Cigarettes careened and snorted like fighting bulls.

Cal stood in front of the Strand Palace Hotel, tired and wet. He had limped the length of the broad street twice but hadn't seen anything vaguely resembling a sign that said: The Ocarina. All he had noted was that the hurrying Londoners seemed to appreciate he was lame, stepping aside, often saying "Sorry, my fault!"

He was convincing himself to try again when above the traffic din he heard it: the thin haunting strains of "Danny Boy." He listened, trying to pinpoint the player. Then he saw him, an old, one-legged man, strands of grey hair sticking out every which way on his large head that jerked from side to side. His fingers skipped nimbly across the openings in a fat little penny whistle held inside one large red-raw hand. His crutches stood against the wall of Moody's Irish Bar. A shapeless peaked hat lay on the sidewalk, catching coins dropped by passersby.

Cal's brain clicked: Penny whistle equals ocarina.

It was a long narrow saloon. And the high, darkly polished wooden bar ran almost its full length. He pushed through the partly frosted door. The good-natured babble of a hundred men, eating and drinking and talking while they stood, flooded into his ears. Slowly, because his hip was hurting from the strain of a long walk with his artificial limp, he moved deeper into the saloon. He recognized Heindemann despite a grey goatee and tweed cap that made him think of Sherlock Holmes. The scar was gone.

He ordered mild and bitter. The pain in his hip subsided.

Heindemann was speaking to the man on his right. He sounded more like the Briton than the Englishman. Cal lit a cigarette and sipped beer. Finally, Heindemann looked at him, frozen-faced.

"Regenbogen?" Cal asked, softly.

"Quite. Bit damp, isn't it. Do you think summer will ever arrive?"

Cal shrugged. "Why not. But I really don't give a damn. I just want to get everything over with. And go home to America."

Heindemann smiled. "I see," he said, his lips barely moving as he spoke, staring at his reflection in the long mirror behind the rows of bottles. "And what is your business?"

Cal, hunched over his glass, said: "I'm a school teacher."

"Interesting that you should say that," the German said, still staring into the mirror. "I know of a very important conference on Ludgate Hill, just before you reach St. Paul's, on the right-hand side of the road. Have you heard of it?"

Cal locked in on Heindemann's eyes in the reflection. "No. But I'd like to attend."

"Excellent. It is scheduled for 0200 hours the day after tomorrow. It will be in a condemned three-storey building just as you walk by a very empty lot. You should find it interesting." The German lapsed into a stony-faced silence until he resumed his conversation with the other man.

F'r Chrissakes! Cal thought, grimly. He finished his beer and limped outside. The rain had stopped. The sky behind Fleet Street was streaked with blue. He had heartburn and his left hip was aching again. He walked until he flagged down a taxi. "The Pavo Rojo. On the Kensington Road." During the short ride, he made up his mind: Because he had never attended such a "conference" before, he would study the layout. Early. By the time he had reached his room, he had also decided to be there late that afternoon. And camp out. Or in, depending on the layout. He chuckled: "Whoever heard of a tourist camping out in downtown London?"

Julio Ruiz supplied him with a blue-and-white tote bag, and didn't ask the question "Why?" his black-brown eyes begged. Remembering that even late May nights can get chilly in England, he took a folded blanket off his bed and packed it into the bag. He decided against the shaving gear and toothpaste, but stowed the toothbrush and Adidas. Because he was never comfortable with the Walther in his belt, he also dropped it in, followed by the extra clip.

Food? He made a mental note to pick up apples, pre-sliced cheese, bread and chewing gum. And because he hated apple peelings, he added a paring knife. Plus three small bottles of plain water. Nothing fizzy. He emptied his pockets of all loose change, leaving it on the night table.

Soap? He asked himself. No soap. But toilet paper. He pulled a handful of the double-sheeted paper from the metal container in the bathroom, and hoped that condemned three-storey British buildings had at least condemned toilets. Probably need a penny, he reflected, and I'm not carrying coins. Cigarettes? No, damnit. Flashlight? No.

The open area next to the boarded-up ruins of what had once been a three-storey building had been created by the German air force during the blitz. It had been bulldozed clear of bricks and stone. The uneven ground had been puddled by the rain. Every window was boarded, with bright red-lettered signs plastered across them: CONDEMNED: KEEP OUT.

It was almost three o'clock before Cal figured out how he could near the building without arousing suspicion. He limped back into Fleet Street and bought a Kodak camera and two rolls of Agfa film. He snapped pictures of St. Paul's. Gradually, he worked his way among the puddles on the cleared ground, edging closer to the building. He took more snaps. Then, convinced he appeared to be just another tourist snapping the last vestiges of a war no one was interested in except eccentric middle-aged visitors, he casually stood facing the rear ground floor. It was still scarred by the sudden rupture with its former neighbor, sectioned off like a huge checkerboard where rooms had shared the same brick-and-mortar heavy wall.

Two bobbies peered casually at him as they stepped, side-by-side, down Ludgate Hill.

Still shooting, now at the cathedral, now across the open ground, he reached the back wall. An iron grill guarded a gaping opening where someone had managed to rip off the thick planking. There was no glass in the window frame behind it. Cautiously, Cal closed his fingers around the

THE LAST HUNTER

grill and pulled. It moved slightly, then came away in his hand. Hurriedly, he bent over and, still holding the grill in his left fist, threw his good leg over the brick sill. He dragged the bandaged one behind him. Slowly, holding his breath, he tugged the grill back into place. Flakes of brickwork fell at his feet.

The mixed sounds of traffic on Ludgate Hill barely penetrated the dusty room. Cal stood motionless. My gawd, I'm out of shape, he thought, listening to his own panting breath. Quietly, he opened the tote bag and placed the camera in it, lifting the Walther out. He hefted it in his right hand and stared around him in the half-light. His eyes picked out two British Army blankets on the dusty floor, their War Department markings still visible. Cigarette butts. A flattened box of wooden matches. Dirty kleenex. Slivers of wallpaper. A heap of glass shards had been swept together in one corner.

Bums, he thought. Old boozers shacking up with their cheap port on cold nights. Or damp.

The next room was larger, windowless and darker. Except for dust and fine plaster, it was clean. He wondered why the old bums didn't use it. The hall between the first and second rooms led to stairs at either end. Another door opened into what must have been a shop, running across the front of the building. Sunlight, sneaking between the boarding, reflected off the broken glass littering the planked floor. Cal could make out the broken lines of pedestrians outside. He retreated cautiously and headed for the stairs. Twice he crushed broken glass under foot, so he sat on the lower step and changed into the Adidas.

There were four rooms off a center hall on the second floor with another two sets of stairs leading to the third.

A toilet, its lid against the tank, jammed with paper and excreta, was tucked under the staircase at the rear. Cal's nose twitched. He closed the wooden lid carefully. Ah well, he reflected, the floors don't squeak. And they aren't littered with broken glass. Or sag under my weight. He was halfway across the third room, looking down at the ancient floor boards when he realized two of them were badly warped. There was a bulging three-inch gap before they came together. Down on his hands and knees, he peered into the center of the clean-swept larger ground floor room. He struggled to his feet, gasping.

The roof over the top storey had been badly holed. But tarpaulins, stretched over the jagged openings, had effectively dammed any rain. Staring between the boards and across a small window in one of the back rooms, Cal peered down at the cleared ground he had crossed. We'd have made a parking lot out of that space, he mused. But in the U.K. they just clean 'em up and proceed. Like it had always been that way. Quietly, carefully, he returned to the second floor by the front-end stairs. A rear room, he decided, would be his overnight bunk-in. Because if anyone wants into this damn building, he thought, they'll have to cross the open ground.

In the darkness, Cal wanted a cigarette. He slid another piece of gum into his mouth and rubbed his shoulders against the wall. He dozed fitfully while the night seeped through the shattered windows and gaping cracks. He awoke with a convulsive start when he heard a woman's voice, her words clear and distinct, drifting up the stairwell.

" 'Arry, this place gives me the creeps. Why do you always want to come 'ere?"

Damn it! he thought, I didn't even know anybody was inside the building! He reached for the Walther on the floor beside the tote bag.

"Cuz hit's free, hit is."

The woman giggled. "I guessed that, 'arry. But hits awful 'ard on me bum. I've told you that before."

So much for *old* bums, Cal thought.

" 'Ave you got 'em off yet, pet?"

She squealed. "Off! But coo, hits cold. Even with the blanket!"

Silence.

"Ain't you gonna warm me up first, luv?" she asked.

Cal shook his head.

The woman began to sigh. Then moan. "Now!" she gasped.

Cal stuck his fingers inside his ears. He could still hear her. And he heard them leave.

The night passed slowly and a tower clock outside reminded him, Cal reflected moodily. I didn't even hear a pair of sex-starved lovers get in. And I think I'll be able to pick up the sounds of professional agents entering the building? It was a proposition he didn't like. He wished he was someplace else. Even on the rewrite desk. But the subtle weight of the Walther in his lap reminded him he had a job to do.

In troubled half-sleep, he dreamed and thought of Pamela. Among sand dunes. Seated across from him, sipping red wine. Lying beside him. Until he couldn't distinguish between his dreams and thoughts. He wakened in bright sunshine, sad and uneasy.

It was a long day. He had wanted hot coffee and a smoke, but settled for water and more chewing gum. Restlessly, he changed position each time the outside clock chimed. He had to use the toilet. Returning to his cell (as he had dubbed it), he glanced at a door he hadn't noticed before. Probably a walk-in closet, he thought, absently. He tried the knob. It wouldn't turn.

Eleven o'clock, his wristwatch's illuminated numbers indicated. Twenty-three hundred hours. Three more to go. To what? Cautiously he stretched his cramped legs and rearranged the blanket across his shoulders. He was out of gum, but no longer wanted a cigarette. He craved one. And solid sleep.

From out in the starry night, the clock tolled. Once.

At first, he believed he was hearing things; that his mind was playing tricks on him because he was tired. He heard the sounds again. Low, muffled voices from inside the room below him. At least two, he decided, instantly alert. But how did they get in? He shivered again although he was as tense as a water-soaked drum. Then they ceased. Silence. Sitting upright, his muscles suddenly taut, he stared into the gloom. Listening.

"I have told you many times," a voice hissed in even, distinctly spaced words, "we are to always use American in our conversation. It is good practice before we are posted to the United States!"

Cal couldn't hear the reply. His brain was running ahead

of his ears. But it could "hear" the old concierge at the Bristol saying: "They talked like Americans." A bead of sweat formed on his forehead. He craned his neck. Cautiously, he flattened on the floor and eased his bulk forward until he could squint through the gap in the plank boards.

Somewhere in the room below him a lamp cast a faint, dim glow of light across the floor. It has to be battery-operated, he thought, idiotically. Then his eyes picked out a square opening and the beginnings of steep steps leading into the inky darkness. Its door was tilted backward, resting against a wall. So, he thought, a trapdoor!

A close-cropped head appeared in the opening, rising higher until Cal could make out a set of broad, thick shoulders.

"What were you doing down there?" another voice asked, querulously.

"Taking a piss," the man with the close-cropped hair said. "There, does that sound American enough for you?"

"Have you checked the building?"

The man with the close-cropped hair moved partly out of Cal's sight. His feet were very large. "Yes."

Two, Cal said to himself. Just two. He could count his heartbeats. He was leaking perspiration. He peered at the big pair of feet. Their owner lies, he thought, sarcastically, like most people who are sure they won't be caught. Turning his head, he looked at his watch. Two minutes to two. He resumed squinting through the gap in the planks. What in the name of God am I supposed to do? He cursed. He had to try twice before he could get the safety catch off the Walther. Hell, I can't even hit anybody unless they stand right under this goddamned slit! His mouth was dry. It got drier when he heard a third voice from inside the trapdoor.

"Vil vun off you gennelmen come down here and help me up these *verdammment* steps?" It was a harsh, hoarse order.

The close-cropped man with the thick shoulders answered. "Coming! Coming! Coming Kameraden!" He began to back down the steep steps. The owner of the first voice, moving quickly, came into Cal's view, carrying the dim light to the opening.

"And now you are talking German!" he chided, exasperated. The man on the steps looked up. It was a flat face, heavily browed.

Both of them had to assist the third man. Once up, he walked awkwardly, like a man on stilts—rocking slightly to his left, then right. For a moment, he stood, panting, directly under Cal's eyes. Almost strutting, he walked out of Cal's field of vision.

Cal shook himself. Closed his eyes. And in his own personal darkness he knew the third man was the legless German, Don Juan Ricardo. Or Freiherr Joachim Heinrichs. But he was dead! His face shredded by his own artificial limbs, Heindemann had said. Vividly, he recalled the full-length contours of the body carried on the stretcher in front of 11 Calle San Ramon in Marbella on that sunlit early afternoon.

God! he rasped silently, he *is* the mole! The Judas who Heindemann said had to be trapped before they could hunt down the wildschwein. His breath backed up deep inside his throat until he was sure his lungs would burst.

Cal couldn't see him, but the newcomer was talking in hushed tones. "Of course, I am armed, gennelmen. But I alone vill vait for him. It iss an old thing that I must settle myself. So you vill go out in the hall, unt only return vhen it iss all ober. Bitte!"

"You are quite certain he will show?" Cal thought it was the voice belonging to the thick-shouldered man with the big feet.

"Ja. He iss a most punctual man."

Cal heard a door open, then close faintly. Slowly, he cocked the Walther. He began to breathe again. His eyes ached. He blinked rapidly and tried to shift his shoulders to relieve the cramps in his back. Damn, he thought, rapidly, I should have removed the tensor bandage. Just in case I have to move quickly. For a moment, he wondered if the two "Americans" were padding down the second-floor hall, heading for his room. Seconds ticked until they added up to an agonizing minute. Then, his eyes widening, he recognized Carl Heindemann emerging through the open trapdoor. And he was the Carl Heindemann he had met originally. No make-up. The chimes from the clock tower struck two.

"Ah, Oberleutnant Heindemann, you are on time. As alvays."

Heindemann climbed the last step, stood for a second, then shifted to his right where Cal could still see him. "Old habits die slowly, Herr Heinrichs."

"You are surprised, perhaps?"

Cal pointed the snub-nosed Walther into the slit. He cursed. He couldn't see Heinrichs.

"Not as much as you would expect," Heindemann said.

"But my 'death' confused you. Did it not?"

"Temporarily. It was your sudden 'cremation' that corrected my thinking."

Heinrich's laugh was shrill. "Still, I bought time."

"Joachim. I am very disappointed. . . ."

Heinrichs' voice was sarcastic. "Disappointed? Ach. *You* are a disappointment! Und a fool!"

"Because I trusted you?" The ex-oberleutnant was in clear view.

"Because you belieff in the vest! In the honor of the Fatherland! Vat did it efter giff you? A chance to die? It took mein legs then gafe me a pension. In a hospital in Spain, I had a chance to think. To make sense of this vorld. Unt ven the opportunity came, I accepted the odds—to travel with the Bolsheviks!"

"You mean the Russians?"

"Jawohl. But enough. You asked me to come here. You haff the key information? The prize? Unt I vould like it. Bitte!"

Heindemann held out his hand. There was a small black pistol in it. Two shots sounded almost like one. They were followed by two more somewhere else in the building. Heindemann was driven backward against the wall. He tried to right himself, stood briefly, then slid to the floor, the pistol in his closed fingers.

Cal blinked his eyes rapidly. In slow motion, he watched Heinrichs, sliding his feet forward and rocking slightly, come into view. He bent slightly and pointed a gun at Heindemann's forehead. Cal only had time to squeeze off one shot at the back of the legless man's shoulders. The Walther's recoil surprised him and he instinctively closed his eyes then opened them again. Heinrichs was sprawled across Heindemann's body, twitching.

There were two more shots. Again muffled.

Cal jumped to his feet and, almost cartwheeling on his one good leg, headed for the stairs. He swore under rasping breath. He struggled one-step-at-a-time until he reached the ground floor, then threw himself through the doorway, landing chest down, his Walther cocked and aimed.

Marc Fauberge was bending over Heindemann. " 'urry, monsieur! The oberleutnant 'as it bad. In the belly!" He faced Cal, tucking a Walther inside his belt. "But first, we mus' get the udder two, an trow them into the cellar. And 'einrichs."

"Where the hell did you come from?" Cal gasped.

"Later, monsieur. We mus' get 'im h'out. 'Elp me!"

Heindemann wasn't bleeding much, but he was fighting for breath as they moved him down the steep steps into the damp cellar. "Close the door," Marc hissed.

"Yeah. Yeah. But not before I get back upstairs and get my tote bag!" Cal wheezed.

"There is no time, mon ami."

Cal didn't listen. He climbed the steps, stiff-legged. He collected the bag, stuffed the hotel blanket and his shoes inside and returned, closing the door over his head.

Marc had the ex-U-boater propped up. Heindemann was conscious, suddenly wracked by a long coughing spell.

"Now?" Marc asked.

Cal sucked in a huge breath. Exhaled it. "If nobody's heard that racket yet, we got until daylight!"

"But the oberleutnant cannot wait!"

The cellar led to a bricked passage into the next building. With Heindemann half walking, half sagging, they made it up another flight of stairs, exiting into a lane that led to Ludgate Hill. "What building was that?" Cal panted.

"Heindemann's. 'E 'as owned it for years. Eet's 'is drop."

The night sky was sprinkled with stars. They stood under a streetlamp. Cal looked both ways, then toward The Strand. "No police, anyway," he panted.

Heindemann went limp for a second, almost dragging both men to the sidewalk. His breath was wheezy as he recovered. "We've got to get him to a hospital!" Cal snapped.

"Impossible!" hissed Marc Fauberge. " 'E cannot. First, we mus' get 'im to the 'otel, by taxi."

Three young men, walking briskly down Ludgate Hill, glanced at them curiously.

"We got to sing. That's it. Sing. And people'll think we're just drunks. Okay, Marc? Sing!"

Arms looped around Heindemann's shoulders and under his arms, they reeled into The Strand. Cal broke into a tuneless "Roll Me Over in the Clover" while Marc tried to follow him.

The driver of the black, humpbacked London cab grinned. "Y're mate 'ave too much t'drink?" he greeted. "Never mind, I'll 'ave you 'ome in a jiffy! To the Pavo Rojo? In the Kensington Road? Right you are!"

The Frenchman took the steps two at a time while the taxi drove away. Heindemann, Cal realized, was losing the fight to stay alive. His breathing was irregular. In the gloom, his face was a pasty white. He twitched spasmodically. And the silence between each terrible, wheezing breath grew longer. His chin slumped to his chest. With a barely audible sigh, he went limp.

"Quick!" Cal hissed, "Quick! I think he's dead . . ."

Cal sat facing Marc Fauberge in the resident's lounge. Across the hall in the Ruiz family's private salon, Carl Heindemann, ex-oberleutnant in the navy of the Third Reich, lay stiffening in death.

A nickel-plated thermos pot of coffee, two cups and saucers, a creamer, half a dozen small sugar-filled envelopes, a half bottle of Black Label scotch and pitcher of water between two glasses cluttered the small table.

The quiet was soothing. Like the afterglow that follows furious love-making, he reflected, when you can literally feel tension draining from your arms and legs. His body demanded sleep, but his mind declined. His hip ached even though he had stripped the tensor bandage off his leg. And his stomach rumbled. He stretched, reached for the scotch and poured three fingers into one glass, nodding toward Fauberge.

The Frenchman shook his head.

Cal ignored his stomach and drank the scotch in rapid mouthfuls, made a face and settled back.

"Okay, my friend, we've done everything we can for Heindemann . . ." he began.

The Frenchman's eyes were heavily lined. "I was in the building with you, since yesterday."

"And you took the other two men out."

"Oui. In the 'all. When the shooting began. I knew you were watching. From the room above." Marc Fauberge allowed a small smile to twist the corners of his mouth. "The oberleutnant 'ad said you would do what you 'ad to."

"And the last two shots?"

"The coup de grace. They were only KGB." Marc shrugged.

Cal remembered dragging the thick-shouldered Russian to the trapdoor and sliding his inert body into the opening until its weight carried it down the steep steps. And standing aside while the Frenchman hefted the second agent and Joachim Heinrichs into the dark opening. *They are for you, Pamela Strong,* he panted exultantly. At the time.

"You're telling me, my friend, that both you and Heindemann expected something like that to happen tonight," he said at last. "Particularly the appearance of that legless bastard, Heinrichs."

The Frenchman poured himself a coffee and sipped from the cup. His eyes were narrow over the rim. "Eet was a trap, Monsieur," he murmured. "The oberleutnant, 'imself, was the bait. You and I? Security, should 'einrich show with 'is people. And when one considers the game, eet was only natural to expect the KGB."

Cal dropped his forehead into his right hand, then peered under his fingers at the Frenchman, frowning. "My God, wouldn't it have been more natural to find Heinrichs, take him, then do what had to be done? Christ, four people died."

"Only one man died. The others? Who cares?"

Cal shook his head. "Okay. You knew Heinrichs was the traitor."

"But where 'e was 'iding was another matter."

"Hell, you managed to get word to him that Heindemann would be at that drop, so why couldn't you locate him?"

"Getting the word to 'im was one thing. Finding 'im was something completely different. But, oui, I passed the word."

Cal grunted. "And now there are three bodies lying in that cellar and enough weapons to arm a bank holdup team."

Marc Fauberge held the cup and saucer in one hand. "The British will discover them. True. And their Makarov pistols. The information will find eets way into an official file somewhere. Questions will be discreetly asked. No one will know anything. And the matter will be dropped," he said.

"And he called it a hunt, played by members of a society," Cal sighed. He closed his eyes tight. Pinwheels of light exploded behind their lids. It felt good when he opened them. "Tell me, Marc, what do you know about the society? Or the hunt?"

The Frenchman's hand trembled slightly when he placed the cup and saucer on the table. He crossed his lean legs.

He said, softly: "Eet was born in the debris of defeat in '45. And while some 'ad served in the Wehrmacht, the majority 'ad been in the navy—the U-boat arm. Dedicated? To destroy the remnants of the Nazi elite? Perhaps. But certainly eet provided the membership with un raison d'être—a reason to exist in those uncertain times."

"And you, a torpedo man, where did Herbert Mueller fit in?" Cal asked.

The Frenchman smiled wanly. "The oberleutnant said you 'ad an excellent memory. I served under 'im. And 'e made that service bearable, even if I was not an officer."

"Yet, you deserted."

"After the oberleutnant 'ad been transferred to the Seekriegsleitung staff. Eet was while in 'ospital I decided that for me—and all of Germany—the war was over. Later, as 'e told you that night in my cafe, we met again." Marc Fauberge spread his hands, expressively. "I felt I owed 'im—the man."

"So you joined up again."

The Frenchman's eyes widened. "You can say eet that way. Pourquoi? Carl visited me in 'ospital before I deserted. And, somehow, I sensed he knew what was on my mind. Yet, 'e said nothing. Later, 'e was aware of Lisette and 'er parents' cafe in the Rue St. Honore." His voice ran down to a whisper.

Cal glanced at the bottle of Black Label. Again, ignoring his stomach, he poured a small drink, adding water. It was tepid. Remembering Les Pyramides, he said: "Okay, so you owed. But let's get back to that society. The first night we met, you'll recall I asked your oberleutnant wherein-hell all the society members were when he needed them. His answer was that he couldn't trust any of them until he ran down the traitor. Yet, you tell me a trap was set for Heinrichs, meaning he knew, or suspected, who it was." He took another sip. "Was the society," he asked gently, "was it only in Carl Heindemann's mind at the last?"

The Frenchman's mouth sagged. "At the start," he replied slowly, "there were many. But time took eets toll. They aged. Some went into the NATO forces. Others continued to provide funds, reluctantly. Such men were always survivors, mon ami. They could read the signs."

"What signs?"

Marc Fauberge exhaled a long, almost wistful breath. "Not too many cared anymore what the Nazis 'ad done. Except, the Judean. An' I'm not convinced the average members of their flocks do, either. For most, what was done was *finis*. Just 'istory. But Oberleutnant Heindemann cared. So, oui, at the last . . . 'e *was* the society."

And because one German still cared, still hunted, Cal mused, ten have died since that warm afternoon Klaus von Hagen was shot and thrown out of a hotel window. Not counting Heindemann or the faceless Spaniard who had been stabbed in place of Heinrichs at Calle San Ramon 11 in Marbella. He was suddenly sad. All over a bloody "hunt," he thought, morosely. "What about that wildschwein . . . still to be hunted?" he queried aloud.

"Eet is still there."

"And who will hunt it?"

"I do not know."

"Do you know, just by chance, where this wild boar is at bay?"

"Non, monsieur. But you do. The oberleutnant insisted you know. When you return to your room, carefully slice open one of your tubes of Pepsodent." Marc Fauberge stood up. "For now, bonsoir, Monsieur Sanders. I am very tired. I need sleep for I 'ave much to do before I return to Paris late tonight."

Cal groaned. He struggled to his feet. The weight of the Walther was heavy in his jacket pocket. He scratched the stubble forming at his hairline."

"I will 'ave the oberleutnant cremated. Privately. And the ashes sent to Frau Heindemann. Those also were 'is wishes, including a desire that a proper obituary appear in the West German journals."

"Fitting. Very fitting."

The Frenchman's face jerked with annoyance. "Eet may also be a signal to the KGB that the 'unt is over. For now. An' provide you with a few days to get what you North Americans term your second wind."

"My second wind?" Cal croaked, surprised. "I'm not a member of any goddamned society. And I don't hunt. Here nor anywhere else. Carl Heindemann is dead. Now, I'm going home. Tomorrow." He paused. "Where did Pamela Strong fit?"

"The KGB owns her."

"Is she alive?"

"The oberleutnant thought so."

"And Anatoley Lebedev?"

"KGB."

Cal sighed. "Can I go home now?"

"Perhaps. But if I were you, I would lie low for a day or two."

THE LAST HUNTER

Cal knew the Frenchman was speaking facts.

Fauberge continued: "Sometime tomorrow, the British will turn the bodies of the three dead men over to the Soviets. Eet will tidy things up un petit peu. And while the KGB will not grieve, Lebedev will zero directly in on 'is last contact: You. That ees 'is policy."

"Why not you?" Cal asked.

"I was the oberleutnant's man, nothing more."

Christ! Cal thought, bewildered, I need sleep.

The Frenchman stood in the doorway. "Bonsoir," he said, again.

Cal's mind returned to the reunion at the King Eddy. The words of an old German naval song haunted him: *Auf einen Seemannsgrab da bluhen kein Rosen.* On a sailor's grave, no roses bloom.

27-5-66   0730 hrs GMT

File: AH 1945

For prime ministerial and presidential

eyes only; to be hand delivered

on receipt.

To: MI 5, CIA, RCMP (Operation Alois

Sibling desks)

Meeting switched to London. A two-two

standoff. Society Leader lost permanently.

Third Party mole fatal suggests missing

Printer has Prize. Immediate that Keepers

go to Red until he surfaces.

Control.

CHAPTER 12

✳

CAL SLIT THE second tube of Pepsodent carefully with a razor blade before he found it. It had been doubled, doubled again and again doubled, before it was ironed flat then encased in a small plastic packet. Smoothing it out under the dim light from the night lamp, he read the neatly typed message: Locate a White Rose that blooms in Ontario during 19 and 63 and you will find the wildschwein at bay at 17, 108 and 10.5 west. He read it and reread it until his weary brain decided it was gibberish. Slowly, he stripped and rolled into bed. I've left my socks on and the light burning, he thought vaguely before he was overwhelmed by sleep.

Orv Harron was the son of a blacksmith. Built like his father's anvil, he had a newsman's instincts. And he had created a tight network of reliable contacts through the U.K. and western Europe that had made it impossible for *The Express* management to move him from the London office.

He was hunched over his old Underwood typewriter, pecking out copy. He looked up and stared hard at Cal when he limped into the tiny Fleet Street office, closing the frosted-glass door behind him.

"What can I do for you?" he asked.

"I'm your replacement," Cal growled.

Harron stood up, puzzled. "Come again?"

Cal repeated his words, using his own voice.

"Harron's eyes recognized him. "F'r chrissakes! Sanders!"

"In the flesh. If not the form."

"How'd you expect me to know you? You've dyed your hair. You're limping. And dressed like some refugee from God knows where!" He laughed raucously, watching Cal hobble to a hard chair and sit down awkwardly, stretching his stiff leg straight out. "You're a wreck, ol' buddy. Where you been? Oh, by the way, I had a query from Limey yesterday. He said if you showed up I was to tell you you're fired."

Cal ignored him. "Still clipping the Brits, I see," he said, glancing at the stack of British dailies piled on a table, topped by a pair of heavy scissors.

"Yeah. And the U.S. editions out of Paris. Plus translated clippings off the continent. Where you been?"

"Lately? Holed up in Lunnon town for the last three days. Did you know London can be as boring as any other city when you're sitting in your room, listening to traffic. Or the BBC."

Harron grinned. "That depends on who was with you . . ." He sat down. "Hurt your leg?"

"Sort of."

Harron had a farmer's patience. "So, don't tell me."

"How's it been going with you the last couple of days?" Cal countered.

"Routine-wise?"

"I mean . . . anything unusual?"

"Such as?"

Cal chuckled. "You're a reporter. Answer a question with a question. I mean, any oddball phone calls? Or strangers showing up at your door?"

Harron's frown was fleeting. "No. Wait a minute. Someone—a woman I think it was—rang yesterday and asked me if this office was tied into the Toronto paper of the same name."

Cal stood up. "What did her voice sound like? American?"

"Hard to tell. It was too hoarse. That's why I couldn't be sure if it was a man or woman."

"Christ! What'd you tell 'em?"

"I admitted it was."

"I knew I was taking a chance coming here. I knew it!"

"Sit down, buddy," Harron said, quietly. "You've got the shakes and you look like you're gonna fly apart. Sit down!"

Cal sat.

"Care to fill me in?" Harron asked in the same tone. He lit a cigarette and passed the pack to Cal.

"I haven't had a butt in five days." Cal got up again, crossed the room and locked the door, returning to the chair.

"Godalmighty," said Harron, "this must be serious."

Cal talked in a low voice for three minutes. ". . . and Heindemann died in the confrontation with Heinrichs. So did a couple of Soviet agents. Just three days ago in a condemned building on Ludgate Hill. And, Christ, Orv, I was there. I took out the cripple . . ." He finished.

Harron's cigarette was burning almost down to his fingers.

"You believe me?" Cal asked.

"Now I know why the limp and funny haircut. Does that answer your question?" Harron was silent for a moment. "How about the broad?"

"She wasn't a broad."

"Okay, I take it back. It was a slip of the tongue." Harron paused, then said, "You haven't seen her since she was picked up in Paris?"

"Nope."

"Or this bird, Lebedev?"

"Nothing since Gibraltar. But he's around, I can smell him. Or maybe I'm paranoid."

Harron half-started out of his chair. The smoking cigarette butt dropped to the floor. He fanned his right-hand fingers. "I think I burned myself!" he squealed. "Goddamn!" He retrieved the butt gingerly and dropped it in an ashtray. "Why wasn't he at the confrontation?"

"According to Heindemann, he's in charge of the operation to 'tidy' up the files on the society. So, I guess he only directs, doesn't get shot at. I don't know."

"So why does he want a piece of you?"

"He believes I have some information. That he wants. Badly."

"Have you?"

"Maybe."

"Then give it to him."

"F'r chrissakes! Orv! I've gone a long way down a rough road. People I got to know—and like—have disappeared or been murdered and you say 'give it to him' just like that! No goddamned way!" He paused. "Besides, I didn't say I had any information."

"You just did." Harron licked his lips. "You took a chance coming here, you know that? Why didn't you phone flrst?"

"In case you were tapped."

"And you figured they wouldn't recognize you the way you are. Right?"

"You didn't."

"Right. So how can I help?"

Cal leaned forward. "I have a hunch Pamela Strong is going to contact you. I think that call you got the other day was from her. Or Lebedev. Whoever it was, masked the voice." He paused. "When she does call again—and make damn sure it's her—meet with her. It doesn't matter where because she'll be watched. Get her an air ticket to Montreal's Dorval. Instruct her to wait there for me. Any airline. Then phone me from a kiosk, not your office. Give me the flight number and departure date. If she goes Air Canada, I'll hop on Lufthansa or KLM and get in a couple of hours later."

Harron reached for a pad of copy paper.

"Don't write anything down. Okay?" Cal's bandaged leg was stiff. He struggled to his feet, and walked slowly along each wall, checking the two lights on the desk. "Have any electricians been nosing around the building lately?"

"No."

"Figures. A wire tap would be less risky."

"You mean no bugging devices?"

Cal nodded. "Here's the telephone number in Kensington." He repeated it several times.

"Got it," said Harron, dryly. "You're getting to be a very cautious man, Calvin Sanders."

"I've had three days to think about it," Cal replied, grimly. "And if I am not, I might not survive to write my story."

Harron repeated the Kensington phone number.

"You got it, Orv ol' buddy. Now, something else . . ."

"Name it."

Cal removed a sheet of paper from his inside jacket pocket. "Call Jim Emmerson. He'll know what the question is all about."

Harron scanned the paper briefly. "Will do!"

"Thanks."

Harron looked at his watch. "It's almost eleven in the ayem. That makes it six back in T.O. Yeah, Emmerson should be on the desk." He dialed.

Cal unlocked the office door and limped down the hall to the bathroom. When he returned, Harron was standing by the window, holding the curtain to one side. "If someone's watching this office," he said, grinning, "it could be any one of ten thousand people on Fleet Street at any given daylight hour,"

"You get Jim?"

"Yes. But it'll take some time to get what you want. When I do, I'll phone. Okay? Good."

"Hold it," Cal interrupted. "I have another favor. Among your contacts, do you have a doctor you can trust?"

Harron smirked. "Even I have to stay healthy."

"Okay. Now listen carefully. I need something, quick-acting that would make someone sick. Dramatically sick. Make it look like it was life or death and insist an ambulance be called at once. Nothing remotely fatal, just scary. If you know what I mean."

"Something that could be slipped into a drink or food?"

"Or taken voluntarily."

"Christ! Do you know someone crazy enough to do that?"

Cal shrugged.

"Liquid or pill?"

"Whichever. Something you can get at a drugstore."

"You mean chemist's shop." Harron frowned, then sighed. "I'll see what I can do. How fast is this—ah dose—supposed to work?"

"Within minutes. But remember, nothing that could be fatal."

"Got you."

"Phone me," Cal said as he started for the door.

"Hold it. What if this woman, Pamela Strong, insists she has to see you. Like soon. In London?" Harron asked.

Two pigeons landed on the windowsill and began pouting.

"Tell her flatly, no."

"Hell, Cal, if I put her on a plane, she's going to have company. Likely this Lebedev. So why not let me arrange something?"

"Sorry, no. And I agree it will likely be Lebedev. But my way, he won't know for certain where I am. Whether I'm already in Montreal or still in London. And if I play my cards right, I'll land in behind them and have a chance to size up the situation before anything can come down."

Harron grimaced. "I hope to hell you know what you're doing," he said. "For your sake."

And Pamela Strong's, Cal added to himself.

Orv Harron rapped his knuckles against the window pane. The two pigeons flew away.

Cal sat in the chair under the floor lamp, staring at the message. He knew the words and numbers off by heart. He waited while an urge to go out and buy a pack of cigarettes subsided. The numbers, he concluded as he had for three days, were highway routes. But why five? Five never merge. Three, perhaps. Maybe the cryptic ex-oberleutnant had been just that: cryptic. Adding two to confuse any possible wrong readers. Yet, he knew Carl Heindemann was a precise man.

The White Rose, he reflected, blooms in Ontario. And Heindemann resided in Ontario, Canada. So, Ontario was where the wildschwein was at bay. No doubt about that. Not Ontario in Ohio or California. Or anywhere else.

"Then I am right in going to Ontario," he mused, "and taking it from there."

Carefully, he refolded the note and slipped it inside his wallet. I'll get a map in Ontario, he thought. Then what? he asked himself. First you have to get there, and who is this wildschwein? He deliberately blanked his mind.

The telephone jangled.

The normally phlegmatic Harron was fuming. "They wrecked the office," he snarled, "yanking every damned drawer out of both desks and files and left 'em on the floor!"

"Who did?"

"How-in-hell would I know? Your KGB friends, I suppose."

"Where are you calling from?"

"A kiosk off Leicester Square." Harron cursed. "Christ! I don't even have copies of wires! What did they think they'd find? You ought to have seen it—paper all over the place. And I had just got my clippings files updated. Cheesh!"

Cal waited for him to wind down.

"Your friend phoned. I'm meeting with her in half an hour."

"Good."

"No change? She still flies out to Dorval?"

"Yes." Cal could hear a taxi honking loudly from near the public phonebooth.

"I think I've been followed. By an Englishman, of all things."

Cal laughed. "Now who's paranoid?"

"He's standing in front of the theater. Bold as you please. I thought these guys were great tails."

"Only in the movies, ol' buddy."

"Any word from Emmerson?" Cal asked.

"No. Talk to you."

The line went dead.

His room seemed stifling, but his mind was in idle. He felt isolated, yet cool. Like he had the first time they went into the attack against a wolfpack. Oddly, he recalled the Ancient Mariner who had gazed from a painted ship upon a painted sea. Beyond the walls of Pavo Rojo, he knew millions of people walked, rode, crawled, even staggered, in millions of different directions for millions of different reasons. But he had only one way to go: To the end of a road he could barely make out. And it would have sudden turns he couldn't predict.

He was asleep in the chair when Harron called. "She wants to think it over," he said. "Let you know tomorrow morning, okay?"

"It will have to be."

"She's some kind of lady, Cal. But I got the impression she's running on nerve."

"If you were taking orders from the KGB, you'd be, too."

"I have that special medicine you requested. Pills. Fifteen of the little buggers. And I mean little. You can hold 'em all in the palm of one cupped hand. They're nitroglycerine tablets. People who have heart problems eat 'em every day." Harron paused. "You still there?"

"Nitroglycerine?"

"That's right. My doctor friend says an overdose of fifteen of 'em—each of 'em point-six milligrams all taken at once—will produce flushing, extreme dizziness and a severe, pounding headache. Within minutes of ingestion. But you won't be able to sneak 'em into a martini. Or soup. The victim will have to throw 'em back, knowingly. And, yes, she'll need an ambulance and some hospital care right quick. He guarantees that unless someone goofs, the victim'll recover nicely."

"Why not barbiturates?"

"He said he couldn't come up with a better approach in such a short time."

"Why not barbituates?"

"Too slow acting. Besides, the victim would only get sleepy."

"If that's the best . . ."

"It is. Who's going to get 'em? The woman?"

"That's my plan."

Harron snorted. "And if she won't take 'em?"

"Then she's against me." Cal stared at the floor lamp standing behind the chair. "After you book Pamela to Dorval . . ."

"If she will go . . ."

"If she won't she doesn't figure anymore. Okay? Anyway, when you book me—and that's a definite, whether alone or after Pamela—leave 'em in an envelope at the flight desk where I'll pick up my tickets."

"That's a roger. Call you tomorrow. When I know who's flying where on which line."

"And, oh, if she decides to take your offer, ask her to wait for me in the mezzanine lounge."

"Consider it done."

Cal assembled his thoughts. Do they "own" her? Or are they using her? he asked himself. "But that's not important," he said out loud. "Coupled with the raid on Harron's office, it means Lebedev is certain I have what he wants. But he doesn't know where I am."

He massaged his leg with the palm of his hand. He touched his shaved hairline. Lisa Fauberge had done a good job. And it offered him an advantage because he understood, with terrible certainty, he and Lebedev would meet. Head-on.

"All I need is the smarts. And a dollop of luck," he said. He hummed to himself while he shaved and showered. He felt so good, he limped down to the Bunch of Grapes. The air smelled better in the Brompton Road than it had three days earlier. The tall young woman who reminded him of Pamela wasn't there. Suddenly, he understood why he had gone to the pub.

It was ten o'clock and gloomy when the phone jarred Cal awake. For a few brief seconds, he stared at it, uncomprehendingly. "Yeah?" he rasped after picking it up.

"It's Orv."

"What are you calling me at this hour for?"

"It's five p.m. in the T.O. city room," Harron said, good-naturedly.

"You heard from Pamela?"

"No. Emmerson. I quote his message: 'She is twenty-three stop an orphan stop only child stop father made fortune in real estate stop uncle executor of estate in seven figures stop uneventful attendance at Californian girl's school until mixed up with campus radicals at Berkeley stop shipped to convent Malaga, Spain stop requested to leave by Mother Superior Xmas stop returned to New York stop dropped out of sight stop uncle says whereabouts unknown stop home Kansas City, Kansas. Regards. End of message.' Got it?"

"Got it. Thanks." Cal hung up. There was no mono, no parents. Only a twenty-three-year-old woman playing a twenty-year-old's game in a make-believe world. He felt like he had been kicked in the groin. Sighing, he lay back on the bed, wide awake. Closing his eyes, he waited for a rage to boil up out of his stomach. But there was nothing. Just an ache that gave way to fear for Pamela, the girl-woman who had come so abruptly into his life. And he could hear her in Gibraltar: ". . . for the first time in my life I know what I have and where I'm going for the next million years!"

Cal dozed until dawn crept through the window, chasing the darkness into the corners of the room, and awoke with a start. He climbed to his feet and went to the bathroom. He showered, shaved his jaw and hairline, then rewrapped his leg with the tensor bandage. Señor Ruiz brought coffee and hot croissants. The phone rang. Cal waited until the Spaniard had closed the door behind him before picking up the receiver.

"Catch you in the shower?" It was Harron.

"Nope. I'm just slow."

"Okay. Your woman, Pamela Strong, has agreed to go to Montreal. I've booked her out of Heathrow, Air Canada—I still want to say Trans-Canada—flight 108 leaving at noon. Today."

Cal looked at his watch. "Christ, it's already after ten ayem."

"Picking her up outside Canada House in a few minutes." Harron chuckled. "I figured return tickets would look better. An' I charged 'em to *The Express*. If that doesn't crank up Limey, it will when he finds out I charged yours, too. Lufthansa. You depart at 1:40. Just a hundred minutes later. Your package'll be at the desk. Okay?"

So, she is going. Cal thought. Because she wants to? Or

has been ordered? He didn't know, he admitted. "You'll see her right onto the plane?" he said, finally.

"No sweat. What about this Russian? What do I look for?"

Cal thought about that. "You won't recognize him. Forget it." He coughed. "Just be damned certain she's on that plane."

"What do you want? A signed pledge?"

"How is she?" Cal asked.

"Still strung out. Like fine piano wire."

"Injured?"

"Not that I could see. Just tied up in knots."

"I owe you . . ." Cal began.

"Keep your head up, Sanders," Harron replied soberly. "That's all I ask." He hung up.

Lufthansa flight 202 out of Bonn and Cologne departed London's Heathrow on time at 1:40 P.M. Cal had settled in the front seats, first class, using the space to ease the ache in his stiff leg. He wanted a cigarette, but declined when the good-legged stewardess with the wide smile offered him a package of Millbanks. He buried his right hand in his jacket pocket until he caught Pamela's engagement ring between his thumb and forefinger. It was cold to touch. And he thought of her, 100 minutes ahead of him, at 25,000 feet, shadowed by Anatoly Lebedev. Was he sitting with her? he wondered. Or three rows behind? Belting back Bols Genevers and water? Or brandy? Coldly watching and waiting.

He tried the other pocket. The small envelope of pills was in place. Oddly, it felt warm.

Stretching, he climbed to his feet and, half turning, casually studied the eight other passengers in the forward area, curtained off from economy class. All men. Their tidy heads buried in newspapers, magazines or stacks of white papers sitting in the lower half of expensive attache cases.

"Before we serve dinner," the stew said, brightly, "would anyone enjoy a complimentary drink?"

No one ordered Bols and water.

Cal sat down and put his mind in order while flight 202

picked up a strong tailwind south of the Irish coast and hurtled westward in brilliant sunlight. He asked for a double Black Label and soda and nursed it through the meal, then dozed fitfully.

He removed the Walther from his bag and slid it between his belly fat and belt before he hobbled off in Montreal.

Neither customs nor immigration officials challenged John Russell's passport. Or searched his one piece of luggage. And he used the ID to rent a Buick after he told the Tilden attendant, "Unfortunately, my driver's license is in my luggage."

"Thank you Mr. Russell. And for how many days will you need the car? Are you visiting here in Montreal?"

"For a day or two. Then I'm driving to Toronto."

"Leaving the car there?"

"Yes. More than likely."

"May I have your address?" She was all business. "There'll be a drop-off charge. You know that?"

"How much is the drop-off fee?"

"Fifty dollars."

"Will you take American?"

The attendant finally smiled. "Certainly."

"Is it topped with gas?"

"Of course."

Skirting the parking lot, Cal drove the round-and-round asphalt-topped road until he found a meter. He threw his bag in the back seat, locked up, and, under a watchful Mountie's eye, bought thirty minutes time with five dimes.

Pamela was in the mezzanine lounge, seated by a large window looking down on the airport apron. She was dressed in the blue skirt, pale blouse and blue jacket. An empty coffee cup sat in a saucer on the table. Without glancing to his left or right, he limped straight to her table and stood there.

She looked up, tentatively. "Yes?"

Orv Harron was right. Her almond-shaped eyes reflected tension. "It's me, Cal," he said, quietly.

"My God!" she whispered, hoarsely. "I saw you come in—limping—and didn't even recognize you! Oh my God! And you've been hurt."

THE LAST HUNTER

He shook his head.

"Your leg?"

"It's all right. Believe me."

Pamela's voice was barely audible. "We're not alone."

Deliberately, Cal stared out the large window. "I know. Where is he? Did he fly with you?"

She said: "He's using me to locate you. Do you know that?" Pamela's eyes were fixed on the empty coffee cup.

"I know that, too."

"And still you came?"

Cal tried to stare through the cloth of his buttoned-up brown jacket where he could feel the Walther inside his belt. "If you knew that," he countered, "why did you agree to meet me here?"

"Because . . . because I didn't know what else to do," she whispered. "And after your friend, Harron, said there was no chance of meeting with you . . ." Pamela Strong lowered her head. "He's here. Somewhere. I can sense it. My God, I've made a mess of things."

He wanted to say "no you haven't, my love," but instead he said, flatly: "Carl Heindemann insisted he was a killer."

She nodded. "And he is convinced you have some information he's desperate to obtain." She was talking to the coffee cup again. "Do you have some information?"

"Perhaps."

Pamela looked up. The pupils of her large eyes were pinpoints of bright light. "Why don't you give it to him? Then it will be done with."

"Did he say that?"

"Yes." It was a muffled "yes."

"I can't. It isn't mine to give."

She was silent.

"What does this bastard call himself? Rheinhardt? Or Lebedev?"

"Anatoly Lebedev."

"How long have you known him?"

"Eighteen months or so. He was with the Russian delegation at the U.N. He spoke to our group. We were . . . students."

"I don't want to know anything about them! Nothing!" he said, rapidly.

She muffled a sob against one hand. "Are you going to lecture me?"

"I'm not a teacher. No matter what my passport says." His eyes shifted from face to face in the half-filled lounge.

"You're in terrible danger, my darling . . ."

"So are you."

"I don't matter any more," she replied faintly.

A CP Air turbo-prop taxied slowly toward the terminal guided by a ground crew man signalling with two lighted bars. Cal watched it come to a stop. Ground crew moved the portable stairs in place and the fuselage door was flung open. Passengers, one by one, two-by-two began descending the metal steps to the concrete, pausing to allow a small tractor towing a high-barred luggage cart to the belly of the cargo bay. Luggage came flying out, to land whichway while handlers stacked them.

"That's a stupid remark," he said. "And you're not stupid."

Again she looked up. Her eyes mirrored hurt.

"All I want is that you come out of this alive!" She began to rise. "Oh, my darling old man, take me for a walk."

"No way. We're safe here. Lots of people."

Pamela sat back. "Where's your friend, Heindemann?"

"Dead."

For a second, Cal thought she was going to bless herself. Instead, she arranged the collar of her blouse. "I didn't like him," she said.

"I know."

"What else do you know? About me, I mean."

"A helluva lot more than I did."

"I still love you." Pamela lifted the empty coffee cup and put it down. "Do you feel it?"

"Yes." Is one of us lying? he asked himself.

"Oh, my God, darling, what's going to happen to us?"

Gently, now, he reached down and lifted her chin up.

"Don't touch me, Cal! Don't! Or I think I'll explode!"

The last of the passengers had left the portable stairs. The crew followed. The small tractor chugged toward the terminal, pulling the luggage cart. Slowly.

Cal edged sideways, sliding one foot after the other, until he was beside her. He sat down, heavily.

"First," he said, "let's have a drink. Maybe something to eat." He saw the waiter the same time the waiter saw him. "I'll have a beer," he said as he came to the table, "and my fiancee would like a . . .?"

"Gin and tonic."

"Yes, madam."

"I have something for you," he said. He held out his closed fist. "Put out your hand." He released the diamond ring.

Her angular face lit up, then collapsed. "My God, what I've done to you!"

You sent a message to Lebedev that cost a faceless Spanish limo driver his life, he thought. But you had no way of knowing. "Aren't you going to put it on?" he asked.

She twisted it the length of her third finger left hand. Her shoulders shook.

"I have a plan," he said, softly, "and you're going to have to trust me."

She straightened up, wiping her nose with a handkerchief that appeared out of nowhere.

She took her first sip of the drink.

"Do you trust me?"

"With my life, my dear old man."

He patted his left-side jacket pocket. "You're going to be violently ill."

"I've been ill since those goons walked me out of that terrible little hotel in Paris."

He grimaced. "I said you're going to be sick."

"I left the ring behind so you would know I didn't leave of my own free will. It was all I could think of . . ."

"Goddamnit! Pamela!"

"You can touch me now," she said, softly.

He trimmed the fuse on his rising temper. God almighty! he thought, she's doing it to me again: switching the pitch.

"I trust you." A half smile formed on her full mouth, then froze. "I'm trying to pull myself together. For you!" she hissed.

Cal softened. "I have some pills. Fifteen. They're quite small. Just gulp them back. As quickly as you can. Then you're going to get sick. Very sick." His shoulders slumped. "And I'll take it from there."

"Then what?"

"If it works, you'll recover in the Royal Vic Hospital here in Montreal where you'll be safe. Until I come for you."

"And if you don't?"

"You'll have to figure that out on your own."

"What about my shadow?"

Cal shrugged. "When this comes down, when the ambulance arrives to pick you up, I'll slip away in the confusion. And you'll go to the hospital where you'll be safe."

"Where are you going? Can't I go?"

"No." He dumped the small tablets in her hand with a quick movement.

"What are they?"

"Nitroglycerine."

For a moment, she held her breath, then blurted, "What will they do to me?"

"Make you perspire. Get quite dizzy. And trigger a heavy headache."

"Do I have to?"

Cal watched her high cheekbones shift imperceptibly when she narrowed her eyes.

"Where are you going?" she asked finally.

"First, I have to shake Lebedev because sure as hell he knows I'm here now."

"And I can't go?"

"It's better this way."

"Do I have to take these things?" she asked.

"You don't have to do anything."

With a motion so sudden it surprised him, she brought her hand to her mouth and, partially chewing and making a wry face, swallowed convulsively. "There!" she gasped. And picked up her drink finishing it quickly while he watched in silence. She extended the empty glass. "May I have another gin and tonic, my dear old man?" she asked. Her eyes were watery.

The woman's voice on the P.A. system seemed to flow out of the cork-tiled ceiling. First in French. The switch to

THE LAST HUNTER

English was smooth. "Ladies and gentlemen," she said. "British Overseas Airways announces that flight 233 to Manchester and London's Heathrow will depart on schedule from gate 26 in exactly twenty minutes. This is the last call for passengers intending to board the flight."

Pamela reached out and rested her hand on Cal's forearm. "I feel so hot," she whispered, "and you're getting to be just a large blur." Her face was flushed. "And my heart is—! God, it's pounding."

He gently covered her fingers with his left hand. The butt of the Walther jammed into his belly when he reached across his body. "It'll be all right, it'll be all right," he repeated. She trembled, violently. For a second, he was convinced she was going to faint. Or have a convulsion.

Harron, he said to himself, grimly, your doctor friend had better have been right-on. "Waiter!" he called loudly, "this woman is ill. She needs an ambulance!"

Pamela's head was lolling wildly on her broad shoulders. She moaned.

The waiter stared at Cal, then Pamela.

"Quick! Call a damned ambulance! Quick!"

"What is it, sir?"

"How do I know! Just call! Now!"

Pamela held her head with both hands and moaned while a hundred pairs of curious eyes watched.

The manager was frowning. "Can I be of assistance, sir?" he asked.

Cal stood behind Pamela, his hands on her shoulders, preventing her from toppling off the chair. "Yes!" He glanced around the lounge. The waiter was at the bar phone. And for the first time, he saw a square-shouldered man on a stool, half turned, staring fixedly at him. The pale glow from a long, shaded, incandescent light reflected off the gold teeth in his half-open mouth. His eyes were narrowed, tightening the lines between his brows. Cal leaned forward. "Yes," he grated softly, "you can help. Make sure this lady is sent to the Royal Victoria Hospital! Nowhere else!" He paused. "You know it?"

The manager was watching Pamela. "Of course! Every Montrealer knows of it!"

• • •

The ambulance, its warning lights flickering, siren wailing, raced toward route 520 to downtown Montreal.

Cal watched for a moment. It was 6:20. Then, absently tapping the Walther in his belt, he limped slowly across the roadway, beyond the taxis and buses, to the Buick. So, he said to himself, Lebedev knows who I am now. There were fifteen minutes remaining on the parking meter when he pulled away. He ran down the window to let the warm evening air fan his face.

Driving the speed limit, he wheeled off the Autoroute to Université and left-turned illegally on to Ste. Catherine. Nobody followed. He needed two minutes to right-turn through heavy pedestrian traffic at Peel and sixty seconds to creep another block to left again into the Place Mount Royale. He braked to a stop, at the Mount Royale's side entrance and sat while the engine idled. He watched a black sedan twice cruise through the intersection where Metcalfe Street crossed the far end of the one-block Place. Satisfied, he U-turned, parked under the hotel's overhead canopy and switched off. The doorman took the key after he told him he would be staying "at least overnight."

Crossing Peel, he limped into the Liggett's drug store.

"Surgical gloves. The finest you have," he asked.

He looked at them. "These the best?"

"Yes sir." The salesgirl watched him, curiously. "Shall I wrap them?"

"No thanks. I'm going to wear 'em."

Her eyebrows wrinkled.

"Now?"

Cal ripped the plastic cover open. The transparent gloves were so thin he could see the lines in his hands clearly. He looked up. "I've got an allergy. When my hands sweat, they break out in hives."

"I'm sorry."

"Not your fault," he said, handing her five dollars.

She rang it up.

The Mount Royale had had its face lifted. Peppermint shaded awnings over the tables and chairs dominated one half of the wide lobby. But the Picadilly Lounge was still in place. Cal accompanied the bellhop to room 909, tipped

THE LAST HUNTER

him and stood inside the door until he was certain he had returned to the lobby.

Standing between the twin beds, he thought of Pamela. In the Royal Vic. It depressed him. Orv Harron's doctor had said that once in hospital—because they wouldn't know she had OD'd on nitroglycerine tablets—they would carefully monitor her blood pressure, afraid she had suffered an aneurysm. Or a stroke. He could recall Harron's exact words: More than likely they would order a lumbar puncture to determine if the spinal fluid was bloody or clear. It will show clear. So don't worry. It will all be over inside a few hours. And there won't be any long-term side effects. It had sounded good then. And still did. But that didn't provide much comfort.

Cal shook himself and reached for the phone. "Long distance," he said, giving his name and room number. "I'd like the North Star Motel. In Gananoque, Ontario. And, no, I don't have the number," he lied, remembering the dozen fishing weekends he had enjoyed while staying at the popular resort.

Cal recognized the owner's wife, Sarah Thomas, when she came on the line. He lowered his voice and spoke haltingly. "Madam," he said, "I am calling from Montreal, but I would like to reserve a room for later tonight. My name is John Russell. R-U-S-S-E-L-L. Some of my friends have told me you have some great muskie fishing on the river, so I'd like to try my hand. How many nights? Let's say two. Or three."

Mrs. Thomas' voice boomed out of the earpiece. "When will you arrive?"

"About midnight. Perhaps later."

"My husband and I like to retire before that."

"Could you not leave the key under, say, the mat?"

"I could. But we don't have 'em." Sarah Thomas chuckled. "What if I left it inside the flower pot by the unit door?"

"That's fine. Which unit?"

"Shall we say 17? It will be eighteen dollars a night. And you can settle up in the morning."

"Thank you."

"We have bait, Mr. Russell. And boats."

"I knew that."

"We'll be expecting you.'

"Thank you."

Softly, his bag hanging from one fist, Cal let himself out of the room and hobbled to the red exit sign. One foot at a time, he descended the stairs. Not only his hip ached, but both buttocks. He was sweating profusely when he walked out the employees' entrance onto Metcalfe St. Crossing through traffic, he limped into Ben's, ordered a beer and one of their hefty hot corned beef sandwiches on rye.

Sitting at the large window, he studied the diners and drinkers. It was the same crowd, he concluded, cabbies, a hooker or two and the odd newspaper type who had been suspended from the Montreal Men's Press Club and all its arabic motif glory in the hotel's basement. Or were between assignments. He sighed and rubbed his aching leg.

The black sedan slowly circled the hotel. It had diplomatic plates. The driver was faceless, the single back-seat passenger lost in the shadows that lengthened on narrow Metcalfe St. His watch said eight-twenty. He stood up, stretched and used the pay phone, then bought an early edition copy of *The Gazette*. It had the usual typos. But the racing results were error free. Outside, he walked slowly down Metcalfe to the intersection and, peering over the broadsheet pages, watched the traffic. The black sedan never appeared. Then, spotting the car jockey deliver the Buick and park it across from the cab stand, he shuffled toward him before he could hand the keys over to the doorman. He slipped him a five, climbed in and dropped the Walther into his open bag. He drove aggressively, reaching the Autoroute in a few short minutes and headed west. He had 160 miles to go.

It began to rain but he made good time until he was eight miles east of Morrisburg where the uncompleted four-lane highway 401 was reduced to two running parallel to an unfinished two-lane gravel-coated roadbed. It was a steady Maytime spray rain that gently washed the green-leaf shrubs and trees on either side of the right-of-way. With it came the night.

In the gloom, his shoulders ached. His stomach heaved

intermittently and he was conscious of an enervating lassitude. Adrenalin, I better start pushing adrenalin, he thought. Just like I did on convoy patrol. Like the pump under the hood pushes fuel to the Buick's eight cylinders. Obediently, because I'm pushing a pedal. He was thinking of Carl Heindemann's cryptic message when the roadside signs warned of another stretch of unfinished expressway west of Brockville. He swung south to Highway 2 and, slowing, neared Gananoque.

The White Rose gas station was still open.

"Fill 'er up," Cal said to the chunky man, emerging from the repair bay, wiping his hands with a soiled rag. "And the oil's okay." He climbed out of the Buick, looking up at the lighted sign. "Say," he added, "you got any road maps?"

"Yep." His overalls were streaked with dirt. He unscrewed the gas tank cap and inserted the hose nozzle. "You want ours? Or the government's? Department of Highways gives 'em away. Ours are half a buck."

"White Rose."

The Buick took eleven dollars worth of high-test to fill up. The man came out of the small office. "And another fifty cents." He handed Cal the folded map. Cal paid absently and looked at it. The mechanic's greasy finger prints smudged the top half of the cover. In fine print across the bottom it said: Copyright, Rolfe Burrows, Ltd. Toronto, 1963.

Nineteen and sixty-three. The numbers exploded in Cal's mind's eye. He heard himself say: "It's a couple of years old."

"No difference," the mechanic said. "They don't change that fast. Except the big one—the 401—north of here."

Cal gazed at the map.

"You want the Highways' map instead?"

"No."

The mechanic watched Cal climb into the Buick and accelerate quickly as he pulled out onto the highway. He shrugged indifferently and started for the repair bay. "I shouldn't stay open so late at night," he said to himself. "The oddballs show up when it gets near midnight."

The North Star Motel faced the St. Lawrence River on

the north side of the highway. It stretched like a gentle crescent behind a screen of poplars broken at either end by an asphalt driveway. The neon sign was out. Cal pulled up into the parking space in front of unit 17.

The lined-off space before unit 15 was occupied by a shiny, blue station wagon. It had Quebec license plates. Quietly, Cal walked the length of the flag-stoned walk, beyond the locked office, to the far end of the motel. Sarah had been correct. There were exactly nine cars. And except for the wagon, they all had Ontario plates. He dug the key out of the flower pot with gloved fingers and, bag in hand, went inside. Closing the screen door, he left the heavy wooden door open and, pulling the lone chair across the room to the foot of the twin bed nearest the exit, sat down heavily and stared beyond the driveway to the highway. Traffic was almost nonexistent. I probably have an hour. Two at the most, he thought.

Carefully, he unfolded the White Rose map. If the date, 1963, explained the numbers 19 and 63, only 17, 108 and 10.5 west were critical. With the map across his lap, he fingered 17 in the Ottawa Valley. Doggedly, he traced it in ink from the Ontario-Quebec line below Hawkesbury, through Ottawa, Pembroke, Deep River, Mattawa, North Bay and westward beyond the Soo.

He located 108 running south from Elliot Lake into highway 17. He circled the junction. He forgot his weariness. And the fact his hands were sweating. His eyes strained, searching for 10.5 west. Or 105. Nothing.

Two cars, one behind the other, raced along the highway, the glare from their headlights flicking between the tall poplars and momentarily stabbing the darkness. He lurched to his feet, startled. Snapping off the light, he stood motionless, listening. The illuminated hands on the dial of his wristwatch told him it was twelve-thirty.

Quietly, following the creases, he closed the map. Ten point five west, he reasoned, has to be ten point five miles—or kilometers, because Carl Heindemann was a continental European—west of the junction of 108 and 17. It must be, he thought, exultantly. And he held his breath, his eyes on the driveway, waiting for a nagging voice to tell him he was wrong. Silence.

It took him five feverish minutes to strip the tensor bandage off his left leg, remove the blankets from each bed, roll them together and arrange them under the sheet covering the second bed. He wanted a shower, but knew he couldn't spare the time. He snapped off the light. Lifting the Walther out of his bag, he stepped over the luggage stand and, turning around, backed into the walk-in closet. It had two folding metal doors on tracks. He pulled them half closed and sat down, gingerly. He had made himself comfortable with the broad of his back against the concrete block wall when he remembered he hadn't closed the heavy wooden door. To hell with it, he muttered to himself, it will look more natural that way. He removed the clip from the pistol grip and checked it. One bullet missing. Enough. He slipped the safety catch off. Now, he thought, all I have to do is stay awake. Oddly enough, he wasn't tired. And despite the warm night air, his hands weren't perspiring any more.

Outside, the gentle hiss of the springtime rain had ceased. He wondered if there was a moon. A lake freighter's horn moaned off the St. Lawrence, like the rolling low of a love-sick cow. Ah, fog, he thought. At least enough to make that skipper wary. Minutes straggled by. Cramps wracked his legs. He jiggled his hips, searching for a more comfortable position. His eyes grew accustomed to the grey-black light.

Cal didn't hear a motor, but the squish of tires rolling through puddles on the asphalt in front of the motel. He was convinced everyone within five miles would respond to the alarm signals racing along his nervous system when he heard a muted noise at the door.

Noiselessly, he cocked the Walther. In the gloom, the aluminum screen door swung open slowly. A blacker shadow formed and filled the darkened doorway. No moon, his tense brain reported. The shadow remained in place. Imperceptibly at first, the dim outline of a head grew. He's straightening up, Cal's brain recorded. The shadow moved a half step. There was a faint odor of cologne. The screen door was closed by a left hand. Without a sound. The right clenched a pistol. Silently, the shadow surged a full step toward the second bed.

Cal liked the angle. Squinting along the barrel of the Walther resting on his right forearm, he whispered: "Don't make any kind of a move! Don't even speak!"

The shadow became motionless.

Cal's eyes were riveted on the silhouette of the pistol. "Drop it! Now!"

If fell to the floor.

"Kick it under the bed!"

The shadow moved.

Cal heard the pistol slide up against the wall under the far side of the bed. "Now walk between the beds. That's it. Lean forward with your hands against the wall."

"Mr. Sanders, you have surprised me," the shadow's voice hissed.

Cal climbed stiffly to his feet. Jabbing the wall switch outside the bathroom, he turned on the light. Without taking his eyes off Anatoly Lebedev, his fingers located the Russian's pistol. He picked it up. By feel, he knew it had a silencer. So, his mind raced, the KGB likes them even if Heindemann didn't. He stuffed it inside his belt.

Warily, at full arm's length, he ran one hand over the back of Lebedev's legs. They were spindly. Then his jacket and the small of his back.

"You are a most enterprising man, Mr. Sanders. For a journalist."

"I try to be." Keeping the Walther fixed on the Russian's back, Cal crossed the floor and closed the inside solid door, turning the self-locking knob.

Lebedev's grey hair was yellowish in the overhead light.

"You tricked me," said Lebedev, hoarsely. "With your long distance call to this . . . this little river town, after checking into the Mount Royale."

Cal grunted. "I figured you would buy that kind of information. And I would buy time. If newsmen can do it, the KGB can."

Lebedev lifted a pale hand to his mouth.

"Keep both hands against the damn wall!"

The Russian spoke to the concrete block. "And the woman is in hospital . . ."

"Safe."

"No one is safe anywhere, if we want them badly enough," Lebedev rasped.

Cal shivered.

"But she is nothing, to anybody."

Cal tried to frame a mental image of Pamela. He couldn't. Twisting his head, he parted the curtains with the barrel of the Walther and stared at the sedan parked against the screen of poplars splitting the highway and the motel's asphalt drive.

"I am alone, Mr. Sanders. And you have my weapon. May I sit down? Perhaps we could talk, like reasonable men." Lebedev shuffled his feet. "I am alone," he repeated.

Cal dropped into the chair. "I know that. You wouldn't have come in first if you hadn't been." He motioned with the Walther. "Okay. Sit. On the bed."

The Russian sighed as he sat. "May I smoke?" He half-turned and ran the fingers of his right hand down the roll of blankets under the sheet. "Such an old ruse, and to think that I, a professional, fell for it." He looked at his wristwatch. "May I smoke?"

The lake freighter's horn sounded again. Farther down river.

"No. Just keep your hands where I can see them."

A thin, brittle smile twisted the Russian's mouth. "You should be on my side of the fence, Mr. Sanders."

Where they teach you a dozen ways to kill the enemy, Cal recalled Heindemann's words. He shook his head.

"You have some information . . . " Lebedev began, tentatively.

And I have about 250 miles to drive, Cal reflected, his eyes riveted on the Russian's burned-out features.

". . . for which my government is prepared to pay a large sum of money. In American dollars."

Cal sneaked a look at his watch. One forty-five.

"And of course guarantee your life and that of Miss Strong."

"Get up!" Cal ordered abruptly.

Lebedev rose slowly, his eyes suddenly narrow. He lifted his hands in a gesture of compliance.

"Now, lie face down on the bed in front of you!"

"Useless," rasped the Russian, evenly. "We have your

license number. And I have friends on the way." He paused. "I will not be a hostage. That is not our way!"

"Lie down! Arms behind your back!"

Lebedev was on his hands and knees atop the bed. He turned his head. "I have a prostate condition, Mr. Sanders. It is imperative that I use the facilities."

Cal hesitated. The thought of a KGB senior agent found tied up, his pants thoroughly soaked, made him want to laugh. He shrugged off the mental picture. "Okay. Get up. Walk slowly, your hands atop your head until you need 'em. Leave the door open. I'll be right behind you!"

Cal yanked the Makarov out of his belt and jammed the Walther in its place as he cautiously followed the Russian into the bathroom. "Move!" He prodded the agent with his left hand. "Until your knees touch the toilet bowl!" He snapped on the light.

Lebedev stared into the mirror, his small eyes shifting from his own reflection to Cal's. He bent his head.

Cal checked the pistol's safety catch. It was off. He shifted his weight to his trailing left leg.

The Russian looked up into the mirror again. He was smiling faintly. His right elbow disappeared in a swift motion as his hand swept upward across his chest.

Instinctively, Cal backed off. The Makarov was pointed directly at Lebedev's wide chest when the Russian whirled, a long glittering knife locked between his right-hand fingers and thumb. He lunged. The 9 millimetre slug ripped into his heart. He went over backward, his head slamming into the mirror, his outspread arms colliding with the wall, before he slumped, to end sitting in the toilet bowl, his chin resting on his chest.

Breath, backed up deep in Cal's straining throat, exploded in short gusts from between his lips. The knife was on the tiles at his feet. He bent and picked it up—slim, tapered and fluted; it could go clean through a man's chest with very little force. Cal shuddered. He pushed Lebedev's lolling head backwards. The scent of cologne rose in his nostrils. He examined the Russian's suitcoat, careful to avoid touching the blue, bloody-red hole in his chest. The knife fitted neatly in a skillfully placed sheath inside the line of buttons where they met the lapel.

The faint moan of the lake freighter's horn rolled through the night.

Cal backed into the room, tugging Lebedev's body by the shoulders. He paused, expecting the owner of the station wagon in the next room to start pounding on the wall. But there was only his own labored breathing. He grunted, shoving the Russian's body under the end bed. Straightening up, he noted one of Lebedev's legs, his polished oxford pointing straight up, wasn't quite under the bed. It jerked. He eased it out of sight with his foot. That's one for you, Pamela Strong. And Carl Heindemann. That's two, he thought soberly, sliding the Makarov next to the Russian's bulk, two I've killed. And he wondered if his innate sense of values had been altered because both had been done without a twinge of conscience. He shrugged the thought off when he suddenly remembered Anatoly Lebedev's rasping words—"and I have friends on the way."

The North Star Motel's outline was stark against the black-blue of night. Cal needed ten minutes to switch the Buick's plates with the Quebecker's, using a thin, worn quarter. Then leaving a pair of twenties under the lamp on the night table, he put the Buick in neutral and laboriously pushed it down the motel's asphalt driveway to the highway entrance. The tight surgical gloves made squeaky sounds as he started it up and swung the wheel, heading west. It was 1:55 A.M.

2-6-66   1845 hrs GMT

File: AH 1945

For prime ministerial and presidential

eyes only; to be hand delivered on

receipt.

To: MI 5, CIA, RCMP (Operation Alois

Sibling desks)

Printer still missing. Field officer

reports Third Party alert eastern U.S.-

Canada. Keepers acknowledge Condition

Red. Urge Allied Van be put in place.

                              Control.

CHAPTER 13

✴

THE SKY WAS starlit. And the warm night air insisted a heat wave was moving in. Highway 400 north was surprisingly busy, but after the Wasaga Beach turnoff, traffic thinned. It was slow going through to Coldwater and north via 103 and 69 to Parry Sound where strings of trucks made passing risky despite all the horsepower under the Buick's hood.

Sudbury's main street was studded with rows of parking meters. Cal walked into a small restaurant while the morning sun peered over the brick-faced post office and glinted off the windows of buses packed with miners. The eight ayem shift, he thought.

The temperature was climbing. The weatherman, stringing off the figures and words out of a small radio next to a row of pies, promised a top of 90. And when that warm air bounces off the Coppercliff slagheaps, it'll get even hotter, he reflected, tiredly. A small dog sat in the doorway, eyeing him curiously.

"Bacon, eggs, toast and orange juice. And could I have the coffee up front?" he asked the waitress.

The coffee was hot, but as flat and tired as he was.

Because food always gave him his second wind, he ate. Even the burned bacon. The monotonous ache in his shoulders persisted. And his eyelids wanted desperately to slam shut while he motored out of the city.

Mindlessly, he turned on the car radio. Just as mindlessly, he twirled the tuner, swinging the slim indicator through bursts of static.

The voice was boyish and fast-paced.

"And this just in," he raced feverishly through the words, leaving Cal with the expectation he was going to announce the Second Coming. "From Gananoque, provincial police report an early morning series of shootings at a nearby Highway Two motel. Two men found dead, one from Quebec, the other a member of a foreign embassy staff in Ottawa.

"While the names of the victims have been withheld, pending notification of the next-of-kin, it is not known if the twin killings are linked, although both men were in adjoining rooms."

Cal froze, easing up on the gas pedal.

"An OPP spokesman said they are asking anyone with pertinent information to come forward. And now from Washington . . ."

Cal switched the off knob. He was wide awake. By now, he thought grimly, the OPP know the Quebecker's plates are missing. Without thinking, his eyes searched the rearview mirror for the tell-tale outline of a black-and-white cruiser. He shut down his conscience, but heartburn churned in his upper chest. Pulling off the highway, he braked to a stop and rested his head against the rim of the steering wheel. "Christ!" he wheezed, "that French Canadian wasn't supposed to die!" The words left a bitter taste in his mouth.

He consoled himself, remembering the old-timers in *The Express* city room. Tough birds, they had broken him in. "When you're after a story," they'd explain patiently, "you go get the facts. No matter who gets hurt. That's the way it has to be."

Shaking his head, he swung the Buick back out on to the roadway. Heat waves rose off the asphalt, distorting the solid and broken white lines splitting the two lanes.

The wooden sign where Highway 108, running south into 17, pointed north to Elliot Lake. Cal slowed again, eased through the tee and rocked to a stop on the shoulder.

The heat in the Buick built up. Fine beads of perspiration bulged on his upper lip until they linked together. He ran his tongue over them, tasting salt.

The mileage indicator read precisely five thousand and fifty.

Well, he thought, it's another 10.5 miles west. Or 105. Or 10.5 kilometers. Or 105 of those damned European numbers. To what? A gas station with a staggered row of one-room shabby cottages behind it? With an outdoor sign advertising live bait, hunting and fishing licenses?

A tractor-trailer swooshed by, the rush of wind in its passing briefly cooling his head and shoulders. He stretched. Who, he asked himself despairingly, would want to hide from the world up in this godforsaken stretch of country? Carl Heindemann's quarry? A wildschwein? With Brazil or Panama or the Argentine as an alternative?

All eight cylinders were purring. He kept one eye on the odometer. Five thousand and fifty-five. He could feel the heat from the outcroppings of granite rock. Five thousand and sixty. That's ten, he reflected. So it should be miles. Unless it's 105. He slowed while the tenths rolled into view and disappeared inside the odometer. Ten point one, two, three . . . four.

The dirt road led north only. The sign read: Camp Curry—UNAUTHORIZED PERSONNEL FORBIDDEN ENTRY.

Stunted evergreens and thick, bright-leafed bushes sprouted from patches of sand and dirt or clung to twisted shoulders of rock on either side of the track. Driving slowly, he covered a mile. The road veered out of view to his left. Gently, he braked the Buick to a stop. For a moment, he listened to the big engine idle. Now what? he asked himself. He stared at a small clearing to his right. If there's something around that turn, I don't need it. Because surprises are for losers, Carl Heindemann would say.

Bush flies rose out of the brush where he parked the car between two pines. They swirled in roiling clusters under the lower branches, humming incessantly. He looked at his bag and wondered if he should take the Walther. Numbly, he shook his head and swung the Buick's left front door wide. The flies rushed inside. Swatting and brushing, he climbed out and slammed the door shut. Frantically, he broke for the dirt road, standing there, staring into the shimmering heat. Slowly, he peeled the gloves off his wet, hot hands, dropping them onto the roadway. He thought of the Walther, shook his head, and clutching his jacket in one hand, started down the right-of-way.

Underarm perspiration rolled down his sides. Absently, he blotted it with his shirt and walked toward the turn. The roadway was sandy and ribbed where graders had scraped it almost flat, banking small ridges of dirt and gravel on either side.

The turn led to a straight 100-yard stretch before disappearing again into the low stunted brush and trees. His vision blurred by sweat, he shook his head, squinting against the dancing, shifting sunlight.

He had covered half the distance when he saw the old man breaking suddenly from the roadside brush. He was wearing a loose-fitting dark grey jacket and darker trousers. Once on the dirt track, he broke into a shambling trot. Only it was more of a reeling walk, his head low on his chest. His arms pumped jerkily. His feet barely cleared the ground as though each weighed hundreds of pounds. Dirty white hair, hanging straight down over his forehead, bounced while he moved.

Abruptly, as if undecided, the old man halted. He stared to his left and right, then down the road, directly at Cal. His face was a blurred speck in the fierce, pale light. His mouth twisted soundlessly. He broke into a crab-like shuffle. One arm, then the other, windmilled.

The sweat-matted hair on the back of Cal's neck and scalp suddenly tightened. He stopped in mid-stride, stunned by an overwhelming sense of horror. He fought rising panic. He tried to blink his eyes. They remained jammed open. He wanted to cry out, but his throat was wound tight around his tongue. It was as if his brain had refused to accept or transmit any willful signals.

Less than a hundred feet separated them. He could hear the old man's garbled croaking cries. Still he couldn't

THE LAST HUNTER

move. Even when he saw a second man, younger and heavy-set, break quickly out of the bush. There was a dull blue-black automatic in his right fist.

The old man, turning sideways, spotted his pursuer. He tried to move faster, but stumbled, falling forward on all fours. For a brief second, he raised his head, shrieking a string of unintelligible words.

His pursuer reached the roadway and quickly closed on the fallen man. He didn't say a word. Reaching him, he bent and grabbed one of the old man's arms. The old man kicked out. His free hand flailed the road, exploding small dust storms each time it flattened against the dirt. He gibbered. Forcibly, his captor lifted him partly free of the ground and began half-dragging, half-carrying him back into the bush.

Shaking his head violently, slowly at first as though he were emerging from a trance, Cal took four strides toward them. He forced his fingers into fists. "Hey! Hey!" The words gargled out of his straining mouth.

He heard footsteps thudding on the dirt track and swung around. Two hard-faced men in dark suits were almost on him. Each had a pistol.

Instinctively, Cal ducked into a crouch and threw a short right-handed punch at the closest. It caught him in the belly. His fist bounced off a hard, washboard stomach. He didn't see the second man's right arm rise and fall in a vicious arc. And he was barely conscious of the numbing pain that streaked through his head when the grip of the automatic raked his skull. He fell face forward into the dirt.

The second man peered down the road until the old man and his captor had disappeared into the brush. He slipped his weapon inside his shoulder holster. He growled and faced his partner, sitting in the roadway, gasping.

"You okay, MacLean?" he asked.

MacLean took a deep breath, let it out slowly and rubbed his belly. "Yeah, yeah, I think so, Keller." He glanced at the fallen Cal. "For his age, that bird packs a wallop," he said in a flat voice.

Keller said: "He's big enough."

MacLean climbed cautiously to his feet. He retrieved his

automatic from where it had landed when Cal's punch connected, then stared down at Cal. "Now what do you suppose he was doing on this road? Can't he read signs?"

MacLean was taller than Keller. But leaner.

Keller shook his head. "Nobody reads anymore, MacLean. Everybody's watching TV." He bent over Cal, rolled him onto his back, examined his head. "No blood. Hope I didn't kill him," he said, matter-of-factly.

Dusting off the seat of his trousers, MacLean shrugged. "Maybe," he said, off-handedly, "he'd be better off if you had."

Keller flicked one of Cal's eyelids back. "The pupil isn't dilated. He'll live."

"Too bad."

"Maybe. But we can't leave him here. Some army personnel could come along." He sighed. "God knows how much he saw." He licked his lips. "Damn! It's hot. That's the trouble with this country, it's either too hot or too cold. Well, he's not going to navigate on his own, so we're going to have to cart him in, until somebody up top figures out what's got to be done."

MacLean stroked his belly again. "You're the boss."
Keller laughed harshly. "An' I guess I'm going to have to do the carrying." He reached down, yanking Cal into a sitting position. It took both men to lift him up on rubbery legs. Keller squatted, buried his shoulder in Cal's midsection and straightened up like a weightlifter making a clean jerk. "Oof!" he gasped, "he's got to be well over two hundred!" He jiggled Cal's unconscious body into a more comfortable position and started slowly down the road, grunting with every step.

Cal's limp arms dangled in mid-air. His head bounced gently against Keller's broad back. The two men turned off the dirt track and plodded into the bush.

Cal opened his eyes slowly and peered into a wavering grey world. He thought he might feel better if he could vomit. He closed his eyelids tight and waited for his heaving stomach to settle down. Then released them. The world was still grey, but it had shape: a stone-block wall with a narrow, barred window high on its face, just below a slate-colored ceiling. There was blue sky between the black bars. Without turning his head—he was suddenly aware of a dull ache inside it—he made out a plain chest of drawers against a windowless wall. Conscious of the slivers of pain rippling across the back of his skull, he stared over the contour of his chest. Two socked feet were turned up at the end of what he understood was a cot. He forced one foot upward. It was his. Then both of them are, he thought.

The room swayed, before righting itself.

His eyes picked out the chest of drawers again. Dimly, he recognized the outlines of a washbasin and pitcher. Next, a closed door. He shuddered. Then he saw a man. He had a rugged, square face. He was smoking.

Cal blinked and tried to raise his head. The pain forced him to lie back. He tried again. Clenching his teeth against the waves of nausea, he made it. Staring first at his feet, he looked down at his dirt-stained trousers, smudge-streaked shirt, dark with sweat. With one hand, he tenderly caressed the back of his head, feeling a running welt.

"If you're worrying about your head, don't." The man in the chair had a flat voice. "It's too hard. The skin isn't even broken."

Cal inched himself through a quarter turn and placed his feet on the concrete floor. "Where are my shoes?" he asked. "Where am I?"

The man's narrow eyes never wavered.

"I asked you, where am I?" Cal croaked.

The man removed the cigarette from his lips. "I heard you." An amused look flitted across his stony face.

"You aren't listening," Cal grated, wrapping his thick fingers around the steel-framed cot.

"I'm a good listener."

Casually, Cal slid his feet under his weight. He groaned, but he had them where he wanted. He measured the distance. "What are you? A cop?" He launched himself in one sudden motion. Surprise opened the man's mouth. But before he could react, Cal was on him, fingers straining for his throat. With one jerk, he yanked him half-forward from his chair until their faces were inches apart. "Now," he snarled, ignoring the throb in his head, "how about an answer?"

The man brought his forearms up swiftly. At the same instant, he jammed a hard knee into Cal's lower chest sending him sprawling backward onto the cot where he rolled quickly, ending up half-sitting. He stared into the round black bore of a heavy automatic pistol.

Cal stopped breathing.

"One little move, Sanders, just one. And you'll never ask another question."

Cal felt the tension leave his arms and legs. His head was trying to explode off his shoulders. And his stomach heaved. "Round one to you!" he gasped.

The automatic never shifted direction. "Wrong again, Sanders. We win all the rounds."

The man backed up, nonchalantly holstered the pistol and walked to the door. He saw the smoking cigarette he had had between his lips before Cal rushed him and stepped on it. Removing a small key from his pocket, he slipped it into the locked door. There was a click. "You want something to eat?" he asked.

Cal nodded.

The door closed.

Cal waited until he was breathing easily and the ache in his head subsided, then crossed to the second door he had noticed. It led into a shower stall. Returning to his bed, he peered under it. No shoes. He searched his trouser pockets. Empty. He found his jacket, hanging inside the bathroom door, its pockets also empty. Climbing gingerly atop the only chair, he stared out through the heavy glass and between the bars. Rocks, sand, scrub pine and blue sky.

What in God's name is happening? he asked himself. He climbed down, rapped his knuckles against the solid wall. What in God's name is happening? he repeated silently.

The man returned with a tray of sandwiches, coffee and a pack of cigarettes. Carefully, he moved the pitcher and basin to one side and placed it atop the chest of drawers. He left without saying a word.

Cal ate hungrily, then, surrendering to a craving for a cigarette, lit up and lay back on the cot. It made him dizzy. He dozed, fitfully. The fading light in the small high window told him it was getting late. The ache in his head was almost gone, but the welt was tender to touch.

THE LAST HUNTER

A light, high over the door to the shower (he hadn't noticed it before) flicked on and off three times then went on. Then, deepening gloom triggered waves of despair which gradually surrendered to a growing terror. He shook himself, coughed, lay back and closed his eyes. For a few seconds he concentrated on a low hum penetrating the room. But the terror remained.

Cal's brain worked while his body slept restlessly. It reflected strings of stark faces in a macabre click-click rhythm: Carl Heindemann's, Joachim Heinrichs', Frau Getz', three putty-featured men whose names he hadn't even known, a faceless French Canadian's, Anatoly Lebedev's. Eerily as the last one faded, he knew he was trying to call to them, but there was no sound, except for his breath rushing in and out of his open mouth.

And the wildschwein? his brain asked. Where is it? His mind's eye searched the green bushes and evergreens. There was no movement.

Sitting up on the cot, both hands gripping the iron sidings so hard his fingers ached, he was slathered in sweat. Slowly, he relaxed and worked the numbness out of his hands. In the silence, there was a low, insistent humming. He cocked his head. Air conditioning, he acknowledged. He dried his sweaty hands on the sheet and reached for a cigarette. He lit it. His shoulders slumped.

I'm getting old, he mused. Too old.

It was midnight when Keller, humming tunelessly, opened the door into a long narrow room almost filled by a table. MacLean sat at one long side, thumbing slowly through a sheaf of thin papers. At the far, narrow end was a third man, sucking on an empty pipe. He was older, with thick, short, brown hair and a ruddy, almost pleasant expression. His black eyes were evenly spaced below thick eyebrows.

Overhead, incandescent lights bathed the room in a garish glow.

"The Printer is quiet. And secured," Keller said before sitting down.

"And the car?" asked Fields.

"Completely out of sight."

"Did you check the plates?"

"I did," said MacLean. "They belonged to that Quebecker. As you surmised. A check through Transport Quebec verified. Plates and serial numbers match."

"What was the poor bastard's name?"

MacLean glanced through the papers. "I've got it here. Somewhere."

"It doesn't matter. He's dead. And so is the Russian agent. Lebedev." Fields scratched a match into flame and pulled on his pipe.

"The Printer did in the Russian, but who killed the French Canadian? Did he? For his plates?"

Fields blew several small puffs of smoke, then content the tobacco was lit, waved the match out. He shook his head. "No, he didn't. But—as smart as he was—the Printer didn't realize that when the KGB reinforcements arrived, they would mistake the Montrealer for him and do what was expected of them. Remember, KGB soldiers aren't known for their intelligence. In the meantime, we have a problem."

"The Printer?" asked MacLean.

"He's part of it," Fields replied. "We're in Condition Red, standing by for Allied Van."

"How soon? And where?"

Fields smiled. "Control never signals the destination. Hell, we aren't even sure where we are when we get there. But you can bet your pension it will be isolated. Even after we get used to it." He removed the pipe from between his teeth. "Allied Van is standard, but this time it's an emergency move."

"And the Printer complicates it," said MacLean.

"What do we do with him?" asked Keller. "Obviously, he can't go along." He answered his own question.

"Control will decide. At least, it will relay any decision."

"What are the odds they'll indicate he just disappear?" queried MacLean, grinning wryly.

Beyond the complex, a night bird sang a melancholy song.

"Let's find out how much the Printer knows, first, eh?" said Fields, "before anyone lays odds."

Cal heard a door click shut, arched his back, blinked and

sat up. The outside world was bright with sunlight. He was alone. On the floor, four steps inside the door, was a tray of food: one cup of steaming coffee, boiled eggs and toast.

Hungry, he bolted it down then sipped coffee. It warmed his throat and made him feel good. He stared around at the grey walls. Nothing had changed. But something was missing. No hum. The air conditioner was off. He looked at his wrist. His watch was gone. Funny, he thought, I didn't notice that yesterday. Or was it yesterday?

He shrugged. "Time doesn't matter now," he said to himself. "Only how to get out of here in one living piece is important."

Getting to his feet, he padded across the concrete floor and stood at the door, listening for footsteps. Satisfied, he returned to the cot and began tearing the top sheet into long strips. He tested them for strength. They took a hard pull. He grunted and wondered if the cell was bugged. He counted the strips. Six. Again he listened. Silence. Breathing easier, he stuffed them under the pillow, flattening it with his fists to spread it as wide as possible. Then he sat on the edge of the cot and waited.

Cal held his breath when Keller walked in. "Welcome to the royal suite," he greeted.

Keller's face was lined. Tired. "Save the comedy, Sanders; the boss wants to talk to you."

"I'm not dressed for anything too formal."

Keller scowled, motioning Cal through the doorway.

The corridor was narrow. About five feet wide and made of the same stone block construction as the walls. It led to a stairway. Two doors broke the line of the wall on one side, including the one to Cal's cell. The only light glowed from two bright bulbs recessed in the ceiling behind steel mesh.

Cal slowed when he passed the second door. It was also blank and windowless. Keller prodded him in the shoulders. They climbed the steps to a landing, up another short flight into a second hall where several closed doors led off on either side. One, at the far end, was open.

"Straight ahead, Sanders," Keller said.

Two men were at the oversized table in the carpeted room.

"Mr. Fields," Keller said, "and that's MacLean." He pointed to the younger man, blue eyed and cold faced.

The rug felt good under Cal's sock feet.

Fields said: "Sit down, Sanders."

Cal lowered himself into a hard chair. He studied MacLean's face in the brief silence. His mouth was thin. And together with his flaring nostrils, it hinted at controlled violence.

Fields brought his large hands together. It looked like a friendly gesture to Cal. "Now, Mr. Sanders," he began, softly, "we have some critical questions to ask. And we would appreciate straight answers. Is that clear?"

Cal nodded, aware he was sweating. "And I have a few."

"We do the questioning, here," Fields interrupted.

Complete cops. Or soldiers, thought Cal. But they can't be KGB. American? CIA? British? West German security? In Canada? His own questions made him uneasy. Christ! he reflected.

"We could begin with von Hagen's death and your friendship with Carl Heindemann—the late Carl Heindemann. Or your subsequent, ah, tour of Europe. Or your affair with the American woman. Or the shooting in London." He paused. "But we won't, will we? Because you are in enough serious trouble without all that."

Cal sucked in his breath, then said: "If you know all that, there's no point in discussing it." He stared at each man in turn.

"But what about the Quebecker? Shot to death outside of Gananoque."

"What about it?"

"You switched your rent-a-car plates with his. And he's dead. The local police are onto that."

"I had nothing to do with his death," Cal said, stubbornly.

"We know that," said Fields. "But the local police do not. Which leaves you up the proverbial creek. An accessory to murder at best."

"What are you getting at?"

"Simply that you aren't in any position to ask questions."

Cal's stomach heaved. "Who-in-hell are you?" he blurted.

Fields smiled enigmatically. "We are known as the Keepers. But that will mean nothing at all to you. Or anyone else."

"CIA?"

"We know why you were on the Camp Curry sideroad."

Cal's jaw sagged. Against his will.

"Who gave you the highway coordinates?"

"I found them."

MacLean half rose from his chair, staring at Cal. "I could get him to be more civil, Mr. Fields," he grated.

Fields frowned him into a sitting position. "Carl Heindemann?"

West German security, thought Cal.

"I'm waiting, Mr. Sanders."

"I'm not certain. I suppose so. They were . . ." Cal replied slowly.

Keller reached over and tapped Cal's shoulder. "Speak up!"

"I suppose so. I'm not too certain. I found them in my bag."

Fields changed his line of questioning. "Didn't you see the restricted sign?"

"Only at the junction of the sideroad and Highway 17." Cal's eyes shifted again from face to face. "Who are you people?"

MacLean said: "We ask the questions!"

"Let's return to the sideroad," said Fields, smoothly. "Sanders, how much did you see before my people picked you up?"

Cal closed his eyes.

"How much did you see on the sideroad?" he repeated.

"Did you or your people murder von Hagen and Frau Getz?" Cal countered.

Fields' eyes flickered briefly. But his lips remained on a line. "You haven't answered *my* question."

Cal watched MacLean warily. "The road? What did I see? Nothing but an old man. Then I was jumped."

"What else?" It was MacLean.

Cal frowned. "What else?" he repeated. So, he said to himself, the old man is the key. He was conscious of

MacLean's hard gaze. Aloud, he replied: "Somebody collared the old man. Then two more came at me. Keller was one of them. I think. But I can't be sure. It happened too quickly."

"How would you describe the old man?" Fields asked.

They aren't KGB, Cal's mind said. Or I would be dead. The facts collided. And his frantic brain went mushy. "What did you ask me?" he asked.

"How would you describe the old man?"

"Old. Just old. With dirty grey hair. Infirm. There, that's all I know, for Christ's sake!"

"What was he wearing?"

Cal understood Fields was mentally checking off his answers. Tallying them against a larger picture. But he couldn't put his own "picture" together. "Grey trousers and a dark jacket. No. Reverse that."

Fields studied Cal for several seconds, then bowed his head and stared at his hands, still clasped on the table. "Sanders, we are patient men. We dislike rough stuff, so try to be sensible. Give us straight answers."

Cal nodded defensively. He heard MacLean snap: "Now, what were those colors?"

"A dark grey jacket and darker trousers. I can't be any more specific than that."

"That's closer."

"Did you recognize the old man?" It was Fields.

"No! Damn it!"

"Would you recognize him if you saw him again?"

Cal glared at the unblinking MacLean.

"Would you?" prompted Fields.

"No. I told you. I only saw him for a few seconds. I would have needed naval glasses to have seen enough."

MacLean snapped. "I don't believe you."

Cal took a big breath. "Why should I lie?"

Fields chewed on his lower lip. He sighed. "Take him back to his room, Keller. That's enough. For now."

Cal got to his feet and walked to the door. Keller watched him impassively, then followed into the hall.

In the corridor, Cal's mind counted ahead of him: two half-flights of steps; the door to the cell; stand aside while Keller places the key in the lock; two paces into the room;

Keller steps inside the doorway; then spin and hit him as hard as I can. In the pit of the stomach.

"You going quietly?" Keller asked.

"Sure, sure, Keller. I've been tamed." If he doesn't follow me at least into the doorway, he thought to himself, I lose.

They passed the other unmarked door. The muscles in Cal's shoulders and arms tightened. He stood aside to permit Keller to unlock the door to his room. Keller glanced at him. "You're the warden," Cal said blandly.

Cal smiled outwardly. He stepped inside the room. "Thanks, buster," he said. Then he pivoted, throwing a hard, right-hand punch. He had a fleeting glimpse of Keller's contorted face when his fist crashed against cloth and flesh. Cal grunted. Keller wheezed, explosively.

The impact doubled Keller up. His head dropped low. Cal's hard chop came down on the nape of Keller's unprotected neck. He dropped like a large rock.

Panting, Cal bent over him. With one fist cocked, he rolled Keller onto his back, removed the automatic from its holster, stuffed it inside his own belt and glanced into the open doorway. Listening, he fought to control his loud breathing. Nothing. He dragged the stunned Keller deeper into the room and closed the door, softly. Using four strips of sheet, he lashed Keller's ankles and thighs together. Then his wrists behind his back. He removed his belt and strapped his thighs tighter. Keller groaned. Cal yanked the automatic out of his belt and held it inches from Keller's nose when he opened his eyes.

Keller blinked rapidly and gasped: "You're crazy Sanders! This will never get you anywhere." His chest heaved.

"Just keep quiet!" Cal hissed. "I only need a couple of minutes to get out of here." Waving the pistol, he grabbed the last two strips of sheet. One he balled and force fed into Keller's protesting mouth. He held it in place with the second, knotting it behind his head.

Cal straightened up, his eyes darting around the room. The key, he thought, the door's closed. I need the key! Frantically, ignoring Keller's bulging eyes, he fumbled in the trussed-up man's pockets, awkwardly digging between the strips of sheet. "Thank God!" he said aloud when his fingers curled around it. He stuck it in the lock. There was a click and he swung the door open. Without looking at the twisting, turning Keller, he stepped into the hall. The weight of the automatic in his right hand made him feel safe. He took three steps. A hollow voice stopped him in a sudden cold sweat.

"Keller! Keller! You okay?"

The voice seemed to boom out of the lights in the ceiling. Cal stared down the corridor.

"Keller! Keller! Are you reading?" It was MacLean. Cal stifled an urge to break for the stairs. Instinctively, he knew it would be suicide. Even with the firepower he had in his fist. He heard rapid, heavy footsteps in the hall above him. Feverishly, his eyes panned the length of the hall. They locked on to the second door. The clump-clump-clump of feet on the upper hall boomed in his ears. They were on the upper stairs when he reached the second door. He inserted the key. There was a click. He pushed it open, stepping inside and closing it gently. Tighter than a bell tent in a rainstorm, he stood, the automatic pointing at the door. He struggled to hold his breath. Racing feet hurried down the hall. Trapped! his mind shrieked. "Not yet!" he said aloud, turning quickly.

At the far end of the room—three times the size of his cell—an old man was rising from behind a wide desk. Cal recognized the dark-grey jacket and darker trousers. Now, they were clearly blue. His grey hair, parted on the right, ran across and down his forehead. A short, trimmed white-grey mustache bulged over his upper lip and below his nose. His eyes shone dully above sack-like pouches, hanging in loose folds halfway down his sallow cheeks. He tried to straighten up but a permanent stoop prevented it. His left arm flopped almost uselessly at his side as if trying to keep time with his head which nodded, spasmodically.

Cal stood, slack-jawed.

The old man's left arm continued to tremble. He began to speak in a thin, scratchy voice. He's speaking German, Cal's brain told him. But it couldn't comprehend a word. He blinked unbelieving eyes while his heart tried to pound its way out of his chest. "Oh my God!" he managed hoarsely, "it's him! Adolf Hitler!"

THE LAST HUNTER 233

Palsied, stuttering, the old man's voice took on a pleading tone.

Mesmerized, Cal couldn't take his eyes off him. His reason insisted his brain was recording lies. He shook his head. His stomach heaved. He wanted to sit down. And think. But before he could make a decision, he heard Fields' soft voice: "Get your hands up, Sanders, and drop the pistol! Now!"

Cal let the automatic drop. Briefly he touched his stubbled jaw and lifted his hands. Someone (was it MacLean?) half turned him with a hard shove. He watched Keller retrieve the automatic.

Fields spoke softly to the old man in rapid German. Cal caught the words "Mein Fuhrer" and "Bitte" several times. The old man sat down, begrudgingly. His grey hair almost masked his eyes. Once he glanced up at a row of books, then, scribbling erratically, began jotting words on a large pad.

Again Cal was shoved. Like a sleepwalker, he moved sideways through the open door. He was shoved again, almost stumbling into the hall.

"You can lower your arms, now," said Keller.

Fields' pipe was halfway into a yellow oilskin pouch. His powerful fingers, working by feel, tamped the bowl full. He closed the flap. Cal watched him place the pipe between his teeth and light it, flaring a match into flame against a thumb nail. Wreathed in thin layers of smoke, he smiled. And when he spoke, his words were surprisingly quiet.

"Yes, Sanders. You saw Adolf Hitler. In the flesh. Old and sallow as he is."

Cal hadn't been set for the flat admission. *It means I'm a dead man,* he thought. He shifted in his chair.

"Now, perhaps, you can understand why we took such an acute interest in your presence here, eh?"

Cal groped through his pockets. He mumbled: "Cigarettes."

Keller's tight laughter sounded like beads bouncing down a flight of steps. "Here," he said, sliding a package across the table top, "Help yourself." Fields pushed matches toward him. Cal lit up, took a long drag and exhaled a gush of smokey breath.

It was a friendly gesture and Cal breathed easier. "How did he get here? In Canada, I mean."

Fields' complexion was ruddy even in the garish light. "We thought you knew who it was before you arrived."

Cal shook his head. "Just a wildschwein."

"Heindemann's expression."

"Yes."

MacLean asked: "But how many other society members knew what was in the message?"

"I don't believe any did."

Fields paused, then went on: "The action in Europe, the chain of events beginning with von Hagen's murder, it was all triggered by the society's decision to determine who was the mole?"

"You knew about the mole?"

"Yes."

"Christ!"

"Are you telling me that Heindemann's people knew this location before you did—and he—went off to Spain?" Fields probed.

"That's the only conclusion I can reach."

Fields spread his hands. "Ah, yes. There was the matter of Heinrichs."

"But Heinrichs didn't know about this place. That's what he demanded at the drop in Ludgate."

MacLean interrupted: "Are you convinced Heindemann did not know who we were holding? Did you?"

"Christ! No! If I had suspected, I would have sent the army in," Cal blurted. "Did Heindemann? I doubt it, or he wouldn't have worried about eliminating any mole. No matter who it was."

Fields frowned. "That fits. He was a technician who insisted every factor be thought out before acting. But somebody *knew* we were holding someone *here*." He sighed. "Let's begin again. Where did you get the information that led you here?"

"From Heindemann."

"Which begs the next question: Where did he get it?"

Cal said softly: "He was alone. On his own."

"Who was?"

"Carl Heindemann."

"But which member of his society brought it to him?" snapped MacLean.

Cal rubbed the palms of his sweaty hands against his thighs. He was feeling uneasy again. "There was no society; it had folded. Gone with the years. He was alone—the last hunter."

"One man?" MacLean asked, incredulously.

Cal nodded. And his mind went back to the ex-German U-boater. Lean. Resourceful. Operated by a brain that clicked and purred like a computer.

"Then," Fields said softly, "we're back where we started: If Heindemann knew, others did."

And he had the training, the discipline, the instincts and patience of a hunter, Cal thought.

"It makes the only kind of sense I understand," said MacLean.

Only such a man could sift the fragments of available information, the reports, the rumors, then precisely analyse them and plot his course.

Keller sighed. "Frankly, I don't know what to think anymore. But one man? Possessing that kind of knowledge? Why didn't he go public?"

He would run down every scent. Examine every track. Grimly, relentlessly, he would stalk his quarry. Until the kill. "It was a personal thing with him," Cal said, slowly. "He believed deeply the only way to purify Germany's name was to hunt down every ex-Nazi who had stained his idea of his Fatherland's honor."

"And he knew Hitler was alive?" asked Fields.

Cal shrugged. "I'm repeating myself. I don't think he knew *who* was up here. Only that it was someone big. Perhaps Bormann."

The air conditioner kicked in. Except for its low hum, there was utter, heavy silence.

"Interesting, if true," Fields said finally.

"Your people knew about the society?" Cal asked. He felt good again.

"Yes." It was MacLean. "But as long as they only fought the KGB, we didn't give a damn."

"Then *you* are . . . what?"

Keller said: "We are the Keepers. Nothing more than you see."

Cal shook his head vehemently. "What I see is the biggest story since . . . since Creation."

Fields placed his pipe on the table. He settled back in his chair. "Mr. Sanders, because we know more about you than even you yourself, I am going to tell you a story."

"I have my story."

Fields ignored him. "We know where you come from, what schools you attended, your navy record, your preferences and dislikes; your personal and your business lives. For example, we know you pulled together a story—after six weeks of digging—a story that could have destroyed a government and half a dozen of the country's political leaders. It never appeared. We know why. And we know you know. The point is, you kept it to yourself. You didn't even discuss it with your wife. That marks you as a man who can be trusted to keep a large secret."

I'm not going to die, Cal thought, finally. "What do you know about Pamela Strong?" he countered, while he tried to sort out his head.

"She has recovered and remains in the Montreal Royal Vic," said Keller.

Cal grimaced. His head felt better. He sighed.

Fields smiled. "Any good psychologist will tell you a little bit of information will create an itch in a man's guts which will eventually drive him mad. I believe that. So, on that basis—together with what I've already said—listen carefully.

"It began," Fields explained, "during those final days of World War II around the Fuhrerbunker situated near the Reichskanzlei on the Wilhelmstrasse in Berlin. Hitler was already a ruined man. His personal bodyguard and staff, his generals, were living in the concrete complex we would call an air-raid shelter. Joseph Goebbels was there, his wife, Magda, all their children save one, Eva Braun, plus Martin Bormann, the party deputy . . . and Generals Hans Krebs, Wilhelm Burgdorf and others.

"Berlin was in flames. Russian shells were dropping

around the Fuhrerbunker, sited near the Brandenburg Gate in the area now inside the East German portion of the then Third Reich capital.

"While Russian intelligence and U.S. agents didn't know exactly where Hitler was, the British did. They asked themselves what they could do about it. A nameless captain recalled that on September 13, 1943, SS Captain Otto Skorzeny and a picked group of German paratroopers had lifted Mussolini right out of his prison—a resort hotel atop Mount Sasso in Italy's Abruzzi district. Wasn't it possible, he posed, to repeat this operation?

"The answer was a qualified 'yes.' Instead of gliders and paratroopers, a captured German light plane, a Fieseler Storch could be used. It would be piloted by one of two special British agents. They would be provided with bona fide SS uniforms and credentials, culled from the prisoner-of-war stockades rapidly filling up as Germans surrendered en masse to the advancing British Army.

"There was another basis for seconding the plan: the British also knew that on the night of April 28, a German general, Ritter von Greim, and a woman, Hanna Reitsch, had pulled off an incredible stunt. They had landed a Fieseler Storch on the emergency strip roughed out on an east-west axis into the Unter den Linden. If she could get in and out, it was argued, so could determined British agents. Even if time was running short. And the shelling would be more intense.

"The decision was reached at 1900 hours, seven o'clock, the evening of the 29th. It was code-named Operation Alois Sibling."

"Operation what?" interrupted Cal.

"Alois Sibling." Fields smiled. "Alois was Adolf Hitler's older brother."

Cal's mouth opened.

"Most people today don't realize Adolf even had an older brother, let alone his name. In fact, he lived for a time near Liverpool in the U.K. And 'sibling' means . . ."

"I know what a sibling is. A brother or sister. Is that a large state secret?"

"Not necessarily. Some historians and researchers have

known of his existence. Alois, named after their father, preferred to keep it that way as time passed."

"Where is he now?"

The lines in Fields' forehead lifted. "He left the U.K. sometime between the wars. Immigrated to the States. Changed his name. And just disappeared."

"My God . . ."

"At any rate," Fields continued, "after the decision to trigger Operation Alois Sibling was underlined as 'go,' the agents took off at 2300 hours from a former Stuka base at Celle. Two men in SS uniforms flew a German plane fitted with a spare gas tank in the cockpit, still with German markings. Their orders: Capture Adolf Hitler alive if possible, dead if not."

As Fields droned on, Cal had a mental picture of the Storch circling the doomed city, the pilot squinting down at the pall of smoke, the charred remains of ten thousand gutted buildings, the glare of as many fires, the flashes of exploding Russian artillery shells and mortars.

He could also "see" the fragile plane banking through the overcast of night and smoke; the pilot picking up his bearings over the Charlottenburg Chasse, running straight toward the Brandenburg Gate where it became the Unter den Linden.

"The timing was perfect," Fields was saying, "and they made a rough landing without any serious damage to their Storch. They reached the Fuhrerbunker sometime after midnight. The SS guards checked their credentials. They passed easily. After all, they were genuine.

"Escorted inside, they were amazed to walk in on a drunken brawl. All semblance of discipline had disappeared. Introduced to Joseph Goebbels and Generals Bormann, Krebs and Burgdorf—both the latter had been drinking heavily—they insisted they carried special instructions from newly created Field Marshal Walter Wenck at his 12th Army headquarters. They were direct: The Fuhrer was to be airlifted to the Bavarian Redoubt where what remained of the German armed forces would make their last stand.

"To this end, they demanded to be taken to Hitler's quarters. The intellectual Goebbels understood the historical significance; Krebs and Burgdorf were too drunk to argue. But the crafty Bormann, named party deputy-minister only hours earlier, was suspicious. He insisted on accompanying the agents.

"Once in Hitler's apartment, they found Eva Braun dead, after biting a cyanide capsule. The Fuhrer's dog, Blondie, was also dead. And a dazed Hitler stood with a pistol in his hand, either undecided or screwing up the courage to shoot himself.

"In less than two minutes, the doubting Bormann had been eliminated with a shot straight into his mouth that blew away most of his face and destroyed his teeth. That explains why the Soviets had such a difficult time attempting an I.D. based on the body's dental records.

"Then, with greatcoat collar up and cap pulled lower over his face, the agents escorted Hitler through the noisy party, stopping only to accept Goebbels' best wishes for a safe journey."

Fields paused, his eyes on Cal. "You're going to ask me why Goebbels would later announce Adolf Hitler's suicide to a startled world, aren't you?"

Buried in the welter of details, Cal could only manage a croak.

"Well, he didn't survive. So we'll never know for absolute certainty. But think about it. He was a Nazi zealot. Certainly, he found Bormann's body. What happened to Martin Bormann, the crude *lumpen* in a general's uniform, was of no importance. But a Fuhrer who had escaped to fight in a flaming Gotterdammerung fitted every lurid climax his twisted intellect could desire. Faking his death would, I'm sure he was convinced, be a gesture, *his* final gesture, to ensure that *his* leader would have the necessary time to escape and carry on the struggle."

Fields took a long breath and straightened his shoulders before going on: "The return flight to the Celle airstrip was uneventful, although an Allied light ack-ack battery took a few shots at the Storch on the wholly acceptable assumption Germans were flying the aircraft."

With a start, Cal recalled unconfirmed reports that a plane had flown out of stricken Berlin the night of April

29-30 while the city burned. "My God!" he whispered softly, "my God!"

"Hitler," Fields continued, "was officially reported to the world as a suicide the night of the 29th-30th. Some two hours after his abduction. Since then, oddly enough, he has been reported as seen alive in the Argentine, even Antarctica."

Cal said: "But everything I've heard or read indicated quite conclusively that Hitler's body was burned . . . that the SS poured some fifty liters of gasoline over his body, then set it afire."

"True," replied Fields. "But there is a welter of conflicting evidence. As I said, Goebbels announced the Fuhrer had shot himself; that he had found the body. Alone, of all those in the bunker, he had gone in and confirmed that fact. But I've explained Goebbels' actions, and why he told the world it was a suicide.

"On the other hand, one trusted SS officer, Harry Mengerhausen, swore Hitler had taken poison.

"The body, as I've told you, was Bormann's. Take Erich Kempka's evidence. He was Hitler's personal chauffeur. He testified he had helped carry the body into the Reichskanzlei Gardens where it was duly burned. Yet he also admitted under questioning that he had never seen his master's face. Only his boots protruding from under the blanket that covered the body led him to assume it was Adolf Hitler.

"And his valet, Hans Linge, swore he poured two hundred liters of gasoline over the Fuhrer. But again, he too *assumed* it was Hitler."

"Surely now," interposed MacLean, "you realize that the man who was under the blanket was the man who was supposed to have escaped—Bormann—the man with the anonymous face, tried *in absentia* and sentenced to death at the Nuremburg trials."

Fields continued, softly but clearly: "More recently, the Soviets released a picture of a so-called death mask of Hitler's face to East German newspapers. It was, the Russians prompted, taken by an unidentified German soldier, minutes after Hitler shot himself in the mouth. Where did he come from fifteen years later? And earlier, the

Russians went to great lengths to try to establish the identity of the body found in the Reichskanzlei Gardens, then gave up, admitting they were stumped."

The air stuttered with electricity. Fields added: "Capturing him was the beginning of a dilemma that was to grow. What to do with him was next. To have put him on public trial could make him a martyr. Yet, public opinion demanded trials; Goering, von Papen, Jodl, plus several generals, concentration camp captains and guards were tried. But they were mere followers. Hitler, on the other hand, was almost a divine figure to a great many Germans. And could remain so to the Nazis still at large in a defeated Germany. Or anywhere else.

"Therefore: martyr or criminal?

"Washington, of course, had been informed. The Russians were not. Ultimately, it was decided he could not face trial. So, following a dozen top-secret shifts, cloaked in utter anonymity, he was moved to this specially designated experimental radar base.

"Only the Canadian and British PMs and the president of the U.S.—and their successors since the original capture—know the truth."

Cal thought for a minute. "What about the two agents who pulled it off? Or the unknown captain who hatched the plan?"

"Tragically, the agents left that morning for the U.K., flying a Dakota transport. They crashed while attempting an emergency landing in Holland. It was an accident. The captain? He was told the operation had been aborted; it was unfeasible. He died in a remote English village blissfully unaware of the facts."

Cal lit another cigarette. He stared at Fields. "How did the old man escape from his room?"

"The doors are electrically controlled. When the key is inserted, the circuit is completed and they open. There was a short. The back-up system failed to kick in. The door opened. He just walked out."

"Well, he can't be completely crazy. He knew enough to escape."

"I don't think he really knew he was trying to escape."

"Well, he certainly didn't appreciate whoever was trying to collar him."

"It was me. And you don't understand. He's crazy, but still very stubborn. And taken to raging now and then," replied Fields. He studied Cal's face. Then added, quietly: "I know what you're thinking, Sanders. But this can never be a story." His tone was taut, clipped.

Cal heard the words like the drumbeat at his own execution. "Nonsense," he said more smoothly than he felt, "I saw him. I know he's alive."

"You saw no one." Fields spaced the four words evenly.

Cal stared up at the ceiling. There was a finality in Fields' voice that unnerved him. "Are you suggesting I'm not going to be able to write anything? Not a word?"

Keller coughed.

"There's the matter of my rental car. The Buick. Someone will find it."

"Only if that someone is scuba diving in a deep cold lake that doesn't even have a name," MacLean said.

"And what about the rental agency?"

"John Russell signed for that car. He doesn't even exist. And you wore surgical gloves to ensure *your* prints would never show either in Montreal or Gananoque."

Christ! Cal thought silently. But, he understood what his captors were saying. "Then I could disappear. Like the Buick. Without a trace," he intoned, "after you've pulled out."

MacLean said: "You're right on one point. We shall be gone. Long gone. There'll be nothing here, nothing but an abandoned radar site. Us? We don't exist on any document you or anyone else has access to. It will be as if we never were." He knotted his fingers. "It's a huge country, Sanders. All we require are a few square yards of space. Then, in time, the man you think you saw will really be dead. Just as it was reported years ago."

Cal cleared his throat. He didn't want to ask, but he had to. "Okay. What happens now?"

Fields chuckled. "Good question. You've noticed you haven't been permitted to shave or clean up? That there's no water in the basin or shower?"

"Yes."

"In a few hours, you will be escorted down a little-known dirt track that peters out deep enough in the bush for the black flies to be a problem. And left there. When

THE LAST HUNTER

you're found—and you will be—with a tackle box, spinning rod and backpack, you can tell the police anything you wish. But, remember, Cal Sanders can't get too involved: don't talk about John Russell for example. He's wanted as a murder suspect."

"By that time, we will be far away," MacLean said.

"And Pamela Strong? Or the KGB?"

"Miss Strong is of no importance."

Anatoly Lebedev said the same thing, Cal remembered, suddenly.

"You say she is fine?"

"Almost fully recovered, according to our contact." Fields scratched his head. "How did you arrange that rather dramatic seizure?"

Cal shook himself. "Can you get her a message?"

"No. Sorry."

"What happens next? After I'm 'found'?"

"You'll be kept under KGB surveillance. For a time. But I don't believe you will be of any interest to them. Not after you surface. And there's no story. The KGB knows how to cut its losses," MacLean said.

"How long will I be 'lost'?"

"Two days. At the most."

Two days. Forty-eight hours, thought Cal. Enough time to figure out a future with Pamela Strong. Even how to soothe Limey Lewis' growling temper. He sighed. "Fields," he said at last, "and I know that's not your real name. What about something for the record? A few words I could use following Hitler's actual death?"

Fields picked up his pipe and relit it. "You're off track already, Mr. Sanders. Adolf Hitler died in the Fuhrerbunker during the night of April 29-30, 1945."

Cal Sanders was abruptly very, very, tired.

Epilogue

*

5-6-66   2300 hrs GMT

File: AH 1945

For prime ministerial and presidential eyes only; to be hand delivered by 0900 hrs 6-5-66.

To: MI 5, CIA, RCMP (Operation Alois Sibling desks)

Society extinct. Printer neutralized. Third Party action quiet following mistaken hit. Allied Van complete.

                                       Control.

THE EXPLOSIVE #1 *NEW YORK TIMES* BESTSELLER

by the author of the phenomenal multi-million-copy bestseller

THE HUNT FOR RED OCTOBER

Red Storm Rising

Tom Clancy

"Brilliant...staccato suspense." — *Newsweek*

"Exciting...fast and furious." — *USA Today*

"Harrowing...tense...a chilling ring of truth." — *Time*

"A rattling good yarn...lots of action."
— *The New York Times*

—RED STORM RISING   0-425-10107-X/$4.95

Available at your local bookstore or return this form to:

THE BERKLEY PUBLISHING GROUP
Berkley • Jove • Charter • Ace
THE BERKLEY PUBLISHING GROUP, Dept. B
390 Murray Hill Parkway, East Rutherford, NJ 07073

Please send me the titles checked above. I enclose _____. Include $1.00 for postage and handling if one book is ordered; add 25¢ per book for two or more not to exceed $1.75. CA, NJ, NY and PA residents please add sales tax. Prices subject to change without notice and may be higher in Canada. Do not send cash.

NAME_____

ADDRESS_____

CITY_____ STATE/ZIP_____

(Allow six weeks for delivery.)

Bestselling Thrillers—
action-packed for a great read

__ $4.95	0-425-10107-X	**RED STORM RISING** Tom Clancy
__ $4.50	0-425-09138-4	**19 PURCHASE STREET** Gerald A. Browne
__ $4.50	0-425-08383-7	**THE HUNT FOR RED OCTOBER** Tom Clancy
__ $3.95	0-425-09718-8	**SUBMARINE U137** Edward Topol
__ $3.95	0-441-77812-7	**THE SPECIALIST** Gayle Rivers
__ $3.50	0-425-09104-X	**RUSSIAN SPRING** Dennis Jones
__ $3.95	0-441-58321-0	**NOCTURNE FOR THE GENERAL** John Trenhaile
__ $3.95	0-425-09582-7	**THE LAST TRUMP** John Gardner
__ $3.95	0-441-36934-0	**SILENT HUNTER** Charles D. Taylor
__ $3.95	0-425-09558-4	**COLD SEA RISING** Richard Moran
__ $4.50	0-425-09884-2	**STONE 588** Gerald A. Browne
__ $3.95	0-441-30598-9	**GULAG** Sean Flannery
__ $3.95	0-515-09178-2	**SKYFALL** Thomas H. Block

Available at your local bookstore or return this form to:

THE BERKLEY PUBLISHING GROUP
Berkley • Jove • Charter • Ace
THE BERKLEY PUBLISHING GROUP, Dept. B
390 Murray Hill Parkway, East Rutherford, NJ 07073

Please send me the titles checked above. I enclose _____ Include $1.00 for postage and handling if one book is ordered; add 25¢ per book for two or more not to exceed $1.75. CA, NJ, NY and PA residents please add sales tax. Prices subject to change without notice and may be higher in Canada. Do not send cash.

NAME_____

ADDRESS_____

CITY_____ STATE/ZIP_____

(Allow six weeks for delivery.)